To Frenchy.

Thank you x

Contents

Chapter 1 - A Singular Event.

His fingers fiddled idly with the napkin that had been provided as a coffee nappy. Neat and tidy habits negated a need for such precautions. Running his nail around the outer edges, reaffirming the creases, Simon did this unconsciously as he stared deeply into the distance. There were few thoughts inhabiting his mind at the moment and when he became aware of this, he smiled at the encapsulation of his life in this moment. His future was, as he considered it now, just an empty space, lacking direction, lacking any plan. How different things had been only a short while ago.

Long shadows were cast by the late afternoon sun and stretched out down the Muswell hill. Simon counted the seconds it took for him to see a shadow before its owner passed by. He came here most afternoons, always on a Saturday, and used this time to clear his mind of the ever increasing problems his life was collecting. How many times had he sat here considering that hill and the pain that final incline had caused him? Thinking about his bike, and his pursuit of the perfect hill climb, was the only way he could find to forget about what was happening to him.

His coffee was cold. Only half drunk and he hadn't really enjoyed it either. This was, of all the coffee houses in Muswell Hill, probably the worst. Both service and coffee seemed to be stuck in the 1980's when it really didn't matter what the product was like, it was cheap and you should be thankful! Simon came here because of its positioning, because it was quiet, and because he never felt it necessary to be cheerful to the staff or patrons. He'd counted all the way to eight before he realised that this was too long a time for someone to be catching their shadow. Paying a little closer attention he noticed that the shadow had ceased to move, the architect had obviously come to a stop and this had been directly behind him. With an effort, Simon twisted his back in the chair and looked over his shoulder. Eclipsing the sun, creating a chill with its absence, the figure behind him waited patiently for his attention. There was a brief pause as both men anticipated an introduction to a conversation from the other. Dark figure broke the silence "A parcel for you sir"

His voice assured and his action assertive as he placed a small box wrapped in plain brown paper on the table next to Simons coffee. Simon regarded the parcel, no name, no address, no stamp, with some surprise. An unexpected and curious occurrence.

"What's this?" he asked, although the answer had already been given.

Without any perceptible change in tone or manner, dark figure repeated himself "A parcel for you sir"

The intervening seconds had given Simon enough time to consider this curious event and formulate a number of questions. Chief amongst these was identification.

"How do you know it's for me?" he posed, squinting suspiciously at the figure behind him.

"Simon Brown?" came the cold, emotionless reply.

"Yes...." said Simon, but before he could follow this up with further queries dark figure interjected once more.

"Then it's for you!" He said, definitely.

Simon, who had swiveled almost fully in his chair to get a good look at this courier, turned back to regard the package. In the moments that this action took up, and in the time his stuttering mind had taken to question it, the dark figure had gone. He was disappearing into a nearby car before Simons call could reach him...

"Hold on a minute!" he shouted, in time only to see the door closing and the car pull away from the curb. Simon stared after it, to see if he could get a better idea of what the man looked like, but it was gone before he'd had the chance to focus his eyes. All that was left of the encounter was the package in front of him. Without touching it - which would have signalled ownership - he bent over the box to get a closer look. It was about the size of a cigarette packet, plain brown paper wrapped and very neatly folded. There were no distinguishing marks on it, nothing to betray what it might be concealing or who it might have been sent from. Simon shifted uneasily in his chair, looked around himself to see that the world was going about its business, just as it had before this arrival. He was looking for some assistance but none was forthcoming. It was just him and the package. He sat back in the chair considering his options. His fingers drummed on the table either side of the brown box, nervously toying with the idea of opening it. What on earth could it be?

Tentatively, he pushed the box an inch or so along the table with his finger. Checking the weight, getting a 'feel' for what it was like. It slid easily under his touch and presented little in the way of resistance. It wasn't heavy. Carefully, with one hand, he picked it up and turned it over to see the underside. No clues were found and all that he managed to learn from the event was that it didn't rattle. Whatever was inside had been fixed to its position. Once again Simon looked around him, hoping to find some security, someone to share this bizarre occurrence with, but he was all alone. If he had taken his afternoon coffee at one of the trendier and more sociable houses then he'd have had the opportunity to include someone, but here, nobody cared.

Curiosity, and the realisation that no help was going to arrive prompted Simon into action. He could have left the box on the table and simply gone home but that made no sense to him. Having taken the decision, his fingers worked quickly at the outer paper and it was soon discarded to reveal a small, plain box with a lid. Placing it on the table and fixing it with his left hand, Simon gently removed the lid. Inside, filling the space completely, was bubble wrap. He picked this out and started to unravel the sheet from the outside. Something was fixed in the middle of it but he couldn't make out what it was. As he turned it over in his hand he began to see what was contained within. Two earphones were clearly visible, along with their cord, and they were attached to a small, square iPod. Discarding the bubble wrap, Simon held the device in front of him and a slight shiver ran down his neck. It wasn't just an iPod.... It was his iPod. What the hell was going on?

This had suddenly become a far more serious event than he'd given it credit for. What had been a bizarre and curious happening had now elevated itself to feeling distinctly sinister. 'How?' and 'Why?' ran furiously through his mind and the world seemed suddenly to have shrunk everything into focus on this, on his music player. Simon felt his stomach constricted and his throat dried. Pressing the button to turn it on, he held the player between his thumb and fore finger, gazing at the screen. What appeared was the usual 'play' and 'skip' icons, whilst at the top, it simply read 'unknown artist'. He put the ear plugs in, took a deep breath and tapped 'play'.

'Good afternoon Mr. Brown, I trust you're anxious to know what this is all about?' The voice ran. It was a clear and well-spoken man, not a voice that Simon recognised.

'You're not doing so well for yourself these days are you? Lost your business, mortgaged to the hilt. All those creature comforts you used to possess and that gave you such joy, all gone now. How proud you were of the things you had... You used to feel like you were the master of this little world of yours, didn't you? And now it's all gone to shit! Truth be known, you can barely afford the afternoon coffees you take, and yet, somehow, you still manage to feel superior to those around you. All of what you built has crumbled and gone but you still retain that ego. Well, its time to see if you're actually right about yourself. Are you really a cut above, or just some hasbeen that never really deserved what he had in the first place?'

'You were born into greed, born to think of yourself as deserving. Public school education and a silver spoon up your backside. Yours was never a struggle, was it? I've seen your like many times before and I've often wondered if there's any steel in there? What would you do if you were pushed to breaking point, sink or swim? Well, you sunk, didn't you! You had no answers to the problems you faced and now here you are, flat broke and no idea how to change your situation. Maybe I'm your fairy godmother...'

It wasn't exactly what Simon was expecting, really he didn't know what he was expecting but a summary of his crappy situation hadn't been it.

'Let me tell you a story Mr. Brown... Forty years ago, or there about, this world had the misfortune to have spawned into it a child. This creature grew up alone in his family, always the spoiled one, always getting what it wanted. Its parents were too busy to pay it any real attention so they bought its love and created a foul little monster. For this 'thing' love meant possessions, whatever gifts it could get its grubby little hands on and its thirst grew as surely as its contempt for others. It resented the other children it knew for having the goodness that comes from affection and warmth, it did not understand these emotions. At school it bullied and tortured the other children, made them feel weak. When it was fifteen one of those children it mercilessly taunted decided that life really wasn't worth continuing with and was found in the school grounds swinging from a tree. It didn't care... It saw weakness, not tragedy. It gained strength from this understanding of the power it had. It fed.

At twenty-one, at university, it delighted in controlling its peers. Making them dance to its tune and casting them aside when they no longer amused it. One girl, one foolish child, thought she saw some goodness inside it. She loved it as purely and honestly as anyone could. Gave herself completely to this fiend and he ruined her. Defiled and humiliated for all to see, it took her innocence and love and spat it all back in her face. She had the strength to finish her degree, to carry on with life, but she was a shadow of what she once was. Whatever joy and wonder she could have brought to this world had been replaced with cynicism and distrust. It had seen the goodness in her and it had scared him. She, more than anyone before or since, had come closest to unlocking the humanity in it. It didn't allow anyone to get so close again.

In business it was just as ruthless, cutting 'friends' as deeply as enemies and clawing for every last advantage it could find. Building an empire was all it cared about and it went about this with such ferocity that is was feared by those around it. Nothing stood in its way, no one dared. False promises, empty gestures, contracts signed and ripped apart, it cared nothing for its destructive practices, for those that suffered in its wake.

Then, let's say five years ago... give or take, the tide started to turn. Big fish in small ponds never see whats coming. They believe themselves too powerful, too clever, too magnificent to be caught in a net. It was easy! All you need to know when you want to ruin someone is their motivation. Give them what they crave and they become blind, and it was as blind as any man could be. The stronger the motivation, the deeper they will fall in its pursuit. How far did it fall? You tell me....'

The audio paused. Simon had listened attentively to his life being cut into shameful chunks. His blood had run cold in his body. Who the hell was this that had gained such knowledge about him?

'And now it is time for redemption. You see Mr. Brown, you can still win this game. There's still a chance for you to get back what you once had... If you want it?' and again, a momentary pause.

'Five years ago, when things were going so well, you were given a tempting little offer. Someone as voracious and unscrupulous as yourself, someone you respected, showed you an interesting little game. It bargained on those traits in you that you held most dear. Your greed and your belief in your own indestructibility. The stakes, as you saw them, were low and the rewards great but this was not why you chose to play. You did so because you truly believed that you would triumph. That you would emerge as the victor because nobody 'could' beat you. Your ego, Mr. Brown, is what made you do it. You'd conquered

all before you and life had left few opportunities to prove yourself. Do you remember?

A Tontine! How delicious the idea had been. Five people of equal age, equal standing financially, equal belief in their own superiority over others. You would each contribute a negligible amount and stand to gain a fortune.... should you triumph. All you needed to do was survive the others. How could you fail?

Back then, the money was nothing, a mere £100k. Oh, how you must wish you had that money now? But it would have gone with the rest of your things. You'd still be the penniless wretch you are today, I'd have seen to that. Or would you? Would any of this have happened had you not decided to play my little game? That is something you'll have to decide for yourself. What's important now is that I have an offer for you. Your investment in the Tontine has grown Mr. Brown. Today, the entire fund stands at £10million pounds - unlike yourself, I'm not motivated by greed and can see when to invest in a company. You can make more money knowing when something is going to lose than you can knowing when something is going to succeed. So you see, all I've done is filter your money into the pot and now it's time to see if you can get it back? You'd like it back, wouldn't you? You'd like your life back?'

Again, the audio paused for a moment to allow Simon to digest what had been said.

'You have a choice Mr. Brown. If you wish, you can just get up and walk away. Keep your debts and your pitiful existence exactly as they are at the moment and see just what this life has to offer someone like you.... Or.... there's a black cab waiting behind you, a little way up the street. Take the cab and I promise you I'll give you the chance to get your money back. It's up to you.'

And there the speech finished.

There really seemed to Simon like there was no choice at all. It may be better to have loved and lost than never to have loved at all, but that certainly didn't hold true in terms of money. To have had everything and now be left with nothing was, as he saw it, the very worst thing that could happen. Especially to someone like him, who loved the fine things wealth had brought him. Collecting his phone and iPod from the table, leaving no tip, Simon drew himself up and turned towards the cab.

Reassuringly, both cab and cabbie appeared to be completely standard and normal - as normal as a London cabbie could be that is - and so he settled into the back of it with no real apprehension.

"So where are we going sunshine?" he called. Simon called every man he considered his inferior 'sunshine'. It had been his dad's pet name for him and it had always made him feel small. There was no reply, not a flicker from the driver, and no indication that he would get a response whatever he asked. Simon sat back in the seat and thought about the message. Ideas about where he was being driven to and for what purpose failed to occupy him. Who was behind this didn't concern him at the moment either. These things would become clear in the future and there was nothing he could do about them anyway. No, what was foremost in his mind at this moment was the memory of Toby Little. He hadn't thought about Toby for twenty years or more, had managed to file him away in the deepest recesses of his mind, although he never would forget his name.

Toby was a pretty small and ineffectual kid at school, notable only for having an elder brother who was less so than him. He went about his school life quietly and Simon had very little to do with him up until about a month before his death. Toby had suffered the usual abuse from the standard school bullies, usually along the lines of his name referring to the size of his manhood, and other such obvious gems. It was pretty mild stuff and, in the main, Toby was no more bullied and abused than anyone else outside the 'cool' group. Simon remembered the day when their paths collided vividly, he could even smell the cut grass on the field next to the playground. That he'd never felt love from his parents was absolutely true and Simon was smart enough to understand that his behaviour, his performances at school were both a way of gaining respect from the other cool kids and a petty jealousy. This day was just an example of all the worst circumstances coming together in one place and one time. Bad luck, that was all.

Simon often hung around with the bullies from the year above him at break times. They knew they could manipulate him, that he was their puppy and would do pretty much what he was told. It was fun for them to have a toy to play with. Acceptance was love to Simon, even though he knew they didn't give a damn about him really. On this cloudless, hot summers day, Simon and the bruisers were patrolling the yard, spoiling for some cruel entertainment. They'd found themselves a tennis ball and were throwing it as hard at each other as they could, what fun! Then they noticed a group of five or six kids sat outside the science block doors. They were perched on the step, minding their own business and chatting casually. Four girls and two boys, one of which was Toby. Simon couldn't remember who it was that threw the ball first, but he did remember the reaction. The girls screamed as the tennis ball thudded against the locked doors, just above their heads. Toby and the other boy (who Simon couldn't remember) just looked like rabbits in the head lights, knowing they could probably make a break for it, but not wanting to leave the girls stranded. They had but a few seconds to consider which was the least humiliating. Running away and deserting the girls or staying and undoubtedly getting a number of tennis ball tattoos, or maybe worse.

Toby chose to stay, the other boy decided that in all probability those girls weren't interested in him anyway so they could fend for themselves, and off he ran. The girls continued to scream, a couple cried, and Toby did his best to fend off the tennis ball that was hurtling towards them at great speed and little accuracy. Then it was Simons turn to hurl the ball and Simon had a good arm! He'd made the county cricket trials mainly on his ability to heave a ball back from the boundary line with some skill. Simon wound up his body and, like a baseball pitcher, threw himself forward. Projecting the ball flat and low. It was heading directly towards the face of the girl next to Toby when a miracle happened. Flicking his hand out in pure reflex, Toby not only averted a certain impact but actually caught the tennis ball. Shit, Simon had never seen this kid catch anything in his life! It was the fluke of all flukes. The bruisers, to a boy, all laughed at Simon and ribbed him for failing to connect with his effort. Whilst he had turned to face them, crest fallen and babbling some sort of excuse, Toby let fly with a throw of his own. It wasn't anything like Simons effort, no great speed to it but it did have tragic accuracy. The bruisers saw it coming, Simon followed their gaze only quick enough to have half turned his face when the blow landed. Those two events happening together must have been a million to one shot. Toby Little had caught lightening twice on the trot, the unlucky bastard.

The bruisers fell about laughing and suggested that Simon should go sit with the girls and let Toby join the real men! Simons' eye was watering and they suggested he was crying, "poor baby!" His pride had taken a battering and the love he craved from the mindless idiots had disappeared in those two moments of unfortunate brilliance. Marching over with malicious intent, Simon grabbed Toby by the throat and pinned him against the door. He remembered the look on Toby's face.... Pure terror. He was trying to mouth something but couldn't speak as Simons grip was too strong. Words were spoken but they have been lost in history and were irrelevant to the outcome anyway. Simon, whilst holding the bluing boy against the door, brought his long, spare leaver sharply into Toby's lower gut. Now he may well have needed the toilet, maybe he was bursting for a pee anyway, but this mighty blow knocked the piss right out of him. Once it started it didn't stop. Running out the bottom of his trousers and making puddles on the floor, the girls he was protecting now squealed at the sight of his urine and distress. The bruisers squealed with delight too, they'd had such entertainment this fine break time. Simon had rescued some of his 'love' back from the brink of disaster and felt reasonably happy with things again.

That was it.... That's what happened, no more, no less. Had he felt shame for what he had done that day? Oh yes, without a shadow of a doubt. It had burned him deeply. That he would do that just to feel like he was part of a group, that he could do such a thing to another human being.... Yes, it had hurt him very much, but worse was to come. You see sometimes these playground events take on lives of their own. Sometimes the stories become bigger and brighter (or darker) and completely envelop those involved. For the following weeks, Toby was greeted everywhere with pissing noises. Boys would loudly refuse to sit next to him for fear of urine stains. Girls would giggle and make squelching sounds as he passed them in the corridors, even the girls he had tried to help, who were supposed to be his friends, turned, in the tidal wave of hilarity at his expense. It was useless to stand by him, that would have brought scorn and abuse and no teenager actively seeks that out. That most felt heartily sorry for him was probably true, but no one told him this, no one was prepared to stand with him or offer some support. Weeks he endured this until he could bear no more. It's a lonely fucking place being a teenager. It's damn hard even when things are going well, but it's pretty much impossible when the whole world is against you, and that was how Toby saw it. He could take no more.

Tuesday lunchtime, Toby left the grounds of the school - as he tended to do these days - and walked off into the woods. Tuesday evening, around eight o'clock, he was found by a man walking a dog. Ironically he managed to hold on to his pee after choking his life away.

The voice on the audio had said he'd seen only weakness and this was very nearly true. What Simon had taken away from the horrific events is that we all stand alone, we have to look after ourselves and fuck everyone else. Nobody was in Toby's corner and the poor fucker died alone. Well, he wasn't going to *rely on anyone from here on in. Simon vs the world, that's the moral he took from the story and he'd defend that position to his last breath!*

Idly meandering through the London suburbs the gentle rocking of the cab, a place Simon had spent a good deal of time, had a familiar feel. There was nothing out of the ordinary about the experience and he felt, despite the bizarre event, rather relaxed. This in turn, when he considered his state of mind, felt weird. Here he was, being whisked away to god knows where by god knows who to do god knows what, and he wasn't in the least bit stressed? He should be, he felt like he should be, but he wasn't. Who the fuck was this person? How did they know so much about him and what the fuck did they have planned? That they'd known where he was going to be at that time on an afternoon wasn't the most impressive piece of detective work, he was always there. Anyone could have found that out. However, getting his iPod, knowing his history..... Toby and Jo.... How did they know about Toby and Jo? Simons' throat gathered a lump as he thought about the girl with the purest soul. The bastard had even got that right, she had been pure....

Up until he'd met her, Simons relationship with women had been one of aggressive sexual fumblings and drunken encounters of a singular nature. He'd never stayed with any girl for very long, usually less than the time it had taken for the sun to come up. He liked sex, liked to fuck girls the way they wanted it and derived his pleasure from pleasuring them. But once it was done, once the performance was over then the spell was broken too. He'd feel nothing for them, they were simply a conquest. Simon liked to hear that he was a good lover, that they loved his body and found him sexy. It fed his ego and made him feel like the alpha male he was pretending to be. It was a dance that they played together, each having a role that meant something to the other, or at least that's how he had seen it. Those one night stands weren't innocent, they knew what was going on, even if it had been unsaid. They were 'playing' a role just as much as he was, that was how it was between men and women, right?

She'd been the same dumb blond he'd fucked a thousand times before. Smiled and laughed along with his jokes, admired his body like the rest of them. He'd met her in a bar they used to go to at orders and could always get a couple of after hours cocktails or beers on the house. One of his friends was nailing the owner and this had saved them a few quid. It was also quite cool to have the bar to themselves and watch the rest of the drunken idiots pass by the window, wishing they were in on the party! She was a new starter, his own age and obviously one of the students at the university. Tall, slender figure and not overly pretty. Just the type he used to do very well with. Simon could be most charming when he set his mind to it, he'd spent his life pretending to be what people wanted him to be so it was never difficult for him to work out what they liked. They spent the evening together and then the night, it had followed the usual pattern and he thought that he'd keep this one for a while. It made sense, given the bar situation, and she wasn't difficult to be with, in fact, he'd actually enjoyed her company. There was something quite different about her, something delightful.

More time was spent together, not just evenings drinking and having sex, they did stuff during the daylight hours too. He'd never done this before, never had the least interest to either but she had a quality about her that drew him in. Jo was unaffected by life and seemed able to live in that way. She laughed when she found something funny, laughed like a child would, with honesty. She questioned what she didn't understand and never felt embarrassed about not knowing. Jo never tried to play any role other than being herself. She had true integrity, a genuineness that fascinated him. She was who she was, unashamedly and without apology, and this was what he admired in her so much. For someone who had never been himself, never felt like he could, was too afraid of what people would think about an actual 'Simon', he was in awe of someone that truly didn't care.

They'd spent a good deal of time together and she'd asked only for his faithfulness. He'd been an idiot at times and she'd told him so. She'd never tried to keep him by pretending it was alright. Then, one day, they'd had a BBQ. All his close 'friends' were there and Jo had come along with some of hers. It was a glorious summers day and Simon had never seen her look quite so beautiful. He remembered how he had worn his shirt open, to show off his chest. How he'd played football, but only in a 'cool' way, not trying too hard but looking good none the less. He'd smoked his cigarettes and swigged his beers with the attitude of a young stag, lording over his group. She'd paid him no attention at all. Jo had taken herself off with the children one of Simons friends had brought and was enthralled by the games they were playing. She couldn't have been happier and as he looked on he realised something quite profound. All that he was doing was peacocking! It was a performance. Here, on this perfect day, he was trying his best to 'show' that he was enjoying it all more than anyone else. He wasn't experiencing the day, valuing each and every wonderful moment. Taking the time to enjoy it for what it was, great friends and company. She was.

Jo had found exactly what made her feel most happy and had lost herself in that moment. She wasn't missing out on drinking and laughing with the adults, missing out on spending time with Simon. She had found some people who enjoyed life as purely as she did, that understood what it was to be truly happy with what they were doing, and that happened to be playing 'tea parties'. She had the ability to take the joy and wonder that the children felt right here and use that to magnify her own enjoyment. She was blissfully happy and in that moment he loved her like no one else on earth. Simon spent the rest of the day lost in his admiration for Jo and when she left that evening he'd cried. That was the only day, then or since, that he had felt true love for another human being. After that, he stopped calling her, made excuses not to see her, messed around with other girls too. When the time came for her to leave the university she had called round to see him one last time. He knew she had come in the hope that he would say 'they should be together', that they were meant for each other and should never part.... But he didn't. He wished her well, barely got off his seat to see her out of the door, even though it broke his heart to do so.

Back on that summers day, when she had been perfect, he'd realised one painful truth. He would never be able to make her happy. Simon could never be the person she was. He was a performer and she didn't care for that. He was affected, damaged by the life he'd had up to now and the only thing he could do to stop her ruining her life was leave her alone. He'd resent her in the end, he'd be jealous of her purity and drag her down to his level. He'd seen the most perfect flower growing in the field and he couldn't allow himself to stamp on it. He could live with the fact that he was a bastard, this was what life had in store for him anyway, but he couldn't live with the knowledge that he'd destroyed something so wonderful along the way. He had to let her go and he knew that she'd never understand his reasons why. So he played the bastard, that was all he knew how to do....

Lazy evening sunshine flashed into the back of the cab through the gaps in the buildings as they passed through some typical London borough. Nothing to distinguish this place from another and Simon's mind drifted back to the situation in hand. 'Where were they going?' he mused and started to take greater interest in the outside environment. They'd been travelling some half an hour or so now and all that he knew for certain was that they were south of the river. Suspecting his question would yield no response but deciding to ask it anyway, Simon called to the middle aged cabbie "How much further?"

Barely glancing in the rear view mirror, the sullen man continued with the task of driving, uninterested in the passenger behind. He was maybe fifty years old? Simon thought, and certainly typical of the kind of cabbie you'd expect to find. He looked grumpy, purely getting on with the task at hand. Having spent many hours of his days in the city in just this position, Simon had never really paid much attention to 'who' the person was, he really had never cared. Now, he was curious. Was this fella actually a cabbie? Had he been hired by the voice on the audio to simply perform this task and been instructed to remain silent throughout, or was he in the employ of the voice? It wasn't beyond the realms to believe that this guy, this cab and the whole damn set up, was exactly that, a setup. Carefully staged to draw as little attention to what was happening. He'd gotten in the cab with no fuss, he was a typically relaxed passenger for the journey, but as Simon saw the situation, he was, in fact, being kidnapped, in a quiet sort of way. Nobody would know he was missing, there would be no clue either as to where he might have gone. It would be days or maybe weeks before any alarm was raised, such was his social life at the moment. Possibly the only person who might become alarmed by his absence, might notice, was his postman. Those endless bills would eventually clog up the basket behind his letterbox, but even then, would they think that anything was wrong? Considering his position in the world at the moment, the only people who would take any interest in his disappearance would be those he owed money to. More likely than not they would believe he had made a run for it, attempted to make himself disappear. This did cause him some concern.

Taking his phone from his pocket Simon scrolled through his contact list to see if he could find someone to tell about his situation. He also had the idea to look on 'maps' and check his position. No GPS was available at this time.... How could that be? His contact list was a shameful roll call of creditors and ex-business associates. How few of those people would even take a call from him, let alone provide some sort of safety net should this thing turn out to be as serious as he was now suspecting it would be. Three people, from a list a hundred strong, stood out as the only ones that might be useful to him and that was the key phrase 'might be useful...' It struck him right there that this was all he looked for in those contacts, all he looked for in people these days, whether or not they might be useful. Here and now he needed a friend, that was what would be most 'useful' and he didn't have a single one!

'Sarah cleaner' - a woman he always suspected was stealing from him but did a good job keeping the flat tidy. She hadn't worked for him for how long now?

Must be coming up three years? They'd had a very professional relationship, meaning they'd rarely spoken but he couldn't remember upsetting her. She'd probably remember him, but care? Why would she care?

'John fat golf' - the name itself told him this was an unlikely allie. John was a businessman with an overinflated opinion of himself and no great talent for golf. They'd played a few rounds together, told stories of the deals they'd done and how they'd shafted people, oh how clever they were! Two fucking big shots that nobody else liked, and at a golf club that really is some going. He was as arrogant and self-obsessed as Simon, he wouldn't raise a finger to help unless it meant he was going to get something out of it, and at this moment in time Simon couldn't think of any such carrot to dangle.

'Coco paid slut' - curiously, given her title in the list, Coco was the one person he felt most affection for. She was a prostitute he used to use when he'd had a lot of money and he'd appreciated the fact that it was a simple transaction. No emotional crap, no wondering how she felt after the event, just sex and money. It was the only sort of relationship he wanted or felt capable of. 'I don't pay girls for sex, I pay them to fuck off afterwards' someone had once said, and he was in perfect agreement with this. Despite this emotionless relationship, despite the fact that he hadn't seen her in over two years, hadn't had the money, this was the only person who just might do something to help him. They'd got along. He could have used lots of different whores if he'd wished, changed them like hats, but he'd liked Coco and she seemed to like him. Obviously, he was paying her.... but there always felt like there was something more, like they understood each other. There had been times when she hadn't 'fucked off' afterwards and they'd talked, properly talked about the world and how they saw it. They were peas in a pod.

Well, there was no one else... If there were anyone who was likely to help then Coco was it. Simon now had to think about what he would say? "Hi, just a quick text from a guy that used to pay you to fuck. Might have been kidnapped by some psychotic mentalist, please tell the police to scour the surrounding areas of London for some deadbeat ex-rich dude who nobody likes?" What the fuck could he say? If I don't text you within the next four hours then call the cops? I've been invited to play a game to get my money back and have decided to go along willingly but have started to think this is a very bad idea and would like some backup. Oh, and I've no idea where I'm going or who I'm going to meet? Nothing seemed to make any sense. Panicking a little, Simon decided to send -

'I've been kidnapped, please tell the police to track my phone. This is not a joke, you're my only hope!' - That would have to do. He would just have to hope that she took it seriously, remembered who he was and give enough of a shit to pass the message on. What the police would do is anyone's guess?

Hitting 'send' Simon was immediately informed that 'messages could not be sent at this time'. Checking the status of the phone he saw that he had no service. No GPS, no WiFi, no service provider listed either. His phone was completely useless. Somehow the cab was blocking any signal from the outside. He tried to roll down a window in desperation and found that they were jammed shut.

"What the fuck's going on?" he shouted at the driver, who ignored him still.

Simon started kicking at the windows with his heels but just as he did so the cab turned into a large warehouse and the steel doors closed behind them. He stopped kicking and started hyperventilating - this was his way of readying himself for a fight, not that he needed much self-encouragement. Suddenly leaving the bright afternoon sunshine for the total shade of the warehouse Simon struggled initially to make anything out of his new surroundings. His eyes seemed to take an age to adjust to the gloom but when they did, they found a nearly empty space. They'd come to a stop at the far end of this obviously disused area and save for a few remnants of what it used to be in a former life, there was nothing here. Nothing other than a black transit van that is. Twisting and squirming in his seat, darting looks all around but never daring to look away from the cabbie for long, Simon waited for the next move. From the back of the van, a smartly dressed man walked around to greet him. He walked casually up to the driver's window first and Simon heard him ask 'did you have any trouble?', to which the mute cabbie simply shook his head. He looked pleased. Moving slowly around the cab, Simon watching him like a startled rabbit the whole way, he eventually made it to the passenger door. Peering in, Simon could finally see what he looked like. Tanned and rugged, were his first impressions, he had strong features and looked like the sort of bloke you might meet at the doorway of a club. Not one of those gorillas whose size alone is supposed to put one off causing trouble, but the kind of man who would be in charge of them. Simon had always believed the smallest doorman to be the one you didn't mess with at all costs, and this fella looked like one of those. He was clearly in very good condition for his age, around 40 he judged, and his suit had been tailored. One has an eye for these things. Tapping on the glass with the knuckle of his index finger, Simon noticed his watch peeping out from his sleeve. Whomever this was, it was clearly the boss of the situation, this had been betrayed by the tourbillon movement of his 'Vacheron Constantin' timepiece. With a smile Simon was beckoned out of the taxi. Having retreated a couple of paces, as if giving room to a dog to pass without fear, the man waited. Simon eased slowly towards the door and ever so carefully pulled the lever to release it from the lock. He was sweating and absolutely no calmer than when he'd tried to kick the windows out, but there really wasn't an option. Opening the door no further than necessary, with the intention of jumping straight back in and slamming it shut, Simon eased himself out of his prison. He held on to the door frame for comfort as he stood there facing the suit.

"Finally Mr. Brown... It has seemed like an age waiting for you"

It was the voice from the audio, there was no mistaking that.

"Who are you?" Simon asked.

"There will be plenty of time for explanations later, but for now I need you to get into the van. We've another journey to take before we can begin." He said cryptically and held his hand out to indicate the black transit behind him.

"I'm going nowhere until I have some answers..."

"You're in no position to bargain Mr. Brown," the man said casually "the only choice you have is to leave now and go back to your broken life with nothing, or get in the van for a chance to get it all back. It's really up to you. I'm not going to force you to do anything, I've plenty to keep me amused already." and again he smiled and gestured to the van. "This is the crossroads Mr. Brown, this here is where you decide. £10 million pounds is up for grabs, or a life like that you have become accustomed to over the last few years.... Which would you prefer?"

"I need to know what's involved? You can't expect me to choose when I don't know what I have to do to get the money... What do you want?"

"Oh but I do.... No more talk Simon, no more questions... Yes or no?"

Simon stood considering the deal, or at least the two options he had available to him.

"Why me? Why...?" he asked.

Shaking his head the suit simply said "Yes or no? You've five seconds to make up your mind!"

After a moments pause, the suit started counting from five to zero.

"Five.... four.... three.... two...."

"Ok!... ok... I'll do it!" he said, and let out a long breath that took some of the tension from his body.

"This way Mr. Brown, let me show you the van" and the suit half turned and moved off to the doors at the back. Opening them and nodding his head towards the contents.

Simon moved carefully over to where he was standing and as he passed the rear door closest to him he looked around the corner to see inside. It was darker still than the gloomy warehouse but as he focused his gaze he managed to make out four people sat down at the front of the van. Their hands were tied behind them and they had gags and blindfolds on. For a brief moment, Simon's guard had dropped as he tried to make sense of what he was looking at. He didn't 'feel' the blow, only heard the thud as the lights went out completely.

Chapter 2 - Awakening

Lola slowly became aware of herself. Her first 'feelings' were the softness and comfort of the bed she was laying on. She was warm and sleepy, and her head throbbed which seemed odd. She was 'hazy' and at this moment she didn't understand why that would be. All she did know for certain was that having her head on the pillow was infinitely better than trying to raise it up and look around. Like one of those hangovers that need a double nap to make the world 'contemplatable' again, she needed that pillow to ease the ache inside.

Maybe a minute passed, maybe an hour or two, she had no idea, but this time when she awoke she came to with a much greater clarity. Sitting bolt upright on the bed and immediately clasping her hands to her forehead, pressing it to keep her brain from bouncing around, Lola let out a pained expletive. Jesus her head hurt badly. What the fuck had happened? What could she remember? She'd taken a ride in that cab, found herself in the warehouse and the voice from the iPod had been given human form and wanted her to get in the van. She remembered that..... He'd given her a choice, get in the van or leave and she'd chosen to leave. How had she ended up here and where the hell was here? She remembered getting back in the taxi and it pulling away to drive out of the warehouse. She'd felt awful sleepy, dog tired. They must have knocked her out, gassed her? Whatever they did it had left her with a terribly thick head.

First things first, where was she and how could she get out of here? The dullness was slowly clearing from her head and with it, the sharpness of her quick brain was returning. What could she see? 'List the room and be methodical Lola' she told herself. She'd always been one for order and reason, control was the world she trusted and believed in, she needed control always.

'Four poster, 18th century and most likely French' she mumbled to herself, 'fine linen bedding, too fussy, like what a man thinks a woman would like'. 'Large, square bedroom. Obviously, a large house of at latest Victorian in period, fabulous cornicing and original ceiling rose, quite beautiful if you like that sort of thing?' Lola appraised the fixtures and fittings, judging each and making notes as to what they might tell her about the owner of this grand old place. 'Fire place, large and original, possible escape route... if there wasn't a fucking fire in the hearth!' The sudden thought of escape prompted movement towards the heavily shrouded windows. Pulling back those luxurious tapestry curtains she noted, with little surprise, that the windows were barred. He'd taken very

good care of every other detail, it was folly to think he would have left such an easy route out of here. Far from being put off, Lola moved around the rest of the room checking each and every detail for possible escape routes or weapons. What she hadn't noticed at the start but had become aware of now, was the lack of furnishings in the room. No fire pokers, no reassuringly heavy vases to crane off someone's head, a distinct lack of anything more dangerous than the pillow her head had so gratefully been resting on only some minutes before. Turning back towards that bed, and its heavenly comfort, she noticed, pinned to the bottom panel, a note. With a certain amount of trepidation, Lola walked carefully over to the base of the bed and picked it off.

Perching on the end of the bed Lola unfolded the note and scanned the contents. Written in a clear hand, nicely printed on thick, good quality paper, it read as follows -

'Your presence is required at dinner, follow the arrows outside your room for directions. There are clothes and shoes on the chair next to the fireplace, you need to be wearing these. Dinner is at eight o'clock, do not be late, do not attempt to stay in your room or run away. If you do, you will be killed and we wouldn't want that now would we Lola?'

Unsigned, it was short and to the point. Glancing at her watch she noticed it was now 7.45. That didn't leave a lot of time to formulate a plan of attack, didn't leave much time to do anything other than follow the instructions and go to dinner. She suddenly realised she was hungry, she hadn't eaten for a good long time, she needed food and had never been good without it. What had he left her to dress, what might befit such an occasion? Evening dress and some fabulous heels? Apparently not...

On the chair, she found a pair of running tights, a short sleeved gym top, pair of used trainers and a headband. All of which, she noted without alarm, were her own. 'Well, at least they'll fit' she thought to herself. What was he planning to do with her? Well, the fucker better be ready because she would fight like a wildcat, that's for sure!

Lola slipped off the business suit she always wore when she wasn't exercising, even now when she had no need for such attire. It was the one thing that made her feel like she was still fighting, still in the game. Standing in front of the large mirror on dressing table, she looked at herself.... She'd lost everything, everything except her figure. She was hard as nails!

5'8" and 62kg's of lean and strong muscle, she'd back herself against any woman, and most men for that matter. She'd always prided herself on her physical abilities, she had even given herself the nickname 'staffy' because she felt like a bull terrier, felt she had to be like a bull terrier. Full on, totally committed and never backing down. Her eyes were drawn to the tattoo just above her knicker line, a badly drawn dog. It was supposed to be a Staffordshire bull terrier, it was supposed to signify her attitude and philosophy, how no one would ever take her for granted, how she would never be bested, how she'd win at any cost and fuck those that might be stupid enough to stand in her way. That all seemed a little silly now. She'd had it done when she was just 17, the day after she left home and set out to make her fortune. The day after she buried her mother and disconnected herself from the family. It was a rebirth for her, the start of a new chapter. Gone were the days of watching her mother beg and scrape her way to a living, sucking the cocks of those fucking 'uncles' who'd always cop a feel of Lola if they got the chance, the dirty bastards! She'd spent her life watching her weak assed mother begging from one fix to the next, crying and shaming herself, and the rest of them, for a few quid to feed her addiction but not her children, fucking whore! She'd hated her not for being a whore, but for being a weak whore. For bowing to those men, letting them abuse her and her children. Lola was actually glad the day she overdosed and disappeared from her life, rejoiced in the end of this woman who'd done nothing but cower to men, she'd never be like that!

She was the youngest of four other gutless bastards. They'd had dads who'd stuck around for varying amounts of time and with varying motivations for doing so. Lola had been fucked by a couple of them and beaten by the others, all her 'family' had. What was different about Lola was that she never backed down. The rest of the spineless fuckers would try and cry their way out of a beating or meekly accept the abuse when it came their way, not her! She'd fight and bite and scratch and scream the fucking street down every time. Even when they asked if she'd had enough she'd muster any energy she had left to fly at them with all she had. Never give up, never give in! That had been her motto, that had been the philosophy that had got her through her childhood and made her the ferocious business woman she was.... Or rather, used to be. She regarded the sad tattoo, blurry and poorly done, as a metaphor for how she now felt. That fire in her belly, that grim determination and refusal to give in had gone. She couldn't claim to be the girl that deserved that tattoo anymore, she was more a fucking poodle than a staffy. How had it come to this? How had she allowed herself to be broken when no one had managed to do so before?

They'd all thought she was tough as old boots, those snivelling bastards at the bank. At the beginning, she'd been sneered at for her background and the thick London accent she possessed. They, those privileged and happy few, thought they could bully her into submission, they didn't know what bullying was! Cheap jokes and snide remarks were nothing to Lola after the hell of her childhood, water off a ducks back. She would show them what she was made of... and she did. As she went about her business with the tenacity and commitment of the tattoo she kept on her belly, those rich boys from the playing fields of England's finest schools soon changed their tune. She was a force to be reckoned with and knew the job inside and out. They never knew about the tattoo but would refer to her as 'the pitbull' purely as a coincidence and she loved it from the first time she over heard one of them talking about her and using the term. Soon it became her name, used quite openly and with the greatest of respect. This was, after all, a dog eat dog world that she inhabited and a pit bull was the king of all dogs in a fight! But they didn't know everything about her, they hadn't seen the real Lola.

Every day, as she walked from her cheap bedsit through the streets she grew up on, dirty and harsh, Lola passed a little park for kids to play in. It had been the brainchild of one of those 'do gooding' dickheads at the council. Give the scumbags somewhere to play and they'll stop dealing drugs and killing each other.... What a joke! It was only there to ease their conscience and help them sleep better in their Park Lane mansions. 'They'd done all they could!' would be the phrase, 'if those types insisted on behaving like that then what could they do?' They were a different breed, an alien species to the likes of those government nobs, sat in their West Minster towers. But as long as they could say they tried then that's all that mattered. Lola stuck out like a sore thumb in this borough, her only concession to the job she had and the money she was making was a number of fabulously sharp suits. She knew she had to look like them, even if she didn't sound like the others. So she would walk, every day, through the shit and the grime, broken bottles and needles strewn around. Through this park, that had been wrecked the moment it was finished and used almost exclusively by the dealers and prostitutes. Here, at six o'clock in the morning, it was silent and entirely without menace. She would only walk this way in the mornings, tough as she was even Lola wouldn't risk going home in the same fashion. Someone looking the way she did, 5'8", blond, sharp suit and not at all bad looking, was certain to be mugged or worse, and she didn't need that. It grated a little that she did this, avoided the quickest way home, paid for a taxi instead - if she could find one that would take her! But she wasn't about to throw it away through something as silly as pride.

Every morning she walked through the park and every morning she encountered only one other human being. All alone, dirty and with the glare of a feral animal, she would see him playing in the skate park. At first, he would move to the other side of the concrete slopes, warily eyeing Lola as she passed, she must have appeared quite the curiosity, something he'd never seen before. Over the days they began to get used to each others appearance, began to accept the fact that they would see each other. Lola pitied the boy. Why was he out here, in all weathers, at this time in a morning? How could he be so dirty before the day had even begun? It was his clothes that made him look so bad, ill fitting and worn through in all the contact areas. Those trainers were hanging off his feet and he was a collection of hand me downs and freebies from the local charity shops. He was always to be found in the skate park too, even though the boy had no board. Sometimes, when he hadn't noticed her approach, she'd caught him pretending to have one. Careering up and down the sides of the slopes making noises he imagined a board would make beneath him. This would bring a tear to the eye of the bull terrier.

Once she'd left a sandwich for him, he looked so pale and under nourished, just placed it on the side of the park as she passed. Hadn't said a word, just put it down and carried on walking. But, as she passed through the bushes she had stopped to see what he would do. He'd regarded it with suspicion at first, but then hunger had taken over and he'd devoured the offering greedily. She could see how the meal had been difficult to swallow, as if he wasn't used to eating food, at least, not this much food, and she'd wondered just how many times this boy had felt a full belly? From then on she never left the flat without some sustenance for the child and in time he began waiting at her side of the park. She remembered clearly the first morning he spoke to her, "thank you" he'd said, in a meek and unsure way. Later that morning she had disappeared to the toilets and cried, the scene still playing in her head. Weeks passed and they began to have a few words together, he'd gained confidence and would greet her with a "hello", sometimes mention the weather, sometimes tell her she looked different to everyone else "in a good way...." he'd supplement, aware enough that his words might be mistaken. Then, one morning, she carried her bag, the sandwich, and a parcel. Long and heavy, wrapped in shiny blue paper.

As she approached the boy she could see the wonder in his eyes, it was nearly Christmas and he recognised the parcel as a gift.

"What do you have there miss?" he'd asked, after taking the sandwich and tucking into it with eager delight.

She loved the way he called her 'miss', she felt properly important and grown up.

"It's a gift for someone special" she'd said and smiled warmly at the boy.

"Oh wow, it looks ace!" said the child, wiping his mouth with the dirty sleeve of his jumper. It was freezing but he had no coat.

"I'm hoping he'll like it," she said, before placing it on the ground before him "here.... it's for you!"

She could have said '...and now you're president of the world...' and not got a bigger reaction. Food dropped from his open mouth as he gazed in disbelief at the parcel and then at Lola. His arms fell to his side and some more of the sandwich detatched itself from the bread and dropped to the ground. For a while, he just stood in awe of the gift.

"Open it..." she said encouragingly, conscious of the fact that she didn't have long to spend here and she wanted to see his face when he found out what it was.

Carefully, like a man disposing of the outer casing of a bomb, the child removed the shiny blue paper. Inside, gleaming and new, he found a skate board. It happened, coincidentally, to be the very one he'd always wanted from the shop across the precinct. 'Matts Boards' had has this in the window for the last month now, it was the best one in the shop and way too expensive for the kids around here to buy. It was a proper 'pro' board. He'd dreamt of it, but not in a realistic way, he'd dreamt of any board if truth be known and never actually thought he'd get one. Now here it was, the ultimate.

He was struck dumb again, like those first few meetings, and could do nothing but gaze in wonder at what was in front of him. Gently, she clasped her warm hands to his cheeks and kissed him, "Merry Christmas" she said and walked away.

Lola never saw the child again. She could only guess at what had happened and the thought that the board she had bought had played some part in it caused her great pain. Even goodness... kindness, was ruined in this place. Taken and made filthy with the rest of this horror, she wouldn't be kind anymore.

At work she rose quickly through the ranks, they couldn't help but give her those promotions her success demanded and Lola made fortunes for the clients she serviced. Soon she had climbed as far as the top brass were ever going to let her. Lola knew that she'd never end up on the board, that was a closed club to girls and certainly never an option for some snotty kid from the rough end of town. She'd known this from the start and had saved every penny she made to use for her own portfolio. Just as she made those rich bastards in the hills of Monaco richer, she also gained a hell of a lot of money for herself. It was all done under a ghost account, she didn't want anyone finding out what she was doing, and the intention was to make enough by her 35th birthday to chuck it all in and retire somewhere hot and luxurious. Hawaii was the place to go, that was where she wanted to spend her time. When she was a child her favourite program was 'Magnum'. It was the contrast between those golden beaches and blue skies and what she saw outisde her own window, the life she was living. It seemed idylic to her, like a paradise on earth. For a long time she thought places like that, places with smiles and sunshine, didn't exist. She also loved the justice of the show. Someone always needed help and Magunum and his friends would somehow manage to come through in the end. Before the show finished, the bad men would get what was coming to them and good would win out. It was nothing but a fairy tale to her, but she clung to it as hard as she could. One time she remembered one of her 'uncles' taking a fancy to her and she just let it happen, hardly kicked or screamed at all. It had been only a few moments before the show was going to start and she didn't want to miss it. All she could think at the time was 'get on with it and finish so I can watch my program'. He had and she'd rushed straight to the manky sofa, blood dribbling down from her nose and one eye clsoing, to catch it. It was one of the very few things in her life that meant something to her and that was why she would live there one day, and everything would be right again. She'd been well on her way too, it had all been going to plan until around five years ago.....

What had the voice said on the audio? 'the bastard child of a drunk whore...' and 'apples never fall far from the tree!' Had he been wrong? She'd hated her mother for the things she had done, for what she had let happen to them, but was she really that different? Glenda - Lola always referred to her mother by her name, she hadn't said 'mum' since she was eight years old or less - had, by the accounts of her auntie Jane, been a good mother in the beginning. She'd fallen for the wrong boy early and fallen pregnant not much later. He'd been a toe rag 'wannabe' footballer, trials with West Ham - hadn't everyone? who'd promised so much but delivered little but rose tattoos and contempt. Whilst she'd worked hard trying to keep a job and raise a kid, he'd done everything to drag her down and make her feel shitty. His failings, his self-loathing was better transferred to her. Whenever he screwed up, and it was often, it was her fault in some way or other. He controlled her in every negative way and reduced what was once a vibrant and engaging young woman into a shell of her former self. She wasn't allowed out of the house, save to go to work and even then he'd walk her to and from the supermarket. Often she'd see him spying on her whilst she worked and if she were pleasant to a male customer then he'd give her what for that evening. Once he'd spotted her laughing with her manager, nothing more than a joke shared between colleagues, and later that evening he waited for the bloke in the car park. It was a terrible scene and even if she'd had the nerve to go back to work afterwards she'd have probably been sacked anyway. As much as they liked Glenda, you can't have your staff living in fear of attack every time they need to speak to someone. And so it was that the downward spiral began. He'd gotten into drink and drugs, selling some but consuming more. It was a habit that needed feeding and he insisted on his dutiful wife following suit. Soon their home became a den for the dregs of society and no place for a toddler... or a mother with another baby on the way. Auntie Jane believed that if it hadn't been for the intervention of both social services and a welcome prison break, Glenda would have lost both the baby and her life in no short space of time.

With the tormentor out of the way, she was free to get her life back on track, but the scars he left were not so easily healed. She'd lost her confidence as well as her 'normal' friends - categorised simply as 'those people who didn't abuse her'. Glenda had a small child, another on the way, zero self-esteem and a group of people around her that did nothing to change that situation. It's human nature to associate yourself with people you see as your equals and, tragically, Glenda thought no better of herself than these serial abusers. When husband No.1 did get out of prison he wanted nothing more to do with her and you may have thought this a blessing, but the damage had already been done. She lurched from one scumbag to the next, collecting children, scars, and further confirmation that she was a worthless soul, no better than the life she was living, if you could call it a life? Lola had been the last of the litter. Soon after her birth, Glenda had been beaten up so badly that she'd had to have a hysterectomy. This over an argument about a pair of shoes she'd bought for her eldest. Money was in short supply and should be used for drugs before any consideration of the children!

She eventually got free of this latest abomination but not of the life she was leading and so she began to sell the only thing she had left. There's not much business for a woman in her thirties looking like a hag in her fifties, unless, of course, you're willing to put up with certain 'kinks'. Those men that visited the house now were the very worst of people. Vile acts for little more than the next fix, and they didn't care for kids. The rest of the story Lola knew first hand.

As she stood there, nearly naked in the mirror, she could see elements of who her mother used to be. They were a similar height and although Lola was athletic and toned, they had a similar body shape and structure. Some of the fire had gone out of Lola's eyes too. These last few years had taken their toll and she had lost that fight she had always prided herself on. She'd lost all that self-confidence too. Lola had seen her life turned upside down, been beaten and broken by the things life had thrown at her, and standing here now, she finally understood how her mother had felt. Shit, she'd lost her money and her status, lost the job she'd loved and hadn't had the fortitude to start again. The way she saw it, life hadn't dealt her half the shitty cards it had Glenda and yet she hadn't been able to handle it. 'Fuck that!' she said to herself.

Whatever this bastard had in mind, she was up to it. Whatever he wanted to throw at her, she was going to take it and push through. She'd show him what she was made of and he'd regret the day he thought he could get the better of her! Some motivational speech came washing into her mind - 'life isn't all sunshine and rainbows, it's a very mean and nasty place and I don't care how tough you are, it will beat you to your knees and keep you there if you let it. You, me or nobody is going to hit as hard as life, but it ain't about how hard you hit, it's about how hard you can get hit and keep moving forward, how much you can take and keep moving forward. That's how winning is done. Now if you know what you're worth, go out and get what you're worth, but you've got to be willing to take the hits and not point your finger saying you ain't where you're supposed to be because of him or her or anybody. Cowards do that and that ain't you... You're better than that!' And she was.... she was better than that. She'd been knocked down and kicked around and had forgotten who she was supposed to be, well not anymore. Setting her jaw and lifting her chin high, Lola put her clothes on, tied her hair back and glared at herself in the mirror once more. She felt taller, stronger and full of hell.

Chapter 3 - The Gathering

'Dining Room' the sign read, 'well this must be it' Daniel thought to himself. Pathologically early for everything, he checked his temperature compensated Sinn UX watch. Ten minutes early, not bad for him! Usually, he was a good twenty five or more. He'd once been late for his Sunday paper round, his father had ensured that he never was again. Some may have said that his father was nothing more that a sadist and a bully, a child beating bastard with deep lying psychological issues that would take a thousand shrinks a hundred years to unravel. Dan chose to look upon the memory of his systematic abuse as training for the big, bad world. His disgraceful old dad was a hero who'd taught him what he needed to know in order to get on in this world. He was strong and had tried to build that strength in his children. That he'd died in prison after leaving them motherless was hardly his fault. She'd failed to understand what was required and had needed 'correcting' just one too many times.

Steeling himself for the unknown, he pushed open the large, solid oak door and marched into the room like he owned it. This was a trick he'd employed a thousand time before, back when he owned the marketing company. Always act like you're the most important man in the room. Walk tall, head high, take no shit from nobody!... There wasn't a soul to be seen.

Surveying the room Daniel looked for exits and danger points in equal measure, finding plenty of one and none of the other. Large and oblong in shape, it was typical of what you would expect from an old country mansion. Lots of dark wood panelling, leather chairs and side tables, lush Persian rugs and a bloody enormous fire place. Big enough, he thought, to roast a human, should it be necessary? It had a bloody enormous fire crackling away in its hearth too, so no chance of escaping up the chimney. As with the windows in the room he had awoken, there were sturdy steel bars putting pay to any hopes of freedom. Daniel walked around the centre piece, a fabulous burr wood table of giant proportions, exactly what one needed for such a grand dining area. Decorated with fine china and crystal glasses, it was all set for dinner.... dinner for six. So there were five others, well, discounting the host, which he judged to be the place setting at the head of the table, four other people were to be expected. He could see cards set out in front of each place too, so being a curious soul he wandered round to see.

First up, walking anti clockwise to the table, he found himself, Daniel Ferris - Marketer/Charletan. Fair comment, he thought, he'd always felt that way anyway. That was the essence of the job! Next came James Evans - Lawyer/puppet. What the hell did that mean? Daniel didn't even try to make sense of it, he only cared that he was a Lawyer, and Daniel had never cared for Lawyers! Next up, Thomas Dean - Designer/Cockmunch. 'Ha!' Daniel chuckled to himself a little, he'd much rather be a charlatan than a cockmunch! So far he felt like the best one there. Moving along, Lola Cooper - Investment Banker/Slum whore. 'Oooh, now she sounds delightful' he mused sarcastically, 'wasn't it always the way, the cockmunch gets to sit next to the only bit of totty in the place!' Finally, Simon Brown - IT/Posh wanker. Well, that was the competition was it? A Lawyer, a puff, a bitch and a toff, this should be a fucking breeze! If he couldn't get the better of this bunch of tossers then he didn't deserve the money. God did he need the money! Those wolves had been at his door, found a key under the mat, let themselves in and were having tea and biscuits in his dining room....

Daniel was snapped out of his thoughts by the creaking of the dining room door. Slowly, and with the sort of entry Daniel scorned, a man emerged from behind the great lump of oak. Glancing around the room furtively, before fixing his eyes on Daniel the man crept tentatively into the space.

Taking his opportunity to gain the upper hand, Daniel spoke "So who do we have here then, the Lawyer, fruit or toff?" he asked, in a superior way. "Come in and join the party"

Shading six feet in height, the man had very short black hair. It was only cut in that style because its better days were behind it. Daniel judged that this fella was probably a deal younger than he looked but the balding head and paunch in the belly added a few years to his appearance. He was the kind of man who should be thin as a rake but had added some bulk through an inactive life.

"What?" he asked in reply, before adding "Who the fuck are you? what's going on here?... Where are we?"

"Slow down chief!" he said, raising a hand as a visible clue "Let's do this one piece at a time and given I asked first, let's start with who the fuck you are!" Daniel only knew the answer to one of those questions anyway but he wasn't about to start this conversation being the 'answers bitch'. "Jim, yes?"

Looking suspiciously at Daniel, pausing a moment to collect his thoughts, he said: "How did you know?"

"Process of elimination old man, it would appear that there are five of us for dinner" and he gestured towards the place settings.

Feeling a little braver about the situation, he walked around the table scrutinising each card as he passed. Daniel gave him some room as he did so and went to lean against the fire place.

After reading each card twice, he asked: "So which one are you then?"

"Have a guess old man" Daniel said with a smile, pleased he had this boy off guard for the time being.

"First up, I'm not an old man! Second, I'm not the guessing type, so why don't you quit with the nonsense and tell me who the fuck you are?" there was a good deal of irritation in his voice.

"Easy Jim.... No need to get shirty! I'm only playing with you..."

"Yeah? Well, I don't play!" he said with authority.

"Ok chief..." Daniel still kept the attitude of the one in control "Name's Ferris, like the Bueller, but you can call me Dan" and he smiled like a crocodile, all teeth, and no eyes.

Just then, striding purposely into the room came the next of the five.

"Somebody better have some fucking answers..." he announced as he glared at the two men in front of him.

Daniel regarded this guy as a much bigger threat, full of attitude and authority. Trying to knock him down a peg he said "You must be Simon? Have to say, you don't sound that posh to me?"

"What the fuck are you talking about? My names Jim... Who the hell are you?"

Any feelings of superiority Daniel had, left with that admission. If this was Jim, who was the other guy? He stared at the mystery man for a second before answering.

"Dan.... I'm Dan but I've no idea who this dude is?" and he regarded the man by the table with a critical eye. "Why don't you tell us who you are?"

"Awww, don't you wanna to guess no more?" he said in a mocking fashion before turning to the new comer "The names Thomas Dean, apparently I'm the 'cockmunch', although you wouldn't guess to look at me, would you Dan?" and he laughed.

"Alright slack arse, don't get fucking clever! You should be pleased I didn't think you were a chutney...." Irritated by the fact that he'd put one over on him, Daniel decided to be offensive.

"Oh, so there's something wrong with being gay is there? And which fucking century are you still living in, Mr. Troglodyte?"

Before hostilities could really take hold, James interrupted the flow "What do you mean 'cockmunch'? and what's going on?"

The two men glared at each other for a moment before Thomas turned to answer. He also took this opportunity to properly appraise the new man in the room. Around 5'8" tall and stockily built, he didn't look anything like what you might expect from a lawyer and certainly didn't seem like he'd be anyone's puppet. He was the sort of man you'd see on 'ninja warrior', giving it a go but failing. More because of age than ability and that would be the exact reason for him being there. Jim was all of about fifty but was fighting it as best he could.

"It seems that we all have place mats with two pieces of information on them. Apparently, there are five of us and there's a place set at the head of the table for whom I assume will be the man with the plan, and the answers. What exactly it is that we're expected to do is anyone's guess at the moment?"

"You'll be hoping for a cock sucking competition I bet..." Dan sneered, still peeved that Thomas had pulled the wool over his eyes. He really didn't care about someone's sexuality, he was just pissed off he'd been made a fool of.

"Well if it is, then my money is on the marketing bitch!" he sneered right back. "Scratch that, tits Magee has my vote!"

Lola had just entered the room and was stood a few feet behind James, feeling like she'd been set up. All the others were dressed in suits and she was head to toe in lycra.

Just then Simon hurried in to make an uneasy five, the three at the door all feeling a little too close for comfort. Before anything could be said, the chime of the grandfather clock at the top end of the room indicated it was eight o'clock on the nose. They all stopped and looked at it, waiting for something to happen.... and something did.

A bookcase, one of two either side of the grandfather, moved slowly backwards into the wall. From behind it emerged the man of the hour, the host for the evening and the possessor of the voice on the audio, Mr. Jon Ayres. He wasn't an overly tall man, maybe six one at best, but he was quite an imposing figure, beautifully clad in fine cloth that had been tailored to a high standard. They were all used to seeing expensively attired people, but Jon was as perfectly turned out as any man could be. Not fashionable, 'classic' is what you would have said and he wore it well. Hair slicked back from his head and neatly parted from the left, he had a chiseled appearance that this particular style accentuated. Clean shaven and bespectacled, he gave one the appearance of a politician, only one of those shadowy types that's always in the picture but no one knows exactly who he is. Private advisor to, or personal assistant of.... The sort of man you'd suspect was actually running things. He walked into the room accompanied by, none other than, the taxi driver. Only his appearance had changed somewhat. Instead of presenting himself as the typical 'casual cabbie' he was now bedecked in similar garb to the master. He'd not pulled it off quite so well and was clearly the subordinate in the partnership, but he still cut a fine figure and now that he was seen upright, an impressive one at that. Easily six three in height and almost as wide, he was not the sort of man to trifle with. As different as his appearance was, his economy with the spoken word remained the same. Jon addressed the crowd.

'Good evening lady and gentlemen' he said genially, opening his arms out in a welcoming fashion. 'Pray, take your seats and we may begin the evening with some answers, I'm sure you're all desperate to know more'

'Just tell me where the fucking exit is.... that's all I want to know' Simon said, but his voice held none of the certainty that he had hoped it would.

'Oh, Mr. Brown... I do hope your head isn't causing you too much discomfort? I fear I may have struck you a little harder than was necessary'

Simon felt the back of his head with his right hand and winced a little as he touched the tender lump that the cosh had left there.

'Don't worry about that, it's fine, just tell me how to get out of here...' but he knew there would be no positive answer to this question.

'As you suspect Mr. Brown, as you all do, there is only one way out of here but we'll come to that in a while. Please take your seats and I'll give you the necessary details about tonight's activities.' Jons demeanor remained that of the dinner party host. He motioned to the cards around the other side of the table and took his seat at the head of it, some fifteen feet away. His right-hand monkey adopted a position directly behind him, standing with his arms behind his back, in front of the clock that had signalled their arrival.

Suspiciously, the five took their place at the table, each eyeing the others in a critical way. They eased themselves into the chairs ever so carefully, making sure they weren't the first to sit squarely at the table. The silence in the room at this moment only added to the tension they were all feeling.

"Why are you here?" Jon broke the silence with this clearly rhetorical question.

"Because you're a fucking nutcase?" Thomas muttered, half under his breath.

"No!!!" Jon slammed his hand down on the table, sending his cutlery dancing into the air and very nearly overturning his crystal wine glass. It was the first show of irritation from the host and they all sat up and took notice.

"No, Mr. Dean," he said, after collecting himself and allowing a little time for the colour to leave his cheeks "you're here because you're broke and you don't like it," he said quietly "you're here because you thought you were invincible. Your egos have lead you along this path, I simply dropped the breadcrumbs."

There was silence in the room. After his show of emotion, those gathered felt the best way to get to the bottom of this most unusual event was to give their host/captor the time to speak. Afterall, he'd want to tell them what it was all about wouldn't he? That would surely be part of the fun? Jon picked up his glass and appraised the aroma of the fine Burgundy within before checking its 'legs' and colour.

"I suggest you fill your glasses and remain quiet, this is a rather fine drop and I have a lot to say."

Simon, after part filling his glass and talking himself out of the 'it's probably poisoned' theory, sniffed the wine with the confidence of a connoisseur. He'd secretly enjoyed the previous irritation and thought he'd see if he could further annoy the man holding all the cards.

"Smells like a pretty standard Malbec to me... Mendoza, not much age... tannins could do with another year or two in the bottle I'd say..." Seeing the look on Jon's face he couldn't help but curl his lips in delight. 'Score one for me' he thought to himself and settled back in the chair. He was damned if he was going to cow down to this bastard!

Whispering in his ear, Lola said "slick move dick head!"

The others just looked daggers.

With some effort, forcing himself to remain calm but failing to prevent a display of extreme displeasure, Jon hissed "This, Mr. Brown, is a fucking 'Richebourg 85' you god damn heathen!"

Before he could continue Simon quickly interjected with "couldn't you afford the 'Romanee-Conti'?... cheap bastard!" and laughed.... Nobody else did.

Jon, realising he'd been goaded and taken the bait so cheaply, recovered his poise. "Well done Mr. Brown, you had me there. Now if you'll allow me to continue?..."

Simon simply raised his glass and smiled. Lola, again in a whisper, said: "you're a dead man!"

"As I was saying before I was so amusingly interrupted. You're all here because you chose to be. Each one of you used to be on top of your world, you had it all and now you've lost it. You miss those days, that money and the things you had and you want them back. When I offered you the opportunity, you all came willingly. Let us not forget, before we go any further, that you chose to be here. Chose to take part in this for the chance to get back what you once had."

One dissenting voice from the group spoke up. "I didn't! I wanted to go back and you gassed me in the taxi"

"Alas yes, Miss Cooper, that is true. You see this evenings entertainment had been set up for five participants and I couldn't have that spoiled by one of you ducking out. Getting you into the taxi was always going to be easy, into the van was the tricky bit. But let's not get caught up in that right now. You're here and you have a game to play, there's no turning back"

"That leads us neatly to 'why you'? Why did I pick you five to play this game? Truth is, I didn't..." Jon had stood and was walking around the table. "What I did do was have the idea. I'd really no clue as to who would be here this evening? You see, you all thought you were so fucking special, unique. You believed in your singular abilities and fed your own egos with each minor victory along the way. You became so wrapped up in your own little worlds that you believed yourselves the masters of them... but you weren't! This is what I wanted to show you, just how pitifully small and insignificant you are."

Stopping behind the back of the table and resting his glass on the mantle of the fire place, Jon continued "Tell me.... Who amongst you has anyone, anyone at all, who's going to miss you?" he left the question hanging "Who is going to raise the alarm when you don't go home tonight? What if you never went home, would anyone care? Would anyone notice? You built your lives and pinned your successes on business deals, on money and beating the next guy. All those trinkets and symbols of status you treasured so much and told you how special you were... What do they mean to you now? Once they were gone what did you have left to show for your wonderful lives? Nothing! Not one of you ever did anything good with your money, never formed any sort of meaningful relationships..."

Thomas Dean decided to cut into the monologue "I've got my baby, he'll miss me if I don't get home tonight."

"Oh yes, that snivelling little-pampered rat of yours..." Jon was obviously unimpressed with this offering "...that's the best you can do gay boy!" he spat before continuing "well take heart, it's a good deal better than any of your competitors"

Collecting his glass, he began circling the table again. "You thought you were special and you are, in a way. You see we started this thing five years ago now with over fifty targets. All high earners, high achievers you might say, and all with egos to match. There are thousands like you in London alone, millions across the world, and we wanted to find the worst kind. People with families were discounted, even if they didn't really care for them. People who showed compassion and understanding were scratched off too. We cut out all those who actually made a contribution to this world and were left with fifty. From there it was a case of who'd take the bait. Many refused to enter into the tontine, some we simply couldn't ruin. They were hard nosed bastards but they didn't leave themselves as open as you. You five... You were the only ones who chased so hard and so blindly, had such unflinching belief in your own supremacy over all others, that you couldn't see it coming. You are special in that you're the greediest and most narcissistic fools we could find. And so you ended up here."

James, who had remained silent up to this point, decided to speak "But you still haven't told us why? I'm not going to argue with you about my character, what I've done and what that makes me... I'll live with that, but why, why did you 'collect' us?" He was cool and collected, James had been in some rough situations with the clients he'd represented and had become accustomed to displaying a detached attitude. He'd seen people have their fingers cut off right there in front of him. Knee cappings, brandings, it had made him sick to the stomach at first, but he kept telling himself it wasn't him that was doing it and if he didn't take the money then some other ruthless, cold bastard would.

"Let's say I'm a humanist..." Jon grinned "and it feels like my duty to rid the world of those creatures that cause nothing but pain to others. For you have caused pain and suffering haven't you?"

Jon was back at his chair. Refilling his glass, he made himself comfortable, leaned back and put his feet on the table.

"You Mr. Evans..." and he pointed his glass "...you've seen plenty of pain and suffering haven't you. Seen it, stood by and done nothing about it. Just took the money all the same."

"I didn't do any of that stuff, it wasn't me that hurt them" he returned.

"Oh no, but you didn't try to stop them did you? Remember a girl, maybe ten years old? The daughter of a greengrocer who owed your 'clients' money."

James looked away, muttered under his breath "Yes... I remember her very clearly" There was a faint break in his voice as he said it, caused by the pain of the memory.

"Do you know how much he owed?... Two grand Mr. Evans, probably less than the suit you were wearing that night, and what was it they did to that child?"

James shook his head, it disgusted him to think about it. This had been the night that he had lost himself to it completely. After witnessing that... that horror, nothing else touched him again. He'd become desensitized to all of it, like a robot simply performing its programmed duties. They'd made him go, to make sure he would never cross them, implicate him in the deed and own his silence from there on.

"Cat got your tongue?... Who do you think got hers?" Jon asked. Then, addressing the group "That little girl, Katie was her name, used to sing and dance. Dreamt of being an actress in the west end, had talent too, so I heard. Not anymore. They cut out her tongue in front of her father and broke both her ankles over two lousy grand and he just stood there and watched!"

It was one of the reasons James had never married or had a family. He was too afraid of what might happen to them should his 'association' go bad. He kept a packed case in his wardrobe with a passport and some money, but he was pretty sure he'd not see it coming if the worst were to happen. These people didn't mess around.

"You sick fuck!" Daniel moved his chair away from the table, repulsed by the man next to him. "I've never liked lawyers but you've taken it to a whole new level"

James said nothing, there was nothing he could say. What had happened was indefensible and he knew it. He didn't care what the rest of them thought about him, they couldn't think anything worse than he already did about himself.

"Let he who be without sin cast the first stone Daniel, you're hardly an angel yourself now are you?"

"Maybe not, but I've never hurt a child or had anyone's life ruined like that," he said contemptuously.

"No?... Is that actually true? Talk to me about Africa then Bueller!"

Daniel didn't reply, he just stared at the host as the colour left his cheeks.

"A person falsely claiming to have special knowledge or skill - charlatan. It seems like a fairly innocent thing to say about someone doesn't it? But it's a matter of context. If one were to, let's say, falsely represent a companies product and make claims that were not only untrue but absolutely the very opposite of what was needed. If one were to claim to fix a problem that didn't exist, bribe government officials into allowing this deceit. Pay trusted people to

endorse the use of a product that would, in time, become a necessity to those who could ill afford it. Devise a strategy that would hook those most vulnerable into using this product before making it so expensive that families would have to choose which child would get the drug and which would perish... Then it doesn't sound quite so innocent, does it Mr. Squeaky fucking clean? No child's blood on your hands? I don't think so. Just because you weren't there to witness it, doesn't mean you're not responsible. No one else would touch the campaign, would they? But you took the money gladly..."

Jon glared across the large, wooden table but Daniel refused to make eye contact.

"I.... I didn't know...." was all he could muster.

"Didn't know you'd be killing little African babies?...." Jon posed "Oh but you did Mr. Ferris and you didn't care one jot. Made enough from that job to buy yourself a Ferrari I believe. Blood red, by any chance?"

He let the words hang in the air for a while, let the impact of what they had done sink in. To have the very worst of you laid out before strangers, to be judged in that way, made the memory burn.

"Before the rest of you become all high and mighty about this, let's just say that none of you are innocent. You've all got blood on your hands whether you like the fact or not."

"Hang on a second..." Lola said, a little affronted "yeah I've screwed people over to get ahead, but I never hurt no one who was innocent, those bastards at the bank would have done the same to me in a heart beat, I was just quicker and better at it than them."

She was indignant and flatly refused to be lumped in with these scum bags.

"I did wonder if the gutter trash would object" and his voice held a spiteful tone "you're quite wrong though."

"Oh yeah, who did I hurt then Mr know all?"

"Ahh, now here's a real sad story!" There was more than a touch of smugness about the way he said it. "With the other two, the motive was very clear, money! That's all it was for them but sometimes our motives are different. Guilt, shame, regret, these all play a part in the things we do but often we don't

admit them to ourselves. We like to pretend that we are doing a good thing for goodness sake, but... deep down, we know that this isn't true, don't we Lola?"

"I've no fucking idea what you're talking about?" she said, quite genuinely.

"Really? How's the family Lola? When was the last time you saw any of them? Do you even know what they are doing now, if they're alive or dead?"

"Sorry, but I fail to see what my useless family has to do with any of this?"

"Then allow me to enlighten you..." and he held both his hands out in front of him, palms up, in a mock religious gesture. "...you see when you got out of that slum and away from your brothers and sisters, you vowed never to look back. You cut all ties with those people that loved you and struck out on your own. Not once did you consider going back and helping them out. Never did it cross your mind that you should, that it was your duty. You were going to succeed and to do that you had to banish the past, banish your own family too. This you did quite skillfully and with very little trouble of conscience until one day you met a scruffy little urchin in the park. He reminded you of your past life didn't he? Brought back those memories and you considered what his life must be like. Probably he was stuck in a very similar situation. More likely than not he was going through just the same things you had, all those years ago. He made you remember your family and how you had abandoned them, shamed you didn't it? And so you befriended him. You fed him and gave him kindness, maybe for the first time in his miserable little life. You even bought him a skate board for Christmas."

"Yep, still not seeing where I'm the bastard in this?" she said.

Jon eyed Lola steadily before continuing "No? Motives Lola, motives!... You didn't do this for the child, you weren't being kind, you were trying to ease your guilty conscience, that's all. You were 'helping' him in order to feel better about what you had done to your own flesh and blood. But you never saw him again after you gave him the present, did you? Why do you think that is, you must have wondered?"

"I've really no idea, maybe he moved away?" but she didn't sound convinced.

"Crap!" he said sharply "You were from the same background, you know what happened..."

Lola looked intensely at Jon and spoke very deliberately "I've no idea what happened.... All I did was buy a little boy a present to make him happy!"

"Well if you're not going to play along then I best tell you what happened after. Little boy appears with an expensive 'gift' in a house that's not got a pot to piss in. Some half baked tale of a woman in a suit buying it for him. It comes out that she's been feeding him too. Poor little bastard gets kicked all over the house and his precious present is quickly sold for a quicker fix. He's never allowed to go to the park - his only sanctuary from the hell that is home - again and comes to the conclusion that nothing good will ever happen to him. Oh, his home life isn't your fault, you can't be blamed for that. But you knew fine well what would happen to him when you gave him that board, knew but didn't want to admit it. You didn't buy it for him, you bought it for yourself and in doing so you hurt that child as surely as if you'd beaten him with your own hands. You can't claim ignorance here Lola, you grew up in that environment. You can tell me you didn't know, tell yourself too, but you did... You knew fine well what would happen but you did it anyway."

Lola had only allowed herself to suspect what had occurred and quickly banished these thoughts for kinder, rosier pictures. She did know, deep down, the trouble that present would cause as well as knowing why it was that she needed to give it. She had dressed it up in kindness but that wasn't what it was really about. With her chin raised and her lips set firm, she said: "You're a bastard!"

"You've no idea..." he said in return.

Time was moving on, these little side tracks were eating into the evening and there was a schedule to keep. Jon waved a hand at the former cabbie behind him and after a whispered instruction he disappeared out of the room.

"What's next then? More tales of dastardly acts against humanity? Is this the grand plan for the evening? doesn't sound too thrilling to me" Simon said with a forced smile.

"No no Mr. Brown, we've got a long nights activities to come but you'll need feeding beforehand. My associate has just gone to fetch your suppers. When he returns I'll tell you what we have in store and you can fill your bellies whilst you listen."

Soon the cabbie/henchman returned with a large silver bowl, steaming under its lid. Placing this in the middle of the five he removed the top to reveal a vat of porridge and chopped bananas. The group regarded this offering quizzically. In answer to those looks, Jon called out

"Complex carbohydrates people, keep you going for hours. Lots of energy in those little oats and I suggest you fill up because you're going to need them."

"From Richebourg to groul, what is this, some Dickens-Gatsby fusion?" Simon looked around the group but no one raised a smile, miserable sods!

Ignoring the comment Jon began to speak as they filled their bowls dutifully.

"You know 'why' you are here and you know why 'you' are here, but you don't know what you have to do here. Allow me to explain. Each of you entered into a 'Tontine' believing you would be the winner, or if not then you would be dead and it wouldn't matter anyway. Well, that's not quite how it's going to work. Those rules, as you understood them, were that the last surviving member of the pact would be the one that collected the investment. This is exactly right, only, instead of nature taking its course, I've decided we're going to speed things up a bit. By the end of the night, one of you will be ten million pounds richer. By the end of the night, only one of you will still be alive."

It was what they had all suspected, at one point of the day or another, but hadn't wanted to hear.

"We're going to see which one of you really has that killer instinct. Who has the will to win above all else. You all think you're special, or at least you used to do, well we're going to find out which one of you really is."

"With a porridge eating competition?"

Simon was really starting to get on Jon's nerves!

"No Mr. Brown, with a series of games. With the knowledge I have, I've devised an individual 'game' for each of you. You will attempt to win this game in isolation from the others. If you fail, and some of you most certainly will, then you will die. However, you have my word that you each have the capacity to win. Whether you have the heart, only time will tell."

Jon waved a hand in the air which set the butler/cabbie/henchman in motion. Silently, he moved around the table and deposited an arm band in front of each member of the group. James eyed the curious item with suspicion. It appeared to be made of the sort of material you find in wet suits - he'd done some diving in his time - with a dark screen, about two inches square, in the middle of it. In total, it was about five inches long with a Velcro fastener to adjust it to the thickness of one's arm. Casting an eye around him he noticed that all of these things were the same. All of his competitors seemed to be going through the same mental appraisal too. No one had, as yet, picked one up or attempted to attach it to an arm.

"These bands are for your benefit and you must wear them at all times. If you remove them at any point then you will be disqualified from the game and, consequently, lose any chance of winning the money. Is that clear?"

John waited a moment, expecting at least one dissenting voice or question, but none came.

"They have a display that will be very useful for you. Not only will it give you a guide as to where you need to go once you've completed your game, but it will also tell you, through a series of dots, how many people are left in the game. If you get within ten feet of another player then their dot will start to flash on your screen."

"Hold on a minute..." said James "what do you mean 'where we have to go after the game?'"

"Mr. Evans, you have entered into a 'Tontine', it is possible that you will all complete your games with your lives in tact. Only one of you can win the money, so... Once you've finished the game and have been released from your room, you will need to make your way to the aviary at the other side of the house. This device will give you some guidance as to the way you need to go. If yours is the only dot left on the device then your task is a simple one. If, however, there are other dots still illuminated, you will need to extinguish them before you enter the aviary. Only when there is one dot left can the owner of that device enter the room and claim the prize."

"So you're expecting us to kill each other for the money?" Lola said, hesitantly.

"Oh yes! That's the point of the evening. I'm curious to see which one of you bastards will make it to the end."

"Don't you think that's a little unfair on me? I'm strong for a woman but I'm not as powerful as these fellas."

"That is why, Ms. Cooper, I've left a little present in each room to even things up a bit. You'll all have a weapon to take with you, should you make it past the game."

Thomas Dean, who had suddenly come over quite pale and nauseous, stammered "I'm not going to kill anyone..."

Simon, who had remained quiet for a surprising amount of time, decided to pose a question "What if we all decide not to play your sick little game then? What if we decide to kick the crap out of you and Odd Job there and break out of this place instead?"

John took out a remote control from his pocket and press a button in the direction of the fire place behind them. Noiselessly, the large portrait of some old dead guy on a horse rotated slowly and was replaced with a TV screen. They all swivelled in their chairs to see.

After a momentary pause, the screen flickered into to life to reveal a small, curly haired dog tied to a pole on a short lead.

"Cujo!" said Thomas, and quickly looked around at John "please!!!.... please don't hurt him!"

"This is Thomas' dog, 'Cujo', and he's very much like all of you. Just a small fucking dog sat wondering what is going to happen to him. Unfortunately, for Cujo, he doesn't get the opportunity to save his life by playing our games tonight. He is simply here as an example of what will happen to you, should you decide you don't want to play.... So let's see shall we?"

The picture panned out to reveal a yard with a number of cages at the far side of it. In those cages were at least six snarling hounds. As they watched, two of the cages opened and the inhabitants of each rushed out and made swift progress across the yard towards Cujo. Simon and Lola both looked away in horror, they had no stomach to see what was about to happen. Thomas screamed at the television before burying his head in his hands.

Daniel and James watched and felt sick to the stomach as the poor wretch was ripped to pieces in a matter of seconds. They all fell silent.

"Now, Mr. Brown, do you really think I've gone to all this trouble to get you here. Set all this up without considering some form of dissent in the ranks? I'm the big dog here you little prick and I say you fight. If you try anything you'll end up in Cujo's position, I promise you that! Now put the fucking arm bands on before I get annoyed and throw you all to the dogs."

When they turned around again to face the host they noticed the henchman was now armed with some sort of automatic rifle and was waving it in their general direction.

"He's an excellent shot and I can assure you that he'd do nothing but incapacitate you. Your actual death would be much more painful and drawn out. So once again you have a choice, thrown to the dogs for certain, painful death, or put the devices on and see if you can win this game. It's up to you."

Thomas' eyes were red from the tears that had been rubbed harshly out of them "You fucking bastard... I'll kill you for this, I'll fucking kill you!..."

Calmly, without a hint of emotion, John replied: "Well you better win the game then hadn't you cockmunch."

They each attached the device to their arms and when the last one had completed the job John pressed another button on his remote. They sprang into life. As stated, each displayed five dots at the top of the screen and they were all flashing, given they were all within ten feet of each other. In the middle of the screen, their was another flashing dot that they were told represented their position within the building. From this dot, like the 'sweep' on a radar machine, there was a direction displayed to indicate which way to go.

"There's a couple of things I need to tell you about those bands. Firstly, held within the fabric is a small vial of poison that, at the press of a button" and he indicated this on his remote "will inject all of it into your blood stream. It will take but seconds to work. So don't try any funny business on the way to your rooms. Secondly, I've no idea which dot represents which one of you. I'm a man that likes surprises! I'll watch you in your games rooms but once you're free from there then I'll be waiting in the aviary excited to see who makes it. Lastly, those devices are fitted with a heart rate monitor and a temperature gauge. Simply removing the device will not make the dot disappear, you will be presumed alive unless your heart rate stops and your body cools at a natural rate. If you do take it off - and you know you cannot win if you do - your dot will

turn blue. Don't think you won't be found and please don't think your end, once you have been, will be in any way pleasant. Oh, and finally, you have until midnight to win the game and arrive at the aviary, there is a countdown timer on your device to keep you informed. Any questions?" and he looked from one to the next.

"You really are a first class son of a bitch, I'm going to kill you very slowly indeed!" Simon said with grim determination.

"Somehow I doubt you'll get the chance, Mr. Brown."

"There's one thing you haven't considered..." Daniel said with a slight smile.

"Oh, and what might that be Mr. Ferris?" Jon looked perfectly calm about this.

"I'll tell you later..."

Chapter 4 - Snakes and Ladders

"Well, why don't we get you started straight away then, you can be the first contestant Mr. Ferris. If that's alright with you?" Jon looked amused by Daniels comment and not in the least bit worried, but inside his head was a whir of boxes ticked and bases covered. Had he missed something? Could he have made a glaring error and just not been able to spot it?

"Suits me chief, bring it on!" he tried to sound relaxed and jovial about it, but his twitching fingers betrayed him.

Jon waved a hand at the henchman/butler and he silently moved around the table until he stood at Daniels seat. Without a word, he beckoned him to follow and proceeded to the door.

"You'll be taken to your room and everything you need to know about your game will be given to you there. Please don't try anything on the way, it won't end well. As for the rest of you, you'll remain here until my man gets back."

"Couldn't you afford any extra staff? Blew it all on the Burgundy eh?" Simon ventured.

Jon didn't fall for this blatant attempt to gauge how many people were involved, also, Daniels comment had unsettled him a little. "Maybe there's just the two of us, maybe I've an army. All you need concern yourself with, Mr. Brown, is getting through your game. Hope you ate plenty of porridge because you're going to need a lot of energy." He placed his fingers together and drew them up to his face. Smiling, he fell silent and allowed his thoughts to drift to the games that had been so carefully devised.

Outside, in the long corridor, Daniel was dutifully following the charmless monkey with the automatic. Checking his wrist band he noted he was travelling in entirely the opposite direction to where he needed to be to win the money. He didn't concern himself with thoughts of winning, he just wanted to know what was in store for him in the room he was going to. It was useless asking the monkey, he'd not uttered a word all day. His mind wandered off to thinking about how he had gotten into this mess in the first place and the fact was that he'd been greedy. Not just the usual greedy, not the grabby 'push for more than you're worth' type of behaviour that most normal folk could both identify with and admit to. No, he'd been exceptionally greedy. From the moment he discovered what it was like to make money he had become obsessed with the stuff. It had been like a drug to him, never ceasing to pull him in further and further. As with all other addictions, Daniel had become so wrapped up in the pursuit of his 'need' that it had blinded him to the existence of other things. Like the movie had said 'when you're on heroin life is simple, that's the only thing that matters' and money had become that for him. He hadn't started off with those intentions, no addict does. They have a taste of it and like it too much. The difference with addicts is that they don't have an 'off' switch. Where the rest of us will start to see the effects these drugs are having, how they are affecting our lives, addicts only see what they need to do to get the next fix. They'll lie and cheat, fight and claw for all they are worth and never count the cost until it's too late. Well, it's too late now, he thought. He'd been offered an opportunity to invest in a company and all he could see was the certainty of vast sums of money. They'd not been aware, he had thought, of the huge potential of the product. They'd been naive in their plans and saddled the company with overheads that they couldn't service. They were ideas men, not business men. So, for a relatively small investment, Daniel had bailed them out of the hole they'd dug and taken control of the business. He remembered the feeling in his stomach when these kids put pen to paper and signed their baby over to him. It had been the most exciting day of his life. That afternoon was going to be the start of his true empire. Daniel had made lots of money in the marketing game, but this thing was going to be stellar! He'd taken on the business, all its rights and was the sole owner of the whole damn thing. He'd looked only far enough to see the potential for profits and not at all far enough to understand the devastating amount of debts that needed servicing. From the day he took over everything had changed. Suddenly he had become aware of just how much the company had borrowed, leased, promised and charged. They had accounts all over the city. Everything they owned, they didn't. All the stock needed paying for and had already been sold to customers. Nothing had been owned by the business outright. He had orders that needed completing, no stock to do this with and it took all the money he could get his hands on to set the company straight. He'd had to sell the marketing business he'd set up, and had seen him a very wealthy man, but it was going to be worth it. This was going to be the big one! And then, when the books had finally been balanced and everything had been paid for, he got the order he'd dreamt of. Fifteen thousand units to a company in Tokyo. This was exactly what he needed to get the company moving again. They'd paid enough up front for him to charm his wary suppliers into crediting him with the stock and he'd taken on extra staff to work round the clock to complete the order. He'd worked like a dog for this and the most curious thing had happened. For once, he'd found the work he put in to be the most rewarding part. Daniel had actually enjoyed the pressure of the order and all the hours it had demanded of him more than the money that was going to be coming his way as a result. It had felt so strange! Then, as they neared completion, just a day or two before the shipment was due to leave, he heard that the 'Fujibashai' company had folded. Bankrupt. In that moment his world completely caved in. He'd used all his assets to get the company back on track and had then stretched every last penny to get the order completed. Now, with no payment for the work, he was ruined. Once again his company, for which he was solely liable, owed everyone for everything again and there was nothing left to pay them. There was nothing left at all. It had taken him fifteen years to build his fortune through his marketing business and only a matter of months to lose everything here. He'd tried to get back into marketing but 'his' company wouldn't touch him, they had taken a 'new' direction and didn't need Daniels input! No one else gave him the time of day. He'd never made any friends whilst he'd been in the sector and that had come back to haunt him now he needed it. And so it was that he found himself 'somewhere' trying to save his life.

They walked along a number of corridors, each sparsely decorated with pictures of horses, dead people, and country scenes. They were typical of what you might find in such a country pile and gave no actual clue as to where they might be. He'd no idea either about how long he'd been unconscious so they could be five minutes from the warehouse or five hours? He could still be on the outskirts of London or the middle of Wales. If the opportunity to escape did present itself, what would he find on the outside? A barren expanse of moor land stretching as far as the eye could see or a row of boutique shops catering for the well heeled suburban gent? Whichever it may be, Daniel felt it a pretty futile exercise. This sadist had obviously done his homework and planned the thing well enough for any escape to be an almost certain impossibility. Daniels adult life had been spent talking himself into and out of a great many precarious situations and he'd become a master of his trade, but there was nothing he could do now.

They'd walked for what seemed like a long time. Daniels heart racing at the passing of each doorway. When they finally did arrive at the one he must enter, it came as some small relief. At least now the waiting was over, It was time to find out what he needed to do. Anticipation of a terrible event is always worse than the reality, or at least he hoped it would be.

Double M (mute monkey, as Daniel, now referred to him in his head) stood back from the door and flicked the nose of his rifle to signal that this was the place Daniel needed to be. Funny how old habits die hard. Daniel grasped the door handle firmly and strode into the room like a boss. He heard the door close and lock securely behind him. What presented itself was certainly not what he was expecting.

It looked like he had walked into another corridor that belonged to another house entirely. Stretched out in front of him, two white walls, about ten feet high and reaching the flat ceiling. It looked to be about fifteen feet in length before it reached the wall at the end of the room. Decorated on the outer side with a variety of bouldering holds, the type you'd find at any climbing centre in the country. Daniel smiled, Jon had, once again, done his homework. He'd often visited his local climbing wall, it was one of the activities he loved and took his mind off his troubles. Climbing required both physical ability and mental concentration. When he climbed, that was all he thought about.

He was standing just inside the door and there was a marker in front of him on the floor making a square for him to stand in. Behind the door was a chair and Daniel noted that, upon its seat, his climbing shoes, trousers, and a top rested, waiting for him to change into. On the blank wall behind him, as he stood looking at the chair, was a TV monitor which Daniel fully expected to spring into life at any moment and tell him the rules of the game. Glancing down the wall he felt pretty confident about completing this task. He was a bit too heavy set to be a really good climber, but he had a lot of strength and a decent amount of technique. This might not be so bad after all, he thought.

Slipping off his shoes and getting himself changed into those familiar clothes helped focus his mind too. He was going to do this, he told himself and suddenly felt very positive about his chances of completing the task. He even allowed himself thoughts about how he might handle the next part... the killing part. 'Stop' he muttered out loud, keep your mind on what you have to do right now, don't get ahead of yourself.

"Mr. Ferris"

The noise made him jump. It was the monitor behind him and when he turned around he saw Jon's face squarely in the middle of it.

"How do you like your game so far?" it asked.

Daniel was about to start a conversation but the voice began talking again. This was obviously a pre-recorded message.

"The rules are very simple, although the task is not." it continued "You must make your way around the entire outside wall, using whichever coloured holds you like, until you find yourself at the beginning again. Once you have begun, the wall you see with this monitor on will be retracted and you will be able to complete the circuit. The square you see marked is the only part of the room where you are able to touch the floor. If at any point during the task, you fall off the wall, you will certainly die. Once you have started, you cannot return to this square, you must continue along the whole of the course. If you try to return, you will certainly die. There are four different types of hold, each with different characteristics. Behind you, within this square, you will have the opportunity to try each and note their differences. So, turn around and grasp the white holds...." The audio paused a moment to allow Daniel to do as he was told.

Whites were easily the most difficult of the holds here. Daniel had rarely tried them at the centre as they required a better technique than he possessed and, possibly, a lighter frame. He grasped the hand holds as best he could. They were finger end grips and he found it very difficult to keep himself on the wall using both whites for feet and hands. Mixing whites with other colours might not be so bad, he thought.

"These were chosen because they are the limit, or maybe beyond, of your capabilities Mr. Ferris. Now try the blacks...." and again the monologue paused for the action to be completed.

These weren't too bad at all. Still not full grips but a lot better, fuller than the whites. Daniel often attempted and completed black hold courses when bouldering.

"Now the blues..."

Daniel confidently grasped the luxury of the blue holds and stood, sure footed, on them. These were easy! he thought, but just as he was holding himself there he suddenly felt a sharp pain in his palms. Falling immediately off the wall and checking them, he noticed puncture marks in each.

"Those, Mr. Ferris, are too easy to be given to you without a forfeit. If you hold onto those for more than two seconds, hands or feet, you will be stabbed with

fine needles. The more often this happens, the harder it will become to use your hands and feet effectively."

'Son of a bitch!' Daniel said and scowled at the blue grips.

"Lastly, try the greens..."

With a great deal of hesitation, Daniel stood and then held onto the easiest grips of all. These were the types he'd warm up with at the centre and afforded the best holds and the largest area in which to place one's feet. After only a couple of seconds, they started to retract into the walls. Standing down, Daniel watched as they slowly disappeared and the hole that they left was studded with razor blades. 'Nice!' he thought.

"So you see, you can use any combination you like to get round, but each has its own particular 'charm' shall we say." and the face on the monitor chuckled malevolently. "That is all you need to know, you'll work out the rest as you go. There is no time limit Mr. Ferris, but I wouldn't dawdle if I were you. You may begin when you are ready, good luck with your adventure."

There wasn't a trace of warmth in that last comment. Daniel regarded his palms, they were spotted with a small amount of blood. If his fingers were to get pricked then that would almost certainly make the whites an impossibility, the liquid would be too slippy to keep hold of them. He looked down the first wall as far as he could see and tried to plan as much of his route before beginning. He was heartened by the fact that most of the way seemed to be well populated with black grips. Taking a number of deep breaths and muttering positive statements to himself, Daniel reached up for the first black grip. It was reassuringly good.

He stepped up and started tentatively traversing the wall, placing each hand and foot with deliberation. For the first few moves it was simple enough to use the blacks and avoid the other colours, however, Dan decided to try one of the green hand holds just to make sure they disappeared like the practice ones did. He was hoping it might have been a joke by the host and that the other greens would simply be nice, static grips... No! Two seconds he counted before it started to retreat into the wall, leaving a hole that was terrifyingly ringed with razor blades. If he really needed it, he could put his arm in there for a short time but it would be extremely painful. Back on the black grips he inched along steadily and cleared the area that was the practice part he'd stood in moments ago. As soon as he did this a partition wall slowly slid across and blocked any return to the area. Jon had said that he mustn't go back, well he had no choice, there was no 'back' anymore. As the noise of the wall moving into place stopped, another, similar noise, began, somewhere behind the new partition. Dan guessed this was the removal of the wall with the monitor on it that would allow him to complete the course and return to the door. 'Well at least he's playing fair' he thought to himself and took a deep breath.

He was working his way along the outer wall, right side first, and the next grip was a bit of a stretch. There was a simpler way to transfer across but it involved either a blue grip - which he hoped to avoid completely or a white one. He didn't quite trust his technique at the moment, he hadn't 'settled' into the climb yet, hadn't found his rhythm, so he pushed up on his right foot and felt for the grip with his fingers. Thankfully, it was a good hold, the type you like to find when you're making such a 'long' transfer across. Skipping his feet over to balance his body again and remove some of the strain on his arm, Daniel blew out his cheeks. This had been the first tricky phase completed and he was pleased it had gone without any real drama. He was about midway down the first wall and feeling a little better about his chances. If it carried on in this way he'd be odds on to finish it without too much trouble. Another mechanical noise caught his attention now. Looking back towards the start, to see if the partition was moving back again, instead, he saw the wooden floor slowly dropping away. Daniel stood still for a while, curiously watching the new event. It must have lowered a good six feet before it stopped again... Why?

He looked back to the job in hand and began planning his next few moves. Right foot over to the black, left hand across and then pull up to reach for the black near the ceiling. As he did this he heard a sound like gas escaping from a pipe. This produced a moment of panic in his body and made his fingers slip a little from the new hold as his attention had been diverted. Dan grabbed like a beginner for the top black grip and pulled himself across. Resting his forehead against the wall he closed his eyes for a second and breathed a sigh of relief. When he opened them again he was looking down towards the floor. It wasn't an empty space anymore. Four, five, six... six long, olive coloured snakes of varying lengths were slithering around on the wooden base. Was this a demonstration of supreme knowledge on Jon's part, or just a lucky coincidence? Dan had always been fascinated by snakes, used to keep a couple as a kid, and he recognised the ones that were sliding around underneath him. They'd been the most fascinating ones of all.

When he was younger, when his family had been happier and his father more like a dad than a vicious dictator, they'd paid a visit to Knaresborough Zoo. Daniel had pestered for the trip as soon as he'd heard that they were going to visit family up in Yorkshire. No one else had shared his fascination of reptiles, and snakes in particular, but his enthusiasm had won the day. One of the greatest joys of being a parent is being able to give their child something they really, really want, and Daniel had wanted this so much. He must have pleaded his case a hundred times as soon as he found out they'd be near to the fabled zoo. 'Why was it so special', they'd asked, Daniel had been to plenty of reptile houses elsewhere, London zoo had a particularly extensive one. But it was special. To a lover of snakes, it was just about the most special place in England. Mr. Nyoka - the owner - had built a collection that others simply couldn't compare with. Not only did he have the largest collection of venomous snakes in Britain but he had a Guinness World record holder. The longest snake ever seen in captivity, Cassius, a female reticulated python of some 27ft 5ins. But that wasn't the real reason he wanted to go. Knaresborough zoo had something else that couldn't be seen in any other reptile house, a snake that Daniel had revered above all others, the most special snake of all, and here it was underneath him! Compared to a rainbow boa or a gaboon viper, they were drab and dull creatures. An olive colour with nothing of note as far as patterning of the scales, but they were incredible in other ways. He'd heard that they were smart, really smart! They were also the fastest venomous snakes alive, capable of incredible bursts of speed over short distances. They could raise their body up, nearly half of it from the ground, and look a man in the eye. With a coffin shaped head that was most apt, they were, and must still be, the most feared snake in the whole world. He remembered that sunny, summers day, being transfixed in wonder by the creatures. Their vivarium just the same as the other snakes, no great bells or whistles about them and most people just gave them a cursory glance and moved on to the brighter coloured serpents. Not him! Dan stood there for ages just watching them, and he felt like they were watching him back. He hadn't been disappointed by them, they did indeed give the impression that they were clever animals. They disappointed most people though, their name suggested something quite different, so when they viewed them, and because they didn't know anything about them, they just shrugged and moved on. Probably thought the wrong snakes had been put in the tank. 'Black Mamba' - the greatest snake of all in Daniels' eyes. It was true that they didn't look anything special if you didn't know anything about them, but they were to him. That head, those sleek features and keen movements, Jesus, they were terrifying and fascinating in equal measure. What gave them their name was not what they looked like on the outside, but the colour of the inside of their mouths, jet black. If you ever saw that, chances are you were soon to be dead! That afternoon was one of the most thrilling in Daniels life as one of the two glorious examples had come to the front of the tank, looked at Daniel and yawned. He'd seen the inside of the mamba's mouth and lived to tell the tale. Not many people could actually say that.

He'd gazed at the serpents underneath him for some time and noted how they had responded first to the new environment and second to him. Each had taken a turn in trying to climb the side of the wall where he was now stationary. Thankfully, each had been just too short of length to make it to one of the lower grips. Had they been able, he felt sure they would have come after him. Looking down the way to the turn in the wall, planning his route, Daniel saw a partition keeping the snakes in this part of the room. Maybe he only needed to get past this bit and he would be free of them? It was a thought he didn't really believe to be true, but it did provide him with some fresh impetuous. Make it to the end and that's this part over with.

He was feeling strong and had found some rhythm to his climbing. Sticking with the black grips he traversed steadily along, his progress being checked at each point by the eager snakes beneath him. Each time he moved across, they shuffled themselves along to be exactly underneath him. These buggers were keen, he thought and smiled ruefully. Any slip really did mean death. Black grips were plentiful and mercifully full at the moment. Dan was able to move with confidence and didn't feel like he was in any danger of losing his footing. As he approached the corner, he attempted to look into the next section of flooring to see what was in store. He even used the white hand grips to gain some further height, hoping this would allow him to survey the whole area. All he could see, and he could see nearly all of the floor, was one dark brown 'thing' at the far end. It was small and motionless and he couldn't quite make out what it could be, but he was damn sure he preferred it to the mambas!

Negotiating the 90-degree corner, Dan, a little excited by the fact that he would soon be free of these killers, stretched his right foot a little too far. His toe barely made the black hold but his balance had shifted too much to adjust and try something else. He was committed to this move and his foot wasn't going to support it. The black grip he'd had his eye on to complete the transfer was too slight for his needs, he had to find one where he could support his weight and move his foot into a better position. Panicked, realising his mistake, he grabbed for the best grip he could see. It was a green. As soon as he got his fingers in place he could feel it starting to retract into the wall. He had no time to mess around. Pulling hard with his hand, Dan managed to 'hop' his foot fully onto the black and swing his other leg over. There was just enough room for the pair of them and enough purchase to hold his weight. As the green was just about to disappear, with his hand still attached to it and in danger of being cut to bits by the razors, he found a comfortable black for his left and quickly let go of the green. For a second his body wavered, on the cusp of falling backwards from the wall, but his fingers found enough strength to pull him back and allow him to find another grip for his right hand. That was a close call, he thought, and sweat beaded on his forehead as his heart raced.

'Concentrate!' he told himself, 'got to be precise...' that was what climbing was all about to him, balance and precision. That word conjured up memories from his childhood, took him back to a place he had never wanted to visit again. Daniel's father had been ex-army, fought in the Falklands and maybe brought back more scars than were visible on his body? He'd seen friends, close friends die, all so that Thatcher could win an election. Nothing unites a country like a war! Daniel had been too young to understand the politics, all he knew was that the father that had returned from those islands wasn't the man that had left for them. He'd always been strict, ran the home with a military precision, but he'd been fair... and kind. When he returned, that kindness had disappeared, lost somewhere across the ocean. Maybe it was understandable to an adult if they had the knowledge of what had happened over there? Maybe a professional could tell you why he did the things he did, but, as a child, Daniel couldn't. He simply didn't understand why his dad had changed so much and adjusting to the 'new' father, to the new set of rules, had taken some time. His dad had been a stickler for timing and neatness before, up at 0700hrs, dressed and ready for breakfast at 07.15hrs and such like. Room inspections and checks carried out regularly, but within a framework that they could all understand. Living by these rules had been pretty simple and if you made a mistake then you knew why you were in the dog house. But after he had returned those things had changed somewhat. Where a carrot had been the motivating factor for good behaviour, for neatness and precision, the stick was now the chosen method. He'd lost any tolerance for behaviour that lay outside what he demanded, and it was a demand, not an expectation anymore.

Many times Daniel had felt the wrath of his father's new regime whilst trying to adjust. Silly things like his socks not being matched properly in his drawer, shoes left with a five-inch gap between them and not exactly lined, heel and toe, against the wall. These all brought about punishments and reprimands. His mother suffered the same fate. Lateness of meals, streaks on the draining side of the sink, coats not put away in order - and this order changed with whatever he wanted it to be that day, these were all punishable offences. Once, Daniel had been sent to the shop to fetch the paper. On his way back home he'd met a friend and chatted for a short time, maybe five minutes? When he had returned his dad was waiting for him. Daniel remembered the words so clearly, his fathers face, like a sergeant major, reddened with anger. He'd tried to tell him what had happened, explain that he had only stopped for a few minutes, but this had been unacceptable!

"What do you suppose happens when a soldier is late back from a mission?" he'd barked.

He wasn't a soldier, he was just a little boy.

"Corporal Thompson was late getting over the hill with his kit, they didn't have communication with command and it cost Private Kinsella his legs... That's what happens when you fail in the army sunshine!"

It was a paper... just a fucking paper for god's sake and he was five minutes late. But it was useless trying to argue. 'Yes, sir, sorry sir' was his stock response, nothing else would be tolerated. Any dissent in the ranks would only make things worse.

"Thompo was sorry, but not half as sorry as Kinsella! Sorry doesn't get the job done sunshine, sorry is an excuse we don't tolerate in this house!"

His mother had tried to smooth things over, tried to calm him, but to no avail. Dad had taken this as an act of mutiny by his family and stamped it down straight away. Daniel was given his punishment and his mother was given hers, a swelling above the eye and some fingers marks on her wrist. She had spent the rest of the day cleaning the skirting boards with a toothbrush and Daniel had been stripped naked and ordered to stand on a kitchen tile, not tiles... a tile, singular. It had been just about large enough to keep both his feet, but no larger. There was no room for movement and, under his fathers gaze, he spent two hours standing there, naked and terrified. This was what happened when you stopped to chat with a friend. This was how Daniel became a world class liar! He learned to invent the most plausible and convincing reasons for why things hadn't happened the way his dad had wanted them to. Sometimes, not often, but sometimes his father would listen and he'd get away with it. Most of the time he would not, but Daniel still played out the deception in his head. It was a way of coping with the punishment. He'd invent a whole other reality and, in his head, he'd 'live' it to take him away from what was happening.

One day, one summers day when the sky seemed endlessly blue, he was playing in the back garden with a friend. Not many visited him, they'd heard about his father and been warned by their own parents. His mother was in the kitchen, cleaning and making sure everything was in order for 'his' return. Daniel had been relaxed for once, it was a state of mind that could only happen when his dad was out and he was enjoying this time with a friend. He was enjoying being a boy and not a soldier. They were throwing a tennis ball to each other, just a game that kids like to play, and talking about school. Daniel had stopped the game to go inside for a drink of water. When he came back out he noticed his shoelace had become loose and had stooped to fix it, it was how he was programmed these days. At that moment his friend had thrown the ball. He hadn't meant to break it, it was just an accident, but the ball had sailed past Daniel and hit the pantry window. Smashed the pantry window. In that moment all the colour drained from his world. Things seemed to happen in slow motion and he heard no sounds, only muffled noises. Daniel had felt sick to the pit of his stomach and dizzy. Despite his friend's apologies, despite the fact that he had taken responsibility and was prepared to own up to it. Both Daniel and his mother, when she had seen what had happened, told the boy to go home. They were afraid of what might happen to him, and what would certainly happen should the boy's parents come round after the event. They would deal with it themselves and take the punishment that would surely be given. In a way, they were protecting their father from what would surely have been an incident involving the police. They were protecting the 'family', as fucked up as it was.

In those dreadful hours before dad was expected home, Daniel played out what had happened in his head a thousand times or more. Each scenario had ended with the window not breaking, with the world not coming to an end. He'd tried to convince himself that it hadn't actually happened, that it was all just a bad dream. but he knew it wasn't, knew this was the most serious incident of all.

When his father did return, Daniel had been cross examined before being sent to his room. His mother, in those painful hours, had concocted a story involving a washing line and an errant wooden prop. It was perfectly plausible, an understandable accident. It could easily have happened that way and been accepted as a simple mistake, an absent minded moment. Any reasonable person would have been fine with that. She told the doctors, and then the police, that she'd slipped at the top of the stairs on some washing. Four broken ribs, a bust lip, and a badly twisted shoulder were consistent injuries for such a fall. Daniel never said a word about how it had really been broken and, when he saw his mother, felt the shame of coward. Cowardice burns like nothing else and it still burned him today. You don't choose it, it's not a decision you make, it's instinct.

Recovering his poise as well as his heart rate, Daniel made his way past the partition and into the snake free zone. He continued with the blacks and as soon as he was clear of the corner he plotted the whole of the next wall, ignoring the brown thing at the end. Whatever it was, it wasn't a mamba, besides, what he needed to do was climb. Regardless of what was beneath him, if he managed to stay on the wall then he'd make it! Black grips were still in abundance and he was steadily growing in confidence. Dan felt, at this moment in time, that his chances were pretty good.

Carefully and deliberately, each hand following each foot, he made steady progress along the new wall. As he made it about a third of the way along he heard a noise... It was a noise he'd heard before when the wall had emerged at the start. He already knew what this meant but looked back anyway to confirm it. Sure enough, the partition was dropping to allow the snakes access to this new area. Before it had even reached the floor they were all over it and into the corridor. It was now that he realised what the brown thing was. Just in case the serpents hadn't wished to follow him, Jon had placed a dead rat at the end to tempt them. Doubtless, they hadn't been fed in a good while and the smell would bring them slithering along. He watched as the snakes made quickly for the tasty treat, ignoring him clinging to the side. It was the largest one that took the initiative and wasted no time in striking the dead rodent, it was lightning fast! They waited a short while, watching the rat intently for movement, before moving in to eat it. Two of the beasts got hold, one at either end, and fought frantically over the spoils but the largest of the snakes won out, ripping the prize from the others grasp and then quickly devouring the snack. As soon as it was over, they resumed their vigil underneath him, as interested as ever. He hadn't heard it, but the partition had elevated itself back into place, herding the snakes into this pen. Well, it didn't change anything really, he consoled himself. Stick to the climbing and you'll be alright.

It had been a knock to his confidence but Daniel made his way along the wall without a hiccup and with each successful transfer he felt better about his chances. Nearing the second corner, nearing the half way point, he refused to look down the next wall. He'd learned his lesson from the last one, keep in the moment and climb what is in front of you boy! Let the future take care of itself. This time he took the corner easily, well balanced and without the use of a green to help him. Only when he got to the partition did he allow himself a glance down the new wall.

Like the first, it was only around fifteen feet long. Like the second, it had a dead rat at the end to encourage the snakes to follow him, though he doubted this was necessary. But unlike the other two, it was devoid of blacks once you passed the partition. From the moment the new area started, it was covered in greens. Not only this, but half way along the section the grips made a sharp upturn towards the ceiling, over the ceiling and back down the opposite side. He would need to negotiate around eight feet of 'overhang' to get to the other wall. Not only that, which in itself would take some doing, he'd have to complete each move, hands, and feet, in a matter of seconds before the green grip would disappear into the wall. 'Fuck!' was all he could muster. Looking down at his eager audience Daniel suddenly became quite angry about their constant attentions and decided to shout at them. Their heads were trying to peep over the partition as if interested to see what the new wall held for him.

"Why don't you just fuck off!" he screamed, "you can't fucking eat me anyway, so what's the point in following me?"

This did nothing to put them off, in fact, the cursing seemed to excite them even more and they danced together on the other side, jostling for top position.

He knew he had to be calm for this challenge, needed a clear head and a plan of attack. Shouting at the snakes did nothing to stop their attentions, but it did release some of the tension in his body and allowed him to cool down again. If he could climb one foot and one hand at a time then that would give him extra seconds for each bit. Because the grips were good enough, he ought to be able to hold on with just the two points of contact. In order to do this successfully, he would have to know exactly what he was going to do from the moment he started. There was no time for dithering. It was a question of how much he could plan in advance and whether he could execute this under pressure. Left foot, right hand, then right foot, left hand. He imagined that using the opposites would enable him to keep some balance but this idea quickly disappeared as he couldn't see how that would help him move across the wall? What would he do on the ceiling part? Normally you'd try to get your legs up to anchor yourself a little, but with the grips disappearing that seemed like a useless endeavour. Fuck, this was going to be tough. Try as he might, Daniel didn't have the brain power to plot the entire course out in his head, he was struggling to plot the moves that would take him to the ceiling, let alone the rest of the thing. He felt like he'd been presented with a chess problem and all he knew was draughts. How the hell was he going to do this?

He was suddenly aware of how tired his grip was becoming. His forearms were hurting and his finger ends felt like they were losing their strength. He needed to move. He'd run out of time to ponder, whatever he was going to do, he had to do it now. 'Speed!' he said to himself and launched into action.

No plan, no idea what was coming next, he just grabbed for each hold and flung his legs across. As soon as he felt even a little bit balanced again he grabbed for the next. It was only a matter of seconds before he'd made it to the ceiling part and he didn't slow then. Hand over hand he pulled himself across with his knees tucked up into his stomach. Those damn grips seemed to be speeding up in their attempt to retreat into the wall but he was fast enough to keep ahead of them. As he reached the final hold before joining the other wall, Daniel let go with his left hand and spun his body around. His legs flailed against the wall, madly searching for a foothold before his right-hand grip disappeared. His right foot touched one and then slipped off, the contact was enough to start the process though and soon that much-needed contact point would be lost to him. Stretching with his left he made contact with another, but again his foot slipped off the end. Both foot holds were disappearing fast and he couldn't quite reach the hand grip in front of him with his left. Dan felt the blades scraping the skin back from his thumb and the back of his hand, gauging deep troughs as the grip went further into the recess. He felt the warm blood trickling down his arm and still he tried to reach with his left... and failed. The pain was excruciating and the blood flowed freely now. There was only one thing he could do, try to jam his feet into the holes that had been left by the retreating holds, that might give him enough purchase to push against the ceiling with his left hand and steady himself. Kicking both feet out at once, they found their target and he squealed in pain as the razors cut straight through the sides of his shoes and into the flesh of his feet. He just managed to fix his left hand to the ceiling before letting go with his right. It would only be a second or so before his weight would pull him off the wall and down to the floor below. Despite the immense pain in his right hand, he threw it forward to the grip his left couldn't reach... and it stuck! With his body weight on his feet and the new grip quickly moving back into the wall, Dan had no time to stop and assess the damage. He grabbed for the next hand hold with his left hand and yanked his left foot out of the bladed hole. He felt the tearing of the material as well as the flesh, he heard two distinct noises as his foot released from the chamber. One was the sound of leather cutting, the other must be what skin sounds like when it's ripped off the bone. There was no time to appreciate what this meant or look to see what state his foot was in, he had to move quickly. Two rapid hand movements carried him down the wall a little and he now had to rip his right foot from hole but he'd gone too far. It was stuck at an angle and wouldn't work free. The holds were disappearing fast and he couldn't go backwards, he'd have nothing left to complete the course with if he did. One almighty yank pulled it free and nearly took his other foot off the wall completely. Again, there was a hideous noise and the pain that shot up his leg and directly into his brain which screamed at him to let go, to just drop to the floor and give in. But he didn't. Somehow, he carried on and found his way to the corner. Finally, mercifully, he found some black grips to hang on to....

Terrific pain shot through his body as some of the adrenaline started to leave it. Coming in waves from the base of his feet and travelling the length of him, Daniel felt sick and a little dizzy. He looked first to his hand, the crimson coloured mess. Those gorged lines were flowing freely and the blood had stained the whole of his arm down to his shoulder. He wouldn't bleed to death from this wound, that was for sure, but he'd never seen as much blood, his own blood, before. It was coagulating in places and the thick, sticky liquid was uncomfortable to work with. With his arm bent, it was dripping down onto the floor beneath him. Looking under his arm pit, Dan could see his faithful audience had gathered eagerly and each had been painted in places by the blood, adding to the menace of these animals. His feet hurt more than his hand although less blood seemed to be escaping from them. Daniel couldn't properly assess the damage that had been caused to them but he was relieved that both hand and feet were still very much usable. Only a short wall to go now, he told himself, trying to build some commitment to the task ahead. He was on the inside wall now, so there couldn't be more than ten feet left, he judged. His muscles didn't ache too much, the adrenaline had taken care of that, and his grip was still pretty good. He felt in decent shape for whatever faced him on the final side of the room.

Feeling with his left hand around the corner before leaning his head around to find a black hold, Daniel was careful not to lose his balance. Pleasingly, as if placed there in a friendly fashion, there were two sturdy black foot holds and two more for his hands close enough to be reached and negotiated without difficulty. First, the left grip was found and then he swung his foot around to gain a stable platform. As he attempted to ease his right foot around before completing the move with his hand, Dan caught the side of it on the wall clumsily. God, the pain was awful! He yelled out a high pitched squeal as the tender flesh reminded him of just how much he'd damaged them. Gritting his teeth, he banged his forehead against the wall a couple of times whilst he waited for the agony to subside a little. This it did to a degree which allowed him to continue and he was soon around the corner and facing his final task.

Aside from the ones he was using, there were no black holds on the wall in front. All he could see were a succession of whites and blues. This very nearly brought him to tears. He was at his breaking point and had been given a choice he didn't like one bit. He could either try to climb better than he had ever done before or accept that the pain would continue. Maybe he could mix his foot holds up a bit, some of the whites didn't look too tiny to stand on, but his hands were too tired to try and use them. Also, after the first blue grip, he knew his hand would be useless for anything trickier. Even if it had the strength, the blood would make any attempt at a white completely futile.

As he was considering his path and steeling himself for the pain ahead, an audio message played through an unseen speaker.

'To complete the task...' it was Jon's voice 'you must touch the wall at the end and wait for it to retract. Well done on making it this far Mr. Ferris, must admit I thought the snakes would have had you before now.' and that was all that he said.

Where the prospect of getting bitten by the mambas had been all encompassing over the first two walls, Daniel had almost forgotten about them since. But they were there, waiting, ready to strike should he misplace a foot or a hand.

Daniel looked down the wall and counted. There must only be ten or so blue holds between him and the finish. It would be painful, that's for sure, but he felt he could do it. He would have to use the whites for his feet, he couldn't take any more abuse there and he needed to stand on them. If the blood began to flow from the toe areas he'd never be able to keep them on the holds, they'd be too slippy even if they weren't too painful. Daniel remembered back to the practice part of the exercise when he had tested the blues. Those needles had shot out after about two seconds but.... but, they had gone back inside the grip afterward. Maybe if he could make the hold then remove his hand at just the right time he could miss the needles and keep his hands free from extra pain? There was a blue just to the left of his hand, the first on the wall, that he could try before having to move any further. Daniel hesitantly rested his fingers an inch or so away from the hold, not quite daring to do what he needed to. Twice he tried to persuade his hand to take hold, just for a moment, and twice it had refused him. He laughed at this disobedience. An image of 'Flash Gordon' appeared in his head, the part where Timothy Dalton has to put his hand into the rock and wait to see if it will get bitten. That was exactly how he felt right now. Taking a few short breaths and uttering 'come on' through gritted teeth, Daniel made his hand retake its position next to the grip. This time there was no disobedience, he held it for a minute amount of time before whisking it out of harm's way. Nothing happened! No needles shot out. He'd been too light of touch, maybe too quick. He'd have to sail a little closer to the wind if he wanted this to work.

Grabbing the blue forcefully and trying to count to 'one' before releasing Dan removed his hand just a fraction too late. It was on its way to safety when the needles shot out and punctured the fleshy part of his palm. 'Son of a bitch!' he cried and instinctively shook his hand and pressed it against his hip. Checking for damage he could see five, small blood stained marks. It didn't actually hurt too much and they had only caught him a glancing blow. Now he needed to do it again to see if his theory was correct, only the problem with that was the fact that the needles would hit the exact same spot if they did make a reappearance. Nothings worse than re injuring an injury, you'd take a fresh cut every time over cutting the same place again. This time it felt even harder than the first, same strategy though. Hand on, count to one and get it off before the needles came. Again, Daniel had to gee himself up before attempting the task. This time he hovered less and was more assertive with his digits. He grabbed and released in what felt like the perfect amount of time. Had he been too light of touch again?... Or had he been right about the needles? Were they a one time shot? He did it again to make sure, and this time he definitely didn't hold it too lightly. No needles appeared. So that would be the plan then, use the whites to stand on, where possible, and grab-release-grab the blues as he went.

Daniel was tired! His fingers ached and his forearms felt like they were about to burst, but there was just a short distance to go, he could make it! If he could just get the timing right, he may even avoid any further injury. He was going to beat this damn game after all. Those black, and now red spotted mambas would have followed him in vain. That first blue hold was large enough to get both hands on and Dan swung his throbbing feet over as far as he could. His toe ends were all he could manage to perch on the grips, but it was enough, with the help of his arms, to hold him securely on the wall. At shoulder height, the next blue grip would take him back above his feet, righting his body once more. But for the second time, Dan failed to get his hand away before the needles struck. This time they penetrated three of his finger ends and stung like a bitch! His arm flew backwards with the pain and the momentum took his left foot off the precarious hold it had been desperately trying to cling to. His body was swinging out away from the wall and Dan could feel his right foot twisting on the white stump. Any further and it would surely slip off completely, leaving him dangling by his fatigued right arm, and that wouldn't be enough to save him.

Pulling hard with his core muscles he threw his left hand back at the grip and managed to get two of his freshly wounded finger tips to just about secure themselves. Walking them carefully into the hold, centimetre by agonising centimetre, he regained control of his wayward body and managed to plant his left foot back on the tiny white stump. Dan let out a deep sigh of relief and rested his head against the wall. He couldn't afford to do that again, he simply didn't have enough strength left in his body. Crossing his hands, he used his right to try and diffuse the next hold, up and another foot or so away from him. It wasn't the easiest way to do it but he couldn't bring himself to use those damaged fingers again, they were throbbing and sore. It was awkward, too awkward to be as precise as he needed to be, and the needles were too fast. Dan felt them puncture and push their way into his knuckle joints, felt the ends scrape the bone inside before retracting. This time he didn't even take his hand away, just held on and bore the pain. He didn't do this silently. Dan screamed at the top of his voice, screamed his pain and frustration away and ended with a grit of the teeth and a growl.

Twice now he'd felt the needles and this last one had cured him of their shock value. It was going to hurt like hell, this next five or six holds, but he would have to bear it. Trying to whisk his hand away hadn't worked, they were just too fast, and it had caused him to very nearly fall off in the process. His best, his only real chance, was to grip, hold and take the punishment.

Each fresh needle strike brought with it more agonising hurt. His palms looked like pin cushions and were sticky and patched in blood. There was no chance now, even if he felt he had the strength and the skill to do it, of using the whites and saving his pain. He'd never felt as much discomfort as this, never wanted something to end like he did right now but he carried on, grimly. Each stab brought a cry that reverberated around the corridor and excited the snakes below, they seemed to thrive on the vibrations. Those white foot holds became shallower and less secure the closer he got to the end and he was virtually holding himself with his arms. Finally, he reached the last. Two nubs, no bigger than the end of a table spoon and no wider than a phone, were all he had to rest his toes on but the blue hand holds were good. Dan reached over with his left hand for the final grip and squeezed it as hard as he could. He would not let go! Moments later he transferred his right hand to it and hung there waiting for the pain to come....

To his great surprise, no needles struck. He was stretched up as far as he could be, his feet on the tips of their toes and his arms way up above him waiting to be stung again, but it didn't happen.Touching the wall quickly with his left hand before replacing it, there came a noise that reminded him of the start of this 'game'. It was the noise of the wall moving. Slowly, far too slowly, it dragged its heels across the floor beside him. It would have to be fully removed before he would be able to finally get off the wall and complete the climb and that seemed like a fucking lifetime. From beneath his armpit, Daniel watched the wall and prayed for it to hurry. Stretched out in this way he felt like he was being crucified. Every last inch of his body was burning with pain and fatigue and he wasn't sure how long he could endure it. As he waited, as the wall crawled, blood from his shoes trickled down towards his toes. Sticky, wet blood. Only, it wasn't so sticky when it came in contact with the white holds his toes were resting on. They were curved grips and the moment the blood touched them they became like little nuggets of ice. Each foot slipped off the hold and couldn't be replaced properly and each time this happened it yanked his body down. Dan's hands were so tired... His body was so tired, broken, that he couldn't hold on any longer. He was going to fall.

Each time he managed to get a toe back on the hold it stayed for a second before slipping again and exhausting his body. He had no reserves left, this was the final straw and he felt almost pleased that it was going to be over. Dan doubted, in that moment, that the snake's bite and venom would hurt anything like how his body hurt right now. Believed that the relief of letting go would be greater. He closed his eyes and gave himself a ten count. Ten more seconds he asked of himself, and then it would be ok to give up. Five.... six.... seven.... he counted through gritted teeth and a grimace. Eight.... nine.... that was it, time's up Danny boy, he thought to himself as he felt his grip loosening, his fingers peeling away from the hold. All was quiet, save the noise of the snakes below him and he savoured his last moment.

With only five fingers left on the hold, having given up on trying to place his toes back on the white, Daniel dangled there. He looked up towards the ceiling, readying himself for the fall when he realised that the noise from the wall had stopped. Glancing over he saw that it had finished its task and he was free to do the same. It must have happened when he had closed his eyes and counted. All he need do was swing himself over and drop. He'd been so close to the wall that there were only a couple of inches between him and the safety of the flooring. With a final effort, he levered his feet over to the left and dropped. His right foot was half on, half over the edge and he wavered a moment before his momentum took him to safety. Dan collapsed in agony and cried with relief.

He stayed there, curled in a ball on the floor, holding himself and letting the pain leave his body. His hands and feet were wrecked by the climb, but his physical exertion, the thing that nearly killed him in the end, was subsiding. After each passing second he felt himself recover ever so slightly and once a couple of minutes had passed, Daniel felt able to move again. Gingerly at the beginning, like one testing each part of his body for breakages, but soon a little more assuredly. Five minutes gone and he felt able to kneel and survey his surroundings. Behind the door, next to where the chair with his clothes was, he noticed that a panel had removed itself. With great effort and feeling like a man of nearer ninety than forty, Daniel hauled himself to his tender feet. Hobbling over to investigate he found a number of useful items. First up, and most importantly, was a green first aid box. Next to that lay a hefty metal spanner with a tag on it that read 'weapon'. Finally, resting next to the pair, was a syringe filled with morphine. He knew this because it said so on the note that had been left underneath it. This read - 'here is a shot of morphine sulphate solution, enough to kill you. If you have been bitten by one of the snakes but managed to make it to the end anyway, then you'll probably want to use this'. How lovely, he thought.

Unpacking the first aid box, Daniel appraised what kit he had been given. He had to admit that Jon was a thorough man, everything he needed to patch himself up was contained within the box. Tape, dressings, saline to clean the wounds and he'd even chucked in a couple of codeine to dull the pain. Obviously, Jon wanted a good fight. Daniel hadn't really considered the next part of the contest, he'd been focused on the task in hand, had to be to give him a chance of beating it. Now though, now he did need to think about it. Was he really capable of killing someone? He checked his band and noticed that all the dots were still illuminated. It wasn't going to be just one at this rate. Could he do it?

Washing his arms and hands with the saline and wincing as he dabbed them dry, it hurt like hell but nowhere near as much hell as he'd had to go through in the previous half an hour. This pain he could take all day long! Daniel put the thought of whether or not he could actually kill someone out of his head. 'Stay in the moment and do what needs to be done right now, let the future take care of itself' he mumbled and nodded his head as if agreeing with himself. He unravelled a length of tape to fix one of the dressings in place and stopped dead. Something had caught his eye. Turning his head ever so carefully to look over his shoulder he saw the very end of a nose sticking over the edge of the flooring. Flicking a tongue to taste the air, one of the Mamba's was attempting to climb out of the pit and into Daniels square sanctuary. Watching it for a moment and hoping it would slide back down the wall, he saw the creature get a little purchase on the corner of the flooring with its chin. He was just about to spring over and stamp on its head when he had an idea. Clearly, the snake had no chance of striking from this position, all its efforts were in trying to haul itself up onto the floor, and it was struggling to do so. This was an opportunity to acquire an extra weapon. It couldn't defend itself at the moment and it would be easy enough to grab the thing before it had chance to get away.

He acted swiftly and confidently. One long step and he was at the edge, a foot or so to the side of it. Bending quickly, he grabbed it behind its head with his finger and thumb squeezing it tightly. It thrashed violently and showed Daniel the inside of it terrible mouth, but could nothing about its capture. Pulling the head up to his standing position, but leaving the body dangling over the edge, so not to give the snake anything to push from, he took the length of tape from his dressing and stuck the first couple of inches to the snake's nose. Then, carefully winding it underneath, he managed to shut its jaws and wrap the tape around them a good three or four times. Dan watched as the snake struggle and desperately tried to open its mouth, but it couldn't, the tape was enough to hold it shut. Now what he had was a deadly accessory! But how was he going to keep it with him?

Part of the first aid kit contained a pair of scissors, not large enough to be a weapon, just a surgical pair for cutting and shaping dressings and the like. What he needed now was two free hands, so, with a mighty deep breath, he did what no man has probably ever done before. He stuffed a black mamba down the front of his top. Boy was it furious! It thrashed and fought him every inch of the way, but eventually, it was in there and the tight Lycra gave it no simple means of escape. He quickly tucked the bottom of his top into his climbing pants and tied the draw string tight. Dan then set about the second stage of the plan, making a bag for the beast to be carried in. Grabbing the trousers he'd changed from at the start of the climb, he cut the leg all the way around at the top of the thigh area. Next, he tied the bottom of the leg in a tight knot. He stood on what was sticking out of the bottom of the knot with his foot and pulled the leg upwards to tighten it as much as he could. In that moment he'd forgotten about the damage he'd done to his poor hoof and it soon reminded him when he applied pressure to the trouser leg. Still, it had to be done, painful as it was. Checking it, Dan was satisfied that it wouldn't come loose. 'And there we have it' he said, pleased with his ingenuity. Now all he needed to do was wrestle the snake out of his top and into the make shift bag. It didn't like it one bit, but he managed to get the thing tucked in and tied the top off with some tape. Placing the bag on the chair, he watched as it writhed and wriggled inside, trying to find a way of escaping. Dan smiled to himself, he knew how the poor bugger felt!

Back to attending to his wounds, Dan removed those climbing shoes as carefully as he could but they hurt like hell anyway. All down the sides of each foot, deep rivets had been cut by the razors. Blood had started to congeal around some of the wounds, whilst others still trickled with that sticky dark mess. Each time he applied some saline to clean the area it stung like a bitch and he had to suck the air in through his teeth and grimace. Drying them provoked the same response, but it had to be done, he needed them to be in a fit enough state to at least walk on. Applying the bandages wasn't easy as they kept sticking to the blood on his hands and coming away from his feet before he'd managed to wrap them. Eventually, though, Dan fixed them in the right place and wrapped them tightly, securing it with lengths of tape. By the time he had finished he'd pretty much mummified them, but he was rather pleased with the results. Because of the pressure, they didn't hurt too badly to stand on and this gave him a little more confidence for the task ahead. What didn't was the fact that there was no chance of him putting his shoes back on. He'd have to do this in bandages and bare feet from here on. Wrapping his hands up was a little easier and he was again pleased with the results. His hands felt good, felt like he was ready to go boxing! Dan had made sure his fingers were still usable without skimping on padding for his poor hands. Finishing up, he took the shoe laces from both shoes, tied them together and then to each end of the Mamba bag, this allowed him to sling it over his shoulder and keep both hands free, ready for action.

Whilst he had been performing these tasks, the wall behind him had closed again, leaving him in the tight square he'd started the challenge from. Looking over at it he noticed a countdown clock had appeared on the monitor. 29 minutes 53 seconds it read and underneath it had the words 'door release'. Well, at least he had some time to ponder what he was going to do next. He hoped that, in those 29 minutes, he'd see all but one of those lights extinguished.

Chapter 5 - It's Simple Simon

Simon stared at the host in silence, watching him closely from across the table. Who was this bastard? He'd been pleased with himself for being able to rattle Jon, but really he knew it hadn't gotten him anywhere. Jon knew everything about them and they knew nothing about him, other than he was a sadistic son of a bitch. He held all the cards and Simon didn't like this one bit. He felt that this was all so out of his control, like a rat in a lab being made to do whatever the scientist wanted. At the mercy of his whim. These thoughts were not positive ones. If only he could find something to go in his favour, a little leverage that might just tip the balance his way a bit. What had Daniel known? Was he just bluffing when he'd said Jon had missed something or had he actually clicked on to hole in the plan? If he had thought of something then surely Simon could to, they'd all had the same experience and information after all. And so he sat there reviewing all that he could remember.

There was silence in the room, each one lost in their own thoughts, nervous, apprehensive about what lay ahead of them. Simon appraised his competition one by one. If he did manage to get through his task, which he fully believed he would, then who would be his biggest problem? Could he kill? If it was a case of them and not him then he was sure he could. At least, sitting here considering it purely on an intellectual level he could, it would surely be very different when face to face. Who would be the most difficult one? He could discount Lola and Thomas, physically that is, he was sure he had the power and fitness to make short work of them, should the situation arise. Franky, he'd back Lola against Thomas if it came down to a fight! James was a different proposition. He was fit and strong, no doubt about that, maybe stronger than Simon, but he was a good ten years older. Simon felt this gave him the upper hand. James had been pretty quiet too, this he didn't like. You've got to watch the quiet ones, was what he'd always been told, how true that was he wasn't overly sure, but he'd have liked to have found out some more about James. It was hard to judge just what sort of a bloke he was from the little he'd seen of him. Daniel, on the other hand, had been pretty cocky. Definitely thought of himself as an alpha male and wasn't shy about showing it. He was a similar height, weight and build to Simon, they were probably of a similar age too. Of all the potential rivals, Simon thought Dan would be his biggest threat. He hoped he'd be eliminated before it got to that point.

"So how long do we have to wait for Lurch to come back and which one of us is going next?" he called across to the host.

Stirring from his thoughts, Jon glanced across at Simon with a look that said 'it's always you, isn't it!' before answering the question.

"You'll be delighted to know, Mr. Brown, that you will be next to take your challenge and that will be happening soon enough. My man will be back any time now, so you've little to wait." adding, with that menacing smile "I do hope you like your game..."

"I tell you what I'm going to like..." Simon called angrily "...shoving my boot up your arse and wiping that smug grin off your fucking face sunshine!"

Jon just stared coldly back at him for a moment.

"If it didn't spoil the evening's activities, Mr. Brown, I'd come over there and rip your fucking head off right now, you annoying little shit!" and he was serious "but that's not the way things are going to be done, we have a game to play."

Simon glared back at the host, he'd rattled the bastard again but what good had it done?

"Well tell Jeeves to hurry up, I'm fucking bored with this!"

As the words left his mouth, the door to the dining room opened and the gorilla with the automatic walked in.

"Typical London cabbie, took the long route back did we dickhead?" Simon felt comfortable in the fact that nothing was going to happen to him until he got to his 'room' and used this opportunity to be as offensive as he liked. As he stood up in anticipation of following the monkey out of the room he found the butt of the automatic return him to his seat as it was jammed, heavily, into his face. Simon tried to right himself in the chair but the world started to swirl and somebody turned the lights off!

Coming round with a bit of a start, the first thing Simon noted was that he was still alive. For this, he was truly thankful! It would appear that he had misjudged the situation somewhat and he wasn't, after all, immune to physical attack. Feeling his face, as he lay there on the hard floor, Simon detected two swollen and tender areas. One was around his left cheek bone and there was a similar spot on his jaw. He remembered now whence it had come, the hard wood finished butt of the automatic. This was the second knockout blow he'd received today and his head was really starting to regret its association with his mouth. It was too tender to rub and so he just held his hand to it and surveyed the room from his prone position. Simon wondered how long he'd been out this time, but then gave up on that train of thought quickly as it really didn't make any difference to his reality. Looking around himself he saw a number of points of interest. His room was nothing special, in fact, it couldn't have had any fewer features. Blank, white walls all around in a box shape. Behind him was a door and that was the only punctuation or adornment to be found. In the corner, near the door, was a chair with some clothes on it. He guessed these were to be changed into for the challenge ahead. It was the centre of the room that held the greatest interest to him, clearly the area he'd be occupying for the task he needed to complete. In the middle of a sunken square, there was a static bicycle, like the ones he'd used so often in the gym, only this had extra bits to the handle bars and pedals. In front of that was a large monitor, presently blank, that he presumed was part of the challenge, and that was pretty much it. It didn't look too foreboding and Simon was a pretty good cyclist, so he felt good about what lay ahead.

Taking to his feet, rather gingerly, he looked around the room once more to see if there was anything he'd missed. As he did so, the monitor sprung into life. Jon's face, taking up all of the screen, beamed out at him.

"Mr. Brown... Welcome to your game!" it began, pleasantly enough "on the chair, you will find some gym clothes that you will be more comfortable in for the purposes of the task, I suggest you change into them now" and the video paused.

Simon did as he was instructed and changed quickly from his more restrictive clothing into the familiar gym wear. It was his own stuff and he wasn't surprised by this at all. What did surprise, and worry him a little, was the lack of footwear on offer. He didn't imagine that this was an oversight, so he would be doing this barefoot? This thought left his head as the video began to play again.

"Your task, as you may have guessed, is one of endurance. You will be attached to the bike by the hands and feet and will need to complete a course in the allotted time. Failure to do so will be punished by death. If, however, you complete the task, you will be released from the bike and may continue with the *second part of the night's activities. Please get on the bike" and again the video waited.*

Walking over to the machine, Simon looked more carefully now at the 'boots' and 'gloves' that were attached to it. His feet were to slot into what looked like carbon snow boots that came up past his ankles. On the handlebars, the attachments were similar looking in material and extended a little beyond his wrists. He didn't like this one bit, but there was nothing he could really do about it. Adjusting the seat to a height he felt was appropriate for him, Simon slipped his feet into the boots and found them to be rather comfortable. As soon as he did this they tightened around his lower legs to fit very snugly indeed. There was no way he would be able to free them. Slowly, like a child reaching for a treat they're not supposed to be having, he pushed his hands into the 'gloves'. These too, tightened to such a degree that they were very nearly uncomfortable and certainly too close fitting for him to remove them again. He was now locked onto the bike.

"To complete your task successfully you must pedal at a rate of no less than 75rpm. Should you drop beneath this you will be given a painful little reminder to up your pace. These 'motivations' will increase in their severity each time you fall beneath the requirement, you would be wise not to do so."

Simon's natural rhythm for cycling in the gym was around 80rpm's so he felt pretty happy with the pace that had been set.

"You will follow the course on the monitor and at certain stages, you will be asked a question. There will be three alternative answers to these questions and you must pick the correct one by cycling under that answer. Should you pick an incorrect answer you will receive a penalty in the form of something rather painful. Should you pick three incorrect answers then you will lose the game. There will be ten questions in all and you should know the correct answer to each, they are simple ones for a man who has taken notice of his world. Good luck Mr. Brown, you may begin your game."

With that, the monitor changed to a scene of the countryside in summertime. Simon began to peddle and although the boots were a little restrictive and stiff around the ankle, they weren't too heavy or difficult to manage. His hands, annoyingly, were fixed in a place that gave him an awkward and unnatural riding position. It wasn't that uncomfortable, but it certainly wasn't the position he'd normally adopt when using the statics at the gym. He was more upright and set back on the seat than he'd like to be. Still, he thought, things could be a lot worse. He'd done thousands of hours on these bikes and was in very good shape at the moment. One thing he hadn't sold was his road bike and he'd been doing the Muswell hill an awful lot recently. Simon felt pretty happy with his challenge. Riding along the sunbathed country lane was a most pleasant experience, the gearing was easy and he could keep above the rev requirement at this difficulty all day long. Flat, winding roads passed through fields and along a river, it all felt a little familiar to him, in the back of his mind Simon knew this place but couldn't quite summon up the details. He'd rode this course before, but when and where were, as yet, a mystery to him. Riding easily, finding his rhythm and trying to drag out of the memory banks exactly where it was that he was travelling, Simon switched into a relaxed and absent state of mind. Miles went by without the hint of a problem, it was all a bit too simple.

Fifteen minutes in he saw the first question point loom on the horizon. He could see that there were three lanes in which to pass under the question 'banner' and each had a word written above them. Only when he got within thirty yards of the banner could he see what the question was. That didn't matter, at the pace he was travelling it gave him a good five seconds or so to read it, see the answers and swerve the bike under the right one. Simon had been worrying about what the questions might be, 'if he'd been taking notice' didn't exactly narrow the subject down any, so he was delighted when he read the first - 'Name your childhood dogs'. In the first lane was 'Oscar and Sophie' the middle read 'Oscar and Cindy' and the right-hand one 'Oscar and Betsy'. Leaning his body over slightly to the left the bike joined the correct lane in plenty of time and he sailed under the banner which disappeared as soon as he got there, replaced by a large, green tick. One down, he thought to himself, only nine to go and only need seven right of those to win this stupid game. Oscar and Sophie... he hadn't thought about those dogs for years and years. In fact, he'd almost forgotten that they had been a part of his life at all. But they had, they'd been a very real part of his upbringing. Without ever meaning to, those dogs had highlighted just how little his mother and father had cared about him. They'd bought them on a whim, without consulting him, but then they never did. Simon had come home one day from a friends party and found two boxer pups in the kitchen. At first, he was delighted, any boy would love a dog to play with, especially a boy who had no one else! However, it soon became apparent that he was allergic to them. Physically, if he spent any time in close proximity to them, they brought him out in a heat rash. For the first couple of years, he was mainly itchy, pink with lotion to calm the rash and unable to get anywhere near the two things in the house that might show him some real love. It was a horrible thing to happen. What did mum and dad do when they found their only child was allergic? Dose him up with anti histamines and tell him he shouldn't get too close to them. This wouldn't have been so bad had the dogs not been encouraged to climb on the sofas for cuddles with his parents - something he was never encouraged to do and certainly couldn't do now the mutts had been there. Simon quickly resented the dogs for both the reaction they created in his body and the wedge they continued to drive between him and his parents. It became clear to him that they loved the dogs far more than they loved him. They were kind, forgiving, affectionate and doting over the dogs, all the things he desperately wanted them to be over him... In time his body adjusted to the dogs and he stopped reacting to them in such a dramatic way, but he never grew to love them and his parents never started to love him.

Was this it? Was this really the extent of the game? He was considering this question when he recollected where he knew this course from. His sudden realisation shook all the confidence from his body and drained his face of the blood that had collected and was heating his cheeks so effectively. He was in the lowlands on his way to one of the most famous climbs in all cycling, the stuff of legends that is Mt Ventoux. He'd recognised a bridge with a particularly lovely cottage set by the river, he'd planned on living somewhere like that when he'd made his vast fortune. This was a simulation of the route and he'd attempted this very one about five times before. Back when he had money, back when life was good, he'd spent a small fortune on a static bike and computer set up that allowed him to ride all the worlds most famous stages. This, this was the one he wanted to do the most. For him, it was the greatest stage in the whole history of cycling, the stage that had cracked so many greats, killed Tommy Simpson. Was it going to kill him? Jesus fuck this was real now!

Since he was a boy he'd loved cycling, loved watching it on the television. All the great riders, Indurain, Hinault, Armstrong but most of all, the cannibal Merckx. He'd been seduced by the history, the pain, and suffering, the grand 21-day soap opera that was Le Tour. Above all else, the pinnacle of any professional riders career would be to win on the Ventoux. It had a mythical quality, partly for its terrible history and its savage nature, it had taken the lives of riders and cared nothing for reputations. Cycling, climbing the Ventoux, for Simon was all about the individual. How much pain could you take? How much could you inflict on your rivals, it was the purest form of sport, you against the mountain. It didn't matter who loved you, how many friends you had or how close your family was, on the Ventoux you were alone in this world. Maybe that's why he loved it so much, it equalised everything.... it didn't matter that they didn't care about him here. Well, here he was and it was going to take some supreme effort, maybe the best riding of his life, to get through this.

As these thoughts passed through his head he was making steady progress along the basin towards the mountains foot. That beautiful scenery that had taken his mind off the task at hand, allowed him some respite from the anxiety of what was to come, was just a blur now. Simon noticed none of it. Soon the gradient would steadily increase and with that, his suffering would begin. In the short distance he noticed a fresh banner approaching, the second question would soon be here and his heart skipped a little at the prospect. He hoped it would prove no more challenging than the last one, but suspected that, like the ride, these questions would become steadily more difficult to answer. He was quite right. As the banner approached he could make out what the question was and it wasn't as simple as he'd hoped. In fairness, it really shouldn't have presented any kind of problem, but Simon felt his throat tighten and the blood escape from his panicked brain.

"What colour eyes does your mother have?" it read. Underneath there were the usual three options - left column, green - middle, brown - right, blue.

At least three of the seconds had gone before his brain decided to even start the process of elimination. He knew she was a red head but he had no idea what colour her eyes may be? He'd no time to stop, had to keep those pedals turning at 75+ and there were only a couple of seconds to decide and swerve the right way. He didn't think they were brown and, somewhere in the back of his head, he remembered that red hair and blue eyes were the most unusual combination. Quickly, he tilted the bike to the left and held his breath... One large, green tick replaced the banner and allowed Simon's chest to deflate and his heart rate to lessen to a more relaxed rythym. How could he not have known? Got away with that one! Still, that's two out of ten, not too many to go and he still had all his lives left. He wasn't exactly brimming with confidence but he was pleased about getting a couple out of the way. He knew, however, that life was about to get a whole lot tougher, the road he was travelling had just taken a sharp turn towards the mountain.

As he approached the beginning of the climb Simon checked his condition. Pace was good, a steady 80rpm that felt well within his comfort zone. Body was fine, breathing regular and no fatigue in his muscles at all so far. His only concerns were his riding position, which still felt a little too upright, and his hands were starting to itch with the sweat that was collecting on them under the mitts. It wasn't something that would cause too much of an issue, just a little less comfortable than he would have liked when attempting one of the most notorious climbs in the world.

Hitting the foot of the mountain Simon felt the gradient change... well, he felt the difficulty ramp up a little through the pedals to simulate a hill anyway. It wasn't too much, it didn't affect his rhythm, but he knew this was only the start. This gradient would steadily increase throughout the whole of the climb and become really tough by the end. His mind was focused on breathing and technique, keep it smooth and relaxed, he told himself. No sooner had he started the ascent than the next banner appeared round the corner of the road. This time, and for the first time he felt he'd gotten a break, he had more time to read and get into the right position to answer. Climbing had reduced his speed a little and, therefore, given him more time to think before answering.

"When is your dads birthday?"

Left - 25 Nov, Middle - 23 Nov, Right 21 Nov.

Shit! He knew it was November, had hoped that the options might be the same day and different months, damn it! Simon couldn't remember the last time he'd bought the bastard a present, let alone seen him on the correct day? They'd usually said they'd pay for the next game of golf, each knowing they'd never arrange one, as a convenient 'thought present'. But what was the damn day? He'd only a couple of seconds to pick and no idea which one it was. No bells were ringing, nothing from the deepest reaches of his memory banks, he'd absolutely no idea and this was his father. Much like the colour of his mother's eyes, he really should have known this... Judging that he'd picked the left one for the first two, Simon eliminated this on the grounds of being unlikely to be three on the bounce. With the bike sat squarely between the two other options Simon closed his eyes and rode exactly, as he thought, in the middle of the two. Allowing lady luck to take a turn. When he opened them he'd passed the banner and passed whatever had replaced the banner to illustrate whether he'd been right or not. Bollocks! he barked at himself, now he didn't know if he'd been right or not? Nothing had happened to him, so he judged that he had. Didn't Jon say that getting one wrong would be painful? Those rules of the game seemed a long time ago now and he wasn't entirely sure what had been said. All this 'thought' had taken his mind off his rhythm, away from the cadence he needed to keep up in order to survive and it was only the red flashing numbers on the front of the bike that saved him. Looking down he saw his pace had dropped to 77rpm and this jolted him back to the job in hand. It was only a small drop from 80, almost imperceptible to the unconscious mind, but it had nearly spelled disaster and he cursed himself for his absence. He'd fluked the question, or so he thought, but nearly screwed it all up with the preoccupation of it, stupid sod!

Onwards he climbed, through the lower part of the mountain lined with trees and peasant houses. Soon though, the gradient would ramp up some more and he'd find himself emerging beyond the tree line and into the high mountain areas. He still had seven questions to answer and an awful lot of cycling to do before this thing was finished. Simon was starting to breathe a little heavier now, not hard, but deeper than before and the sweat was beading and running down his body. He'd always been a heavy sweater and had taken care to ensure he maintained his hydration with lots of water and energy drinks. He didn't have this luxury today. He was going to have to complete the Ventoux on a cup of coffee and a glass of Richebourg, not exactly ideal he thought.

Banner number four appeared just beyond the small village he was passing through. As he closed in on the sign he read "What was the name of your 6th form IT teacher?" This was a gift! He hadn't liked the woman, had paid very little attention to her because of that and wouldn't have had any idea what her name might have been, had it not been for the fact that she'd been a very large woman with a nickname. They'd called her 'Boom boom baboon' in reference to the noise she made walking across those old wooden floors, the 'boom boom' bit. As for 'baboon', well her last name was Boon so that seemed natural enough. Once again he was going to get away with the right answer for the wrong reasons. He'd have had no idea should the question have been about any of his other teachers, their names had been lost long ago if he'd bothered to know them in the first place. However, 'Boom boom' had been remembered, but not because he cared but rather because he'd been unkind about her. Simon snorted to himself at the irony. Jon had devised these questions to see if he had paid attention to those who had been important in his life, to see if he had cared, and he'd only known the dogs because he resented them and the teachers because she was fat!

Left - Birne, Middle - Boon, Right - Bone.

Scratch another one off fuck face, I'm coming to get you! he said out loud and the sound of his voice cheered him up no end. It had broken the silence and taken some of the edginess out of his mind, it was a comfort. So much so that he decided to strike up an imaginary conversation with the monitor in front of him to keep those spirits raised. 'So you think you're going to beat me nob head?' and 'I'm fucking crushing this game you shitbag!' were just two of the verbal attempts at sparring with the unmoved and silent screen in front of him. Still, it did make him feel better, more confident about his chances. Simon decided to make the monitor his dad, that disapproving, superior bastard would provide ample motivation. He'd always wanted to shove something up his nose, show him that he was a better man than his dad ever was, so here was the opportunity. He was going to beat this mountain, beat that fucking machine too and show these bastards who's boss!

These thoughts had taken him out of the villages and up to the tree line which bore another banner. Half way there and feeling good, he smiled. There was a fresh determination in his attitude towards the task.

"Who was the captain of your Sunday football team?"

They had a 'captain'? Was his first thought. That team had been so poor that he couldn't imagine anyone admitting to being its leader! Simon remembered playing on that freezing cold mud bath of a pitch with a shiver. It was far too large for kids that age and sloped terribly from one end to the other. When the wind blew, which was always, it felt impossible to get the ball up that hill. But who the hell had been captain? He barely remembered who was in the damn team...

Left - Chris Firth, Middle - David Riley, Right - Grant Holden.

Brilliant... Not a bloody clue! He'd cared little for the team and, evidently, less so for the kids that were in it. His reason for joining had been that his dad had played for the same club when he was a lad and had actually talked to Simon about those times with something close to affection. It was an attempt, on his part, to get his dad to like him, to get some positive attention for once. It hadn't worked. Every time he came home after a match his dad would ask, somewhat absently, what the score had been. Simon, trying to impress him, had always lied and said they'd won, often trying to embellish the story in an attempt to prolong the conversation. His father, however, had simply used the introduction to talk over him about the team he had played in and how brilliant they had been. County champions, first class boys to a man, etc etc. Simon had listened attentively, but his dad hadn't really been engaged in the conversation but simply reminiscing past glories. It really didn't matter if he were there or not.

Then, one fateful day, father dearest had decided to go and watch them. This he'd never done before. It was the local derby with the best team in the league. Maybe it had dredged up some fond memories of when he had played them as a boy? Simon didn't care why he had been so excited that his dad was coming to watch. Finally, he had a reason to be there and an opportunity to show him how good he was because actually, he wasn't a bad player at all, he just never cared enough about it. Despite his position at centre back, Simon had scored a goal, driven the team forward, headed one off the line and kept the league's top scorer in his pocket for the entire match. It was, according to all that had watched the game, a man of the match performance. His crappy team had lost the game 2-1, one of their closest defeats, but had played like lions, none more than Simon himself. Once the match had finished, he'd run to his dad to ask him what he had thought.

After commenting on the qualities of a number of the opposition players, telling him his goal was a fluke, and remarking that the referee had missed a couple of penalties for the other side, he said that Simon had had 'an alright game'. That he hadn't played 'badly' but the other team were much better. That was the last time his dad ever came to watch him play anything, it was also the last time Simon ever played Sunday football.

These thoughts, these memories of how he'd tried so desperately to impress his dad, brought a tear to his eye. Why couldn't he have just said 'well-played son' and looked proud? Even if he hadn't meant it, even if he'd thought he was shit at football, Simon wouldn't have cared. He just wanted to see, just once, some love in his eyes.

Cycling through the middle, because at this moment he didn't know and didn't care who was the fucking captain, Simon was greeted with a large, red cross as he passed. That wasn't the only thing he was greeted with either. His hands, fixed to the handlebars, felt a faint vibration coming from within. At the same time, he could hear what sounded like the noise of a muffled electric toothbrush. Instinctively, he tried to remove his hands from the bars but found them fixed to the spot. Those gloves couldn't be shifted and they held his hands in a 'grip' like the way all around the metal tube. Simon couldn't see what was happening but he soon guessed. There must have been small, metal blades rotating at high speed within the bars and then through some pre cut slots in them. He felt three points of contact on each palm, hot and stinging like someone was holding a scolding knife edge to his skin. These sharp inflictions of pain sliced through the outer parts of his skin and cut deeply into the flesh on each hand. He could feel the hot metal spinning inside his hands, feel the muscle separate and scream at him to remove them from danger, but there was nowhere to go. Simon pulled and shook the bars with all his strength, but the damn thing hardly budged. It wasn't about to be broken but this didn't stop the thrashing around, it was all he could do! Slowly, as slowly as they had made their way into his hands, the metal discs removed themselves and he could feel every millimetre of their retreat until they were gone again. His hands still burned from the blades and Simon felt the hot blood mix with the sweat that had collected in the gloves giving a fresh, 'salty' sting to his hands. He'd been screaming obscenities from the moment he felt them make the first incision and now he was swearing and forcing air through his teeth, saliva dropping from his mouth onto his thighs.

In all of this, Simon had forgotten about his cadence. Unsurprisingly, keeping a nice even pace had slipped his mind when the blades had penetrated his soft, fleshy palms. It was brought to his attention by the flashing red numbers on the panel of his bike. Underneath the RPM readout, flashing 71, there was a countdown timer that, when he noticed it, read 02...01...00. Before his brain had managed to compute what this signified it had hit '00' and without the necessary time to react and increase his speed, his forfeit was issued. Simultaneously, and with great speed, he felt something sharp and hard penetrate his heels and force its way right through to the bone. With a sickening 'pop' of the skin and tear of the flesh, Simon screamed and would have jumped right off the bike, had he not been fixed to the spot. Those 'spikes' felt like large nails being driven straight through into the heart of his heels, chipping the bones, before retracting at equal velocity. Jesus did it hurt! He screamed and yelled at the top of his voice and pressed firmly on his toes to try and bring his pace back up into credit. He couldn't afford any further injury to the very things he was relying on to get him through this and although it hurt like hell, Simon pushed off on the front of his feet for all he was worth. Within seconds he was above 90 revs a minute and way in excess of what was required, but he needed the breathing space, couldn't chance being anywhere near the danger zone.

In a matter of moments, he'd gone from acing the test and feeling almost smug about his chances, to a total loss of confidence. Blood dripped from the finger ends of the mitts and spattered the flooring below, his hands and feet burned with pain as the sweat entered two deep wounds that had been inflicted. Simon clenched his jaw and made a low grunting noise at each exhalation, waiting for the pain to subside a little.

When it eventually did, to a level that allowed him to think a little more clearly, Simon considered his position. He was half way through the questions, maybe a little more than half way up the mountain and, although he'd been damaged, wasn't in too bad a state to possibly see this through. What was certain, in his mind, was that he couldn't drop below the 75 again. His feet were his only hope, if the front of them were to be attacked then that really would be game over. He could ride ok with the injuries he'd received, he was more of a front foot cyclist anyway, so the heels weren't that important. His hands were in a bad way, he felt, but again, they were not so important to finishing the task. As silly/horrific as it sounded to him right now, he would rather get another question wrong than drop below the required RPMs. He must concentrate, therefore, on always keeping those pedals turning no matter what happened.

Steadily he climbed the now sparse landscape and his rhythm had returned along with some determination. The monitor became 'dad' again and he was fucked if he was going to lose! Next question...

"What are your mothers favourite flowers?"

Left - Roses, Middle - Lillie's, Right - Tulips.

With a great deal of relief, Simon stuck to the middle path. He knew this answer because they smelt so bad. He remembered asking what the 'stink' was as a child and having been scolded by the old witch for not appreciating their beauty. Yet another childhood memory where he'd just not measured up. She'd sneered at him, made him feel shit... She always made him feel shit... That monitor now became mum and dad, a superior portrait of the pair of them.

Onwards he travelled with fresh fire in his belly and as the gradient increased Simon's legs were equal to each step. He was driven, focused and convinced his body wasn't going to let him down. It was hard, really hard, and he was breathing heavily now but he wasn't in his 'red zone', didn't feel like he was even close to it yet. Another banner appeared in the distance and he welcomed the next question, it meant he was another step closer to finishing.

"Who is your father's favourite band?"

Before he could see the options Simon had already arrived at his answer. Simon and Garfunkel, he'd always listened to Simon and Garfunkel on a Sunday afternoon. This was the only time he could recall spending any time in his company. Not that they had played together, talked or shared anything other than the same space. As he neared the answers he realised he was in trouble again.

Left - The Beatles, Middle - The Stones, Right - The Animals.

Simon had about seven seconds to summon up the right answer or he dreaded to think what the consequences would be. Taking each, in turn, he reasoned them out as best he could. 'Beatles' - he could remember seeing a near pristine 'white album' in his dad's collection and maybe a similar 'Sgt peppers' but that had been the extent of his Beatles catalogue, surely an avid fan would have had the lot? 'Stones' - the only album he could recall was a greatest hits. It had been well used but again, surely he'd have seen a lot more had they been his dads favourite? 'Animals' - did he have any at all? Somewhere in his head, he thought he had seen one, a dog eared and well-thumbed affair, but he wasn't sure? With the banner only a second or two away he needed to choose. Discounting the Beatles altogether he moved the bike in between the other options, ready to dart towards one of them at the last moment. Stones... must be the stones! and he nearly swerved to the middle when he thought, 'why include the animals?' Surely there were bigger bands to throw into the mix? On a whim, he leaned hard right and just made the edge of the answer as he went under the banner. Holding his breath and unconsciously pulling his hands away from the bars, or trying to, he waited for the result. This time and he was sure it was deliberate, there was a delay of some three or four seconds before a large, green tick appeared on the screen. He puffed his cheeks out in relief and checked his pace. 76... Fuck! He'd lost his concentration once again. Simon was furious with himself.

One consolation, and he was thankful for the money he'd wasted on that damn machine all those years ago, was that he knew he was over the steepest part of the mountain now. It didn't level off from here, far from it, but it was a little easier and given how tired he was becoming, that was the news he needed to carry on. Only three more questions, he told himself and pushed down on those pedals hard.

Was it his imagination or was the air actually getting thinner? Had the sadistic bastard somehow worked out how to simulate the conditions of the high mountain? Simon was breathing heavily, more laboured than he had been before and each gulp felt like it hadn't the oxygen to sustain his efforts. He felt like he was drowning. How much further had he to travel? Each turn of the pedal took more strength than he believed he had and that rhythmical 80rpm's that had been so easy to maintain before had deserted him now. He was flirting with the 75 almost constantly. With each press of the pedal, he grunted like a tennis pro and prayed for the next question to arrive. It seemed like an interminably long time but it did arrive and seeing the banner lifted his spirits once more.

"What did John, your golf buddy, get his wife for their wedding anniversary?"

Simon couldn't recall the little fat shit ever having a wife? All the conversations they'd had were about business deals. Poor bitch! he thought, being married to a pathetic excuse of a human being like that. All he had cared about was money and fucking people over, he probably did the same with her. Bought her shit and fucked her over! Was he any different? They'd been buddies because no one else could stand them. They'd had a lot in common... This wasn't a pleasant thing to think about. Simon looked for the options to divert his mind.

Left - flowers, Middle - Rolex watch, Right - trip to Paris.

Well, it wouldn't have been the flowers! he thought. John was undoubtedly a tight bastard as far as money was concerned but flowers were far too understated and nice. He'd be much more likely to go for the grand 'look what I did' gesture. Not because it was what his wife wanted but because it was what he wanted to tell people. Fucking show off, big shot, little man syndrome cock end that he was!

It had to be the Rolex. In John's mind that would have been the classiest thing to buy and he would have been able to grab her wrist and show people just how fucking generous and rich he was. Simon had bought Coco a Rolex, but that was because he loved her. This admission came as a bit of a shock to him, but it was true, he had loved her. She'd just laughed when he gave it to her and he'd tried to pass it off as a throwaway gesture, but it had meant something to him. She had meant an awful lot to him...

Under the middle answer, he waited in full confidence for the green tick... and it duly arrived. Two more to go, get just one right and you've made it my boy! This time he kept the pedals turning at the proper rate and had no worries about flirting with the 75. To his surprise, the mountain gradient slackened off some more. This, and the understanding that there were only two questions left, gave him the boost his legs desperately needed. Simon's clothing was soaked through, sticking to his skin and irritating him. It was uncomfortable to ride like this but he could do nothing about it. His hands stung, but not as badly as they had done when first cut and his heels were sore. They ached terribly but he managed to ignore them as best he could and stuck to climbing on his toes. Winding up the road, way above all the villages, he could see for miles, should he have looked. All he was concentrating on, aside from his speed, was the top of the mountain which had just come in to view. That final question must be the end of the ride, he judged, and so the ninth one must be just around the corner. Almost doubling back on itself, Simon saw that he was right, there was the next banner.

"How many grandchildren did Sarah (your cleaner) have?"

What the fuck??? he gasped at the monitor. Who the hell listens to their fucking cleaner? This question took the wind right out of his sails. It wasn't fair, how the hell was he supposed to know the answer to this? She was a fucking cleaner that prattled on about all sorts of shit, he hadn't listened to a word of it, had barely even acknowledged her existence. What sort of bloody test was this? Then he realised something... Sarah had been one of the three people he had thought about contacting when he was in the taxi. Three people in his entire life that might have helped him and she, his cleaner, was one of them. Here he was crying foul but she was very nearly the closest thing he had to a friend... and he hadn't even acknowledged her existence most of the time. It was a deeply sobering thought, what sort of life had he lived? What sort of person was he that he'd gotten to this point in life and had no one. Even his parents, whom he despised, had managed to find each other. What a waste.

Maybe it was the fatigue of the climb, the mental torture that had left him drained, or a combination of both those things and the blows to the head, but whatever it was, Simon started to cry. He was completely spent, both physically and emotionally and the realisation of what his life had added up to, what sort of person he'd become, was too much for him right now. He sobbed and shook, muttered pitiful things and took no notice of the options in front of him, he simply didn't care. He did, however, keep pedalling. He pedalled under the banner and didn't bother the look and see if he'd gotten it right. He hadn't...

That muffled toothbrush noise returned and he waited for the pain to begin. Simon was expecting further cuts to his hands, similar to the last failed answer, but that was not what he got. He felt the sensation of the spinning blade cutting into his little finger, close to the knuckle, and bit his lip whilst waiting for it to stop. But it didn't stop. It cut along the crease at the base of the finger and continued through the flesh, through the bone, and out the other side. It cut the whole damn thing off. Simon screamed and hyperventilated with the shock of it. He hadn't expected it to remove his finger and the surprise of the event acted like a cold water bucket to the face. Where he had been absent in his exhaustion he was now fully awake and aware of everything around him. Aware of the fact that when the first buzz stopped another had started up on the other hand. This time it was much much worse as he knew what was going to happen. Knew that the blade would not be stopping until it had removed the finger. It was horrendous! He felt it cut through the skin and the flesh and he had to wait for the joint. It made a horrible noise as it came in contact with the bone and cartilage and he could smell it burning as it forced its way through. This time it seemed to take forever to finish and every single moment was excruciating. When it was over, when he was sure there were no more drilling noises, he gulped the air to try and stop himself fainting. He was dizzy in the head and felt like throwing up, more at the thought of what had happened because he couldn't actually see. Simon threw his head back as far as he could, then forward, then any position where he felt like it would stop him being sick. His head was spinning like a drunks and everywhere he put it seemed to spin faster. It was no use, his body needed to react to what had happened and his stomach emptied itself over his busy knees. All that porridge was no good to him there.

Once he got over the fact that he was minus two digits and his legs were covered in puke, Simon fixed his gaze to the top of the mountain and pedalled for all he was worth. Shock had provided him with some adrenaline and he was using it before it left his system. God knows he didn't have anything else to get him through. He pedalled as hard as he could and used the whole of his feet for extra pain. He was back to grunting like a tennis pro again and spit made its way down his chin and swung off the end as he jerked forwards and backward again. One last effort, one more question to go...

Suddenly, as he hit the brow of a hill, he saw the finish line. It was maybe four hundred yards away now and the road was just about flat from here. He felt the tension slacken from the pedals and the difficulty lessen considerably, he'd made it! Simon started to shout and laugh aggressively at the monitor. He'd done it, he'd fucking done it! What he couldn't quite see from here was the final question, it was just too far away. It wasn't until he got to within fifty yards that he was able to make out what it said.

"Where did Coco dream of going on holiday?"

Simon laughed... out loud and uncontrollably. Of all the questions he could have asked about her, he thought. What Simon didn't know about Coco could fill volumes. He'd no idea how many siblings she had, if any? Parents? Whether she liked Lillie's or the Animals? But what he did know, and had found out thanks to that stupid gift, was where she dreamt of going. He'd found out because of his feelings for her and that's what made him laugh. After all the questions he'd guessed at, all the times during the ride that he'd not known the answer because he hadn't cared about the person, here, at the final hurdle, he'd been saved by actually having connected with another human being.

After he'd given her the Rolex she'd laughed at him, seen the gift for what it was, a 'big shot' gesture from a dick head trying to look cool. She'd seen right through it but had seen also that Simon, in his emotionally shit way, had meant something genuine with it. Coco had casually chucked the watch back to Simon and said - 'if you really want to give me something to treasure, take me to the lakes for a weekend' He remembered the way she had said it, how she had looked quite vulnerable for the first time. He'd laughed it off in an arrogant way and suggested they go up on the train and camp for the weekend... She told him that was exactly what she wanted to do. All the bravado, the piss taking, and cynicism that had encapsulated their relationship to this point had gone in those few words. She was laid bare and needing him to drop his guard too, but he hadn't. It had scared him, that honesty. Scared him the same way that Jo had and he retreated behind his mask. He did say he would take her at 'some point' but neither of them believed it to be true. It wasn't long after that that they stopped meeting up and Simon felt that pain of loss once again.

He crossed the line to a large tick and a chequered flag. Digital confetti rained from the sky and there was even a fan fair as he came to a halt. Simon slumped over the bike panting and laughing to himself, he'd beaten the bastard. As he caught his breath and tried to cool down a little he checked the gloves and boots, they were still holding him to the bike. Looking up at the screen he saw Jon's face peering back at him, and this was no recorded message.

"Hard lines Mr. Brown, you did so well and put in such a valiant effort..."

Simon scowled at the monitor "What the hell are you talking about? I beat your stupid game fair and square!"

The two-dimensional image laughed "fair and square? You should know fine well that there is nothing fair or square about this life Mr. Brown!"

Angrily, Simon shook the bike, rattled the handlebars with his blooded hands. "Let me out of this fucking thing, I won the game you bastard!"

With a calmness that unsettled him his host continued "Oh you won alright, played the game well and managed to get to the end. Have to admit that I didn't think you'd make it all the way, thought that last question was beyond you. Thing is, and here's the kicker, I don't want you to win..." he paused to let the gravity of what he had said sink in "...as you well know, life isn't fair and I'm under compulsion to be so. You've annoyed me throughout this little exercise and I made my mind up before you even started that you wouldn't be leaving this room..."

Simon, ashen and desperate, interrupted "Wait!... Just wait a minute. You can't do this, you promised you'd let me go on to the next bit if I completed the task... Please!..." He knew he was pleading for his life here.

"Just words Simon, nothing but words! You've told a million lies in your miserable little life, you shouldn't be surprised when someone does the same to you." Jon continued in his emotionless way.

"Please... please don't do this..." was all Simon could muster.

"I've given you the opportunity to consider your life and what you've done with it. You've failed as a human being Mr. Brown and now it's time to end this, you have no value to me" and with that, the screen went blank.

"No!!!... Wait!" he called, but it was too late.

What he heard was the sound of compressed air escaping from somewhere underneath him, what he felt was a tremendous amount of pain. Splitting the seat, forcing its way straight up from its housing within the bike, a large, steel spike exploded upwards. It entered his body through his groin and continued upwards before hitting his spine at the bend. His 'unnatural' position on the bike had been carefully manufactured for this very purpose. To provide the spike with this exact entry and exit point. It ripped through his vertebrae, just above the lumbar region and served his spinal cord before coming to a stop, protruding about a foot beyond his body. Simon could feel, for a moment, the whole thing rigidly holding him in position. Felt every inch of it pushing through his gut and out the other side. When it cut through his spine he lost the sensation from the lower part of his body but still felt the shock of it in his brain. He slumped forward with no control over his torso but the spike, still within him, held his broken body still. It hadn't hit any major organs, it wasn't supposed to, but it had caused massive amounts of damage. As his head fell forward all Simon could see was the blood pouring over the seat post and down onto the floor. He gasped for air and wished for death to come soon. Another mechanical sound pulled the spike back through his body and returned it to the housing within the machine. In doing so, Simon fell forward off the bike but was held to it still by his hands and feet. Those manacles now released him and he fell to the floor. He was bleeding to death and could feel his life force leaving him with every passing moment. All he wanted now was for it to end. His wish didn't take long to come true.

Chapter 6 - James smells a rat

Quietly, motionlessly, James sat in his seat and sipped the fine wine that had been provided. He liked the expensive things this world had to offer and hadn't had a good Burgundy for some time now. He neither engaged the host with what he considered would be pointless questions nor attempted to talk to the others that were left in the room. He was used to keeping his own counsel and felt perfectly comfortable doing so. Having worked for the people he had, James was also used to feeling out of control and because of this, his thoughts were confined mainly to how he was going to die. He was sure that he would, didn't believe one word about being able to 'win' this game. He'd known cruelty and could recognise it in others. Jon was cruel and nothing about what would happen from here would be fair, this he was sure. And so he sat, quietly, awaiting his turn and resigned to his fate.

It was only five minutes or so before the big lump in the suit returned and Jon indicated that James should follow him. Picking up his glass he took one last swill of the wine, savoured its exquisite flavours and replaced the empty vessel on the table most carefully. Let's see what's in store for me then, he mused, and pushed the heavy chair backward. No need for a rifle to the face this time, he followed the lump willingly out of the dining room.

Just as he reached the door, Lola called after him "Oi!..." and he turned to face her "...just so you know, if you make it through to the next bit, I'm going to be waiting for you, you evil bastard!" and she spat at the floor in front of his feet. What he'd allowed to happen to that poor little girl was still fresh in her head and she wanted to inflict as much pain as possible on him. She didn't feel like she had anything in common with her fellow competitors, she wasn't like them at all. It wouldn't prick her conscience one bit killing this scum!

James stared blankly at Lola, then the spit on the floor, and mumbled "stupid bitch" before turning and leaving the room. He didn't care what she thought and was certain they would never meet again anyway. He wasn't 'evil', he didn't feel that way at all. He did, however, feel like he deserved to die for the things he had done, for the person he had become. On the way to his room, James considered the road he had travelled.

He'd been a misfit from the start, born into a family of distinctly average intellect and very little ambition. Mum and dad performed at a very basic level, in work as well as home life, and his siblings had been apples that fell very close to the tree. James' apple had hit the floor and rolled down a large hill to rest as far away from this tree as was possible to imagine. Within a very short space of time, he had usurped his parents and many of his teachers, as far as smarts were concerned, and found himself isolated from his classmates by this gulf in brain power. They were all struggling with the best way to open a pencil case when he was considering the most cunning way to open a chess match. In the playground, those boys and girls of his age were skipping rope and playing army whilst he would sit, all alone, and read about Tesla. This attitude gathered no friends. His teachers were as nervous of his abilities as those children were hateful and his early life in school was not a happy one. James held nothing but contempt for all of them and did not possess the ability to mask this. It's not an endearing quality in a child and, as a consequence, he spent his formative years alone, nosing through the books of those equal to him.

It wasn't until the final year of primary school that someone decided to act on his undoubted talent and seek to find him a more suitable environment. It was unusual, back in the 80's, for a first school teacher to be anything other than a person marking time. Most of them were close to retirement and dreaming of days in the allotment, the others were too stupid to teach anything more advanced than 'how to make a paper hat'. One teacher though, driven by his own motives, fell into neither category. He was principled and enthusiastic about his work, he still possessed the belief that he was making a difference. Mr. Thomas, 35 and a hit with the young mothers in the school yard, had a passion for showing kids the endless wonders of this world. It turned out, some years later, that he had a passion for showing them something a little less wondrous too, but that's another story. He recognised the potential in James immediately and did all he could to keep the boy interested in school life. It became apparent, fairly early, that operating a classroom where twenty kids were within 10% of each other and one was streets, if not counties ahead, just wasn't going to work. Try as he might, he simply didn't have the time to dedicate to James' continued development and it was clear to him that he needed a different environment. James' family were poor, there was no chance of them paying for a better education even if they'd have wanted to, so a scholarship to the local grammar was the only way to go. Mr. Thomas organised the necessary interviews and tests, and was as delighted, if not more so, than anyone else when James was accepted. This, he felt, would be the making of the boy...

Pushing the large oak door ajar, the lump in the suit stood to one side to allow James through. This he did with an air of resignation and no resistance. He'd no idea how far they had walked or in what direction, what was the point? They'd made their way to the room with James taking no notice of his surroundings, or how he might find his way to the aviary, should he complete the task. He felt certain that, if the aviary even existed, it wouldn't be necessary. As he crossed the threshold he heard the door slam behind him and believed, totally, that this would be the last room he would ever be in. Taking stock of what was around him, James noted the curious set up of the room. Devoid of any features around the outer edges, this fifteen-foot square was condensed into six feet of interest in the middle. Surrounded by what looked like a series of boxes that completed a ring, there were three TV screens on a large table in front of a chair in which he guessed he would be sitting. There were metal straps for his ankles and a larger one to fit around his stomach. It was made entirely of metal and didn't look the most comfortable place to be spending his time. Along the seat and back, up the square legs too, were any number of holes and perforations, as if the chair needed these to breathe? Behind those legs and running from the floor all the way up the back, was chicken wire. Again, a most curious thing to be found on a seat. On the table, aside from the screens, there was a mouse. This must be what he would use to play the 'game', he judged. Behind the door was a chair that contained a change of clothing, some shorts and a short sleeved top with a pair of his trainers underneath. James didn't wait for any instructions before removing his suit and donning the clothes that had been set out for him. He felt neither excitement nor trepidation for what was about to happen to him, he'd switched off and was simply going through the motions.

As he was tying his laces the centre screen illuminated with the face of the host. Pre-recorded, it introduced the elements of the task ahead.

'Welcome Mr. Evans, you will find some clothes to change in to on the chair behind the door, please do so without delay...' and it paused. James waited. After a minute or so the video message resumed.

'If you would make your way into the circle and seat yourself in front of the monitors Mr. Evans, I will explain what your task will be' and James followed the instructions without question. Seating himself and swinging first the metal ankle straps and then the body strap into place. They locked into their housings securely and he would not be leaving this chair until the ordeal was over.

'Please fix the straps you can see into their slots and we will continue...' it paused again and he felt a little annoyed by the fact that he had to wait once more. '...good! Let me outline the rules of the game. In front of you are three monitors, each will display a separate chess game that you must play. To win, you must finish with two points out of the three games. You will have a certain amount of time to complete each move and failure to do so will result in a forfeit, continual forfeits will make your life a lot harder, and more painful! Play whichever game you wish first by clicking on that screen. Once the first move has been made, all three games will become 'live', meaning you can make whichever move you see fit on whichever game. In the left-hand monitor you will be white, the middle black, then white again... you can win this game with a clear head.'

James was still unconvinced but quite happy with the task he'd been set, he used to love chess.

'Use the mouse to make your moves and when they have been completed, pass on to the next match. Simple!' And it did indeed appear simple enough. 'Good luck Mr. Evans, I'm counting on you to beat this test'

That was the end of the message and the screen went blank, leaving James to consider his 'task' whilst he waited for it to begin.

Chess had been his childhood saviour, his sanctuary from the cruelty of the world around him. It was somewhere he could escape to when life became too much to deal with. Without it, he wouldn't have made it through that fucking school, wouldn't have made it past the first year...

Mr. Thomas had secured him a future in education that he'd neither asked for nor wanted. He'd done it with the very best of intentions but had failed to see the problems he would face. At his 'normal' school James was an odd fish in a small pond. He stuck out like a sore thumb, it was true, but he was, at least, on the same socioeconomic 'level' as the rest of the kids. His intelligence was the only defining difference between him and the rest of them, and James had gotten used to that. Here, at the grammar, he was both an intellectual outcast and a financial one. Not only was he isolated by his brain, he was viciously tormented for being poor too. That he was 'better' than the other kids in his primary school was something they could accept, as long as he was equal to them in money. At the grammar, those around him felt both inferior and superior to James, and the dichotomy of these two emotions bred a whole new level of bullying that was impossible to endure. He was beaten regularly and ostracised from any and every group he attempted to join. Hopeless at sports, he was made to stand on the side lines in the rain and watch, rather than join in. When the captains, those fucking self-righteous bastards, picked the teams, he was always the last one left and they would compete to give him away to the other side. It was beyond humiliating. James remembered one time when he was picked in the football match and they'd told him to go in goal. He'd taken up his position and, naively, had determined to do the best he could. Had actually believed that if he tried his best, the others would see his effort and respect him for it... It didn't work out that way. Quickly it became obvious that the two teams - each and every member - had collaborated before the match and decided amongst themselves to really show him up. As soon as the match started his 'team mates' just stood by and allowed the opposition to waltz through with the ball. They took it in turns to fire shots at him from close range. Closer and closer they came and they weren't trying to score, they were trying to hurt him. He remembered clearly the loud cheers from everyone on the pitch when the ball hit him and he fell to the floor. James even remembered looking to the teacher for some support and seeing him laughing along with the rest of them. After that incident, he stopped changing for gym and simply sat with a book instead. Nobody tried to encourage him not to, they were all happy to see the back of him. It was then that he 'found' chess. There was a book on Bobby Fischer in the library and he devoured it, it was a fascinating world where intellect was king and no bully could touch you. James immersed himself in the world of the chess grand masters.

Flickering into life, the TV screens displayed three chess boards with timers at the top of the screen and the name of his opponent. In the left screen, where he was white, he saw he was playing Kasparov. In the middle screen, black, he had Fischer and on the right-hand monitor was the name, Sam Westwood. Hahaha.... James laughed audibly at the task ahead, and the opponents he'd been given. Garry Kimovich Kasparov, the greatest chess champion of all time! In his mind, there was probably only one man who could defeat Kasparov at his best and that was the unconventional genius of Fischer, the man in the middle. Then, with a deliberate 'poke' in the ribs he'd been given Sam to finish. How the hell was he supposed to get two points out of this challenge? On the middle screen, where his mouse icon was hovering, were the words 'please select which game to start first'. James sat there for a good few minutes shaking his head and laughing at the absurdity of it. Jon had said he could win this task but he failed to see how. He used to be good, could possibly have become a grand master, but Kasparov and Fischer were a whole other league. Maybe the two greatest players ever to take up the game. He had believed, before he even got to the room, that he wouldn't be able to win, that the point of this whole thing was to make him suffer for his sins and, ultimately, kill him. There was nothing here to make him feel any different, it was impossible! It really didn't matter which game he started, he would lose two of them anyway. Even if he played the game of his life against one of them and snatched a draw, he'd never be able to do that in two matches. Beating Sam would be a piece of cake but gaining the other point needed was beyond him.

As he sat there, as the seconds and then minutes ticked by, James considered not playing at all and just waiting for the inevitable to happen. Why give this bastard the satisfaction of trying and being humiliated once again? One thing stopped him from doing this, there was one nagging question in his head. Why had he been given the option of which game to start first? There must be a reason? Jon had said he 'could' win this if he kept a clear head and there was something about the way he had said it that made James believe him. Was there a clue in the fact that he could start where he wanted? Suddenly his brain kicked into gear, if there was a way then he was going to find it. If he started with Sam then he'd have white against Kasparov and black against Fischer... so what? That didn't seem to present any advantage. Garry could crush him playing from a losing position, never mind just being second to start. If he began with Garry then he would have Bobby as black. Again, he could see no benefit... There must be something, he thought. If he played Bobby... If he played black first, let Bobby make the opening move... That was it! Fucking hell, how stupid could he be? Of course, that was the answer to the puzzle, he couldn't fail to take the two points this way. Ha! He laughed, clapped his hands and drummed them on the desk in front of him. Jon had been telling the truth, with a clear head he could indeed win this task, in fact, it was going to be easy, anyone could do it. All he needed to do was make sure he didn't slip up against Sam, and he wouldn't allow that to happen. Eagerly, with a renewed belief in his chances of surviving, James clicked the centre screen and waited for Bobby's opening foray. This was actually going to be fun!

Fischer started with queens pawn to D4, as expected this was the move that left the greatest number of attacking options for white, concealing which particular 'opening' Fischer was attempting. James waited to see if he was right about the 'cheat' Jon had given him. Once the move was complete, Bobby's clock stopped and his started. But, crucially, it started on each board. This meant he could play whichever turn he wanted next. Yes! James shouted, his theory was correct and Jon had indeed given him the means to win this. He opened with the same classic move against Sam and moved on to Garry. This was the key to it, all he needed to do was play Fischer's moves against Garrys, Garrys counters against Fischer and let them fight it out. If one of them beat the other, then he'd get a point. If they drew, he'd get half a point from each match, either way, he'd end up with two points from the games as long as he beat Sam. The crucial part was that he could play whichever turn he liked when white, as long as the clock count didn't expire. That allowed him to see what Fischer was doing and replicate it against Garry. There was nothing in what Jon had said about taking each game in turn. As long as he was white, the clock was moving on each board and he could play anyone he chose.

His first move, or rather Bobby's, against Garry complete, James waited for the counter play which came within a second. Clicking the middle board he replicated this against Bobby and moved on to Sam's game. This swift play gave him nearly 45 seconds to consider his game against Sam, which, he felt, would be ample time to beat that cretin! He could have played Fischer's opening against both Kasparov and Sam, but he wanted to show that he could beat the crap out of that toff bastard without the need of any help from elsewhere. Those clock counters reset to 60 seconds after each move was complete and the computer opponents only took a second or so to make their moves, he was almost always 'in play' on all three boards. This didn't matter, he was simply exchanging moves in the first two games anyway, that took no time at all. Sam's game was going to take all the brain power here and most of his time. He must be careful not to let the clock run out. James felt distinctly rusty in those opening exchanges, it had been 30 years or more since he last played the game. Thirty years since he learned his final lesson from life.

After the football incident, James had retreated into his own world of chess, learning all he could from the books that were available. Luckily, the library at the school was well stocked with such things and he was able to drink in all that the old masters had to offer. Aside from attending the obligatory lessons, for which he had little interest, James spent the rest of his time in the library reading. It was a great place to avoid the bullies too, they only ever went there when there was a test due, and the librarian was a hard arsed little Irish woman who took no shit from anyone. One lad had tried to humiliate him once, making fun of the books he was reading and pushing him around. She caught him by the sideburns and marched him out of there squealing as he went. She could only have been half his size, but she had the fierceness of a bull terrier. Nobody said shit to him after that, they kicked his bag and maybe mumbled to themselves, but he could handle that no problem.

James learned and played - against himself - all hours of all days and found his brilliant brain was, for once, working in his favour. He joined the chess club at the school, purely to test his skills against someone other than himself, and found it depressingly easy to win. Those members weren't bullies like the others, but they were nothing close to his level of play and he failed to connect with them socially either. His advanced play and lack of humility bred contempt from the only kids in the school that might have befriended him. It was a club full of lads that had been bullied just the same as James, but they were still rich kids. Or, at least, that's how James viewed them and he delighted in crushing them and highlighting their stupidity. In his head they didn't deserve to play the game, it was far too beautiful for such creatures. Soon, no one would play him at all, nor would they acknowledge his presence and so he stopped attending. His skills, however, hadn't gone unnoticed and when it came to playing other grammar schools across the country, first at county level and later at national, he was always the first name on the list. James played, won, and took great satisfaction from the fact that he was now the bully. He even adopted the Kasparov 'hunch'. Making himself large and dominant across the other side of the table, furrowing his brow and playing his moves with aggression. He was only eight years younger than the great man, similar height and build, and he idolised him. Garry had just become the youngest world champion, beating the great Karpov, and James wanted to follow in his footsteps.

Then came the national championships, a chance to show the larger world of chess what he was about. It was a dream come true for James, this was, at last, a world he belonged in. Somewhere he fitted in and felt that he was amongst equals at last. It was his destiny! They were to be held in London and five of the best school kids had been given the chance to compete against the best players in the country. Of those five, James was top ranked. For the first time in his life he was actually excited about something, actually felt joy in his heart. This was going to be the spring board to a life dedicated to the most beautiful game ever invented. His imagination ran wild with the possibilities and glorious opportunities that this would afford him. In preparation, he read like crazy. Learned all he could about those he would be competing against, which, at that time, wasn't a great deal. If only the Internet had been around back in 1986.

James did everything he could to be ready for the event and couldn't wait to get started. Then, on the eve of the tournament, a mere 48 hours before he was due to leave, he got a visit from the headmaster of the school. It was supposed to be one of those 'do the school proud' type pep talks, the old bastard had never taken any interest in James up to this point, never even set eyes on him before. When he did, he didn't like what he saw. James was a scholarship boy and the head despised them. He didn't like poor people, didn't believe they had any business being at his school and couldn't possibly allow one of 'them' to represent Ardwood Grammar at such a prestigious event. People might see! Sam Westwood, a boy of breeding and sound stock, 'old money you know' was hastily drafted in to replace him. That was the last time James had thought about the game, that was the last time he had cared about anything other than money. From that day to this he hadn't even picked up a chess piece, let alone played a game for fun.

Bobby traded blows with Garry and James was fascinated with the way the game was going. It was a wondrous thing to behold, the two great geniuses of chess, toe to toe. Would Bobby play something outlandish and fool Garry, throw him off guard, or would Garry find a way to power through from black to win? He was genuinely excited to see how it would go. For his own game, James had played conservatively from the start but was feeling a little more daring now. As the game progressed he could feel his sluggish brain begin to pick up the pace. It was as if it had been reawakened by an old friend and was rising to the challenge. James was enjoying himself, more than he had done in years. This was better than money, better than all those stupid things he had bought himself to try and feel like one of those arseholes he had despised all his life. Why had he thought that having money would make things better for him? It didn't make the past disappear, didn't make him feel any more a 'part of the club'.

Bobby offered a pawn, it was a simple swap to possibly gain some territorial advantage later down the track and the type of exchange that happened frequently at this level. James couldn't see where he was heading with this move, he might have done 30 years ago, but was curious to see if Garry would accept to offer. He did, and the pair of them traded. As soon as they did so, two 'hatches' opened in the ring of boxes around him and two dirty great rats appeared. James froze to the spot, not that he could do anything other than stay exactly where he was. Rats were his great phobia. They panicked him and muddled his brain, made the outside world swim around and go fuzzy before his eyes. It had always been this way since he was a little boy, back in that dreadful terraced city street. All those feelings and memories came flooding back to him at once.

When he was a boy, the youngest of three, James was always the one that was made to do the worst of the chores. Whilst his sister and brother got away with washing up or cleaning the rugs, he was always given the duty of stocking the coal bucket. They knew he hated going out to the coal shed, knew he was frightened to death of rats, but would make him do so anyway. He'd complained to his mother, pleaded with his siblings, begged to do anything other than but to no avail. Even within his own family, he was bullied for being different and so it was that he would have to make the trip to the shed for coal, no matter what. Often he'd be in tears before he even made it outside, but they didn't care. They just threatened him with the wrath of father, should he not complete the task, and that was only just a little more frightening than the job itself. He couldn't remember when his petrification had begun or whence it came, but the feeling was most certainly a real one. It churned his stomach and made him numb with fear. They were dirty creatures, base animals doing whatever they could to survive. They'd eat anything, including their own, and lived in the most squalid conditions. To James, they represented those children he went to junior school with. Stupid and dirty and terrifying. Like rats, they just bred and fought and took over, infesting the world with their dirty beliefs and stupid thoughts. Dispose of one and ten would take its place, they were an unstoppable force of nature and hateful in every respect.

One day... one cold and dark early evening in the winter time, to be precise, James had been handed the coal bucket by his sister - the chief tormentor. He hated doing it during the daylight hours but it was ten times worse when darkness had fallen. You couldn't see them then, but you could hear the rustling. Hear the high pitched noises they made and smell them close by. That awful, acrid, cloying stench of ammonia that was particular and unmistakable. It used to make him physically sick. In the darkness, he always felt they were going to attack him, that they were readying themselves for an assault at any moment and this day was no different. Off he was sent, into the yard out back, to fetch the coal. In his blind panic, James was incapable of noticing anything other than the task ahead of him. He failed completely to see that, on this occasion, his brother and sister were ever so quietly following him. Failed to see that his brother had something in his hand. Failed to notice anything other than the horror of the situation.

When he reached the door to the shed and had yanked at the rusty bolt to shake it free, the door - as it always did - 'popped' open a little. It had been warped by the rain and was always a shock when it did this and a pain to bolt shut again afterward. Jesus, the whole damn process was horrible! He'd pulled the door open, gingerly, and was about to set down the bucket when he felt a pair of hands shove him into the shed. Falling onto his hands and knees James had screamed for a second before the terror had taken over and removed the ability to breathe. He remembered how he had turned to begin the process of removing himself from this hell, only to see his brother standing in the doorway. Before any words could come out, before any breath had been taken, Dean had thrown into his lap the biggest rat he had ever seen and shut the coal shed door. Later he learned that psychologists call this 'flooding'. Basically, overloading someone with the thing they most fear and leaving them to deal with it. The belief being that the body cannot panic forever and, at some point will have to calm down. When it does this then the object of the phobia will decrease in its fear factor to a point where the subject will be comfortable. When James had heard about this technique he wished, with all his heart, that those stupid bastards could feel one tenth of the absolute terror he had felt that day. It is impossible to articulate just what happens to the brain in moments like that and James felt the experience had gone on forever and would never end. In actual fact, he was shut in that shed for no more than five seconds, but those were the worst of his life. Every one of them filled to the brim with paralysing, heart stopping dread.

When they let him out, white as a sheet, he'd wet himself and could hardly stand. They had to pull him to his feet and were crying with laughter as they did so. James couldn't speak, didn't know how to control his body and was limp in their arms. As it turned out, the 'rat' that his brother had thrown on him was actually just a bundle of old fabric he'd sewn together to look like the animal, complete with tail. He'd made it in his craft lesson that day and had gotten praise for his efforts. Far from being junior psychologists, Dean and Shelley had simply found the idea too hilarious to pass up and didn't see why James had been so distraught. James' mother had been distraught though at the sight of his clothing after his incontinent trip to the shed and had given him a thick ear to go along with his mental scar. It was the worst moment of his life, bar none, and the appearance of those two large rats had brought it all back to him now.

They scurried around the outer edges of the circular boxes, sniffing the air as they went. James could hardly look at them but couldn't take his eyes off them either. He was hyperventilating and completely incapable of focusing on anything else, especially the chess games in front of him. Nosing the other boxes and, seemingly, looking for a way out of the centre circle, the rats paid James very little attention. Not that this eased his petrification one bit. It was as if he were returned to the coal shed, only this time it was daylight and he could see his tormentors coming. All the while, had he noticed, the clocks on the screens were winding down to zero. Each at a slightly different point, but steadily counting down as he sat in complete panic. It was the game against Sam that ran out first. In bold, red flashing numbers the clock ticked away - 4.... 3.... 2.... 1.... 0. When it hit zero, and he hadn't even seen it coming, the whole screen flashed. Something else happened too that managed to refocus James' attention, the chair he was sitting on sprang to life. He felt it 'hum' first, somewhere under his backside, just a small vibration, and the sensation made no real impression on him. He was still entirely absorbed by the furry menace. However, within a second or two, at numerous points on his body, it was hard to tell how many, the chair fired what felt like stinging needles into his skin. They broke through the outer layers and penetrated his flesh with a burning sensation that jolted him back to the present. James jumped in his chair, as one stung by a bee, but found himself firmly held in position by those braces. This biting reminder of the game he had neglected forced him to make a hurried move, lest the chair feel it necessary to provide any further provocation. Quickly shifting a pawn one step further up the board without paying it any real thought of mind, James groaned as he noticed the folly of this move. Quickly, the computer simulation of Sam returned by taking the pawn and advancing its bishop into a most threatening position. It was a disastrous play by James and had put him deeply on the back foot. He had no time to dwell on the matter though, as the other clocks were very close to zero and flashing for his attention. He managed to play his next move against Garry with only a second to spare but was too late to play Garry's response against Bobby.

Two more flaps opened on the boxes in the circle, a reaction to the taken pawn, and the chair made that dreadful buzzing sound again. Two more rats, bigger and meaner it seemed than the first pair, entered the fray and busily chatted with the others. Exchanging information about their environment and planning their next move. This time the chair cut. Tiny wheels of sharp metal sliced first the back of his calves, only superficially but it still hurt a great deal. Then they did the same to the back of his thighs, bottom and back. James felt the blood trickling down his legs and pooling on the seat. Trying to shift his position to alleviate some of the discomfort the cutting had caused, he felt his shorts sticking to the metal. It was a sensation not unlike sweat but it had a thicker, stickier quality to it and James knew it was blood. Moreover, the four fat rats knew it too. They sniffed the air and became quite excited by what they could smell. Where before they had paid him no mind, now, with the stench of his blood in the air, they stopped their reconnaissance of the circle and all stood and stared at him. James could see them watching him, sniffing and looking with those dead, black eyes. It was enough to make him scream. That panic he had felt before paled in comparison to how he felt right now. With every ounce of strength in his body, he shook and pulled at the chair. Tried to break free from the shackles that held him in place. All he could think, all that was rushing through his blurred mind was 'escape!' But there wasn't even an ounce of give to encourage him. Those dirty, furry bastards took a step back at first, alarmed by the commotion and noise. But once they knew he was fixed to the spot, they grew ever more confident in their movements. They crept tentatively closer and grew bolder with each little step. James could smell them now too, their musty damp stink filled his nose and dragged him back to the coal shed once again. That thrashing, the idea of breaking free had left him now as the energy had left his body. Adrenaline had coursed through his veins but he had emptied all of it into the chair and was left with no reserves. One of the rats moved closer. Blood had dripped over the shoes he was wearing and little puddles were forming on the wooden floor around them. As the dirty brown bastard edged its way towards the soles of his feet, James attempted, despite his horror, to kick out a leg and repel it. His foot shifted half an inch or so and that wasn't enough to send the rat running. It sat back on its fat backside for a second, appraising the situation, and when it was happy that James was securely locked into the chair, it moved forward again. This time it moved with certainty and the others followed suit. Sam's timer was running low again, flashing red numbers filled the screen but James took no notice. He was now paralysed by what was happening beneath him and unable to shake his attention away.

They started at the puddles. Big rat number one was the first to lap at the blood that was collecting there and James could see the disgusting creature had smeared its face with it. Its nose and whiskers were oiled in the dark red substance, as were its feet. Soon the others joined in and bathed themselves red. The sight of this, the revulsion he felt in the pit of his stomach, made him sick. Leaning forward in the chair and unable to stop himself, he puked all over the table in front of him. Porridge mixed with Burgundy made a hideous sloppy cocktail and it dripped in globules off the table and onto the floor. Some of it hit a rat and stained its back. This made him throw up what was left in his stomach.

With the clock at zero on Sam's game, and nearing zero on the other two, the chair sprang back into life. This time it drove thick nails deep into his legs and back. He could feel how far they pushed their way in before retracting again and the holes that were left soon filled with fresh blood. Suddenly, all the boxes opened at once and maybe sixty rats escaped into the arena. They all had a hunger, they had been able to smell what was going on and somehow knew exactly what to do. Scurrying quickly across the floor they fought to get to the puddles. Squabbled with each other over the feast that James had offered up and soon became discontented with the slim pickings at his feet. Two, four, six of them started to climb the chicken wire to reach fresh parts of his wounds. James was crying, howling at what he could see but do nothing about. Those filthy, nasty little bastards were all over his legs now, lapping at the cuts eagerly. He could feel their rough tongues on his skin, inside his skin. It wasn't long before one of them took a bite. It was just a little nip at first, but he felt its razor sharp teeth sink into his skin and pull some away. They all seemed to get the message immediately, he was there to be eaten! He had the ability to grab them with his hands, they weren't held by the chair but they were held by his terror. Petrification is exactly the word to describe his state of being, he was frozen to the spot.

All the clocks reach zero, the screens flashed and demanded attention but James had none to give. He was consumed by the rats. They climbed further up his body and, although he screamed at the top of his voice, they weren't put off in the slightest. More buzzing from the chair, more stinging needles, nails and cutting discs ripped open his flesh and the rats worked themselves into a frenzy. They bit hard, confident that nothing would happen to them, and pulled the skin from his body. His arms and legs were a sea of filthy red rats and the blood poured out of him now.

There's only so long that the body, or rather the mind, can take such stress. Only so much blood one can lose before you start to shut down. It was lucky, a mercy really, that James, covered in rats and having his body cut to pieces by them and the chair, passed out. He simply couldn't take anymore and had given up. Slumping forward in the chair that was still ripping into him, he lost consciousness as the dirty, hungry bastards feasted on every inch of him. They'd made their way onto his shoulders now and were gouging deep pits into his neck and face.

James never got to see who would come out the victor between his two heroes, never got to take that long awaited revenge on Sam either. Thankfully, he never regained consciousness.

Chapter 7 - Lola the Honey Badger

"Did you really have to spit on the floor?" Jon asked as the door closed. He said this with an air of someone looking down 'one's nose'.

"Well you can take the girl out of the slum..." she returned, sarcastically "besides, you know what he did, do you honestly think I belong in this company?" and she gave a sideways glance towards cock munch.

"I've absolutely no doubt darling, you're as ruthless and avaricious as any of your competitors, maybe more so? I've a feeling you'll do well if you get past your game" he said with a smile.

"Yeah.... about that, don't suppose you'd like to tell me what's in store? Give me a chance to get my head around it?" She wasn't in the least bit hopeful.

Jon sat back in his chair, extended his right forefinger and wagged it from side to side before resuming his silent contemplation. Lola looked again at Thomas who was still giving the impression of someone who'd recently lost a loved one in a most horrific way. Conversation was going to be thin on the ground. She sat back in her chair and thought about how this might play out.

What she would get for her 'game' was anyone's guess and there seemed little point dwelling on that subject. What would happen afterward was much more thought worthy. She felt certain that at least two of them would make it out of the games alive, otherwise why bother with the whole 'make your way through the house' charade. There would be no need for the wrist bands either and Jon seemed like the sort of sadistic bastard that would enjoy watching people kill each other for money. She didn't for one second believe that he wouldn't be watching their progress through the house, again, what would be the point? He liked surprises? She doubted that very much indeed. He'd be watching alright but would he have any power to intervene? Given her physical disadvantage, what sort of weapon would she get to even that out or was it just a case of taking the others by surprise? That she would be capable of killing another human hadn't really been an issue. Lola was a single minded girl and wouldn't have gotten herself out of that hell hole of a community if she didn't possess the necessary balls to do whatever it took. That she might have to kill to survive this evening.... fair enough! That didn't worry her one bit. They had until midnight to get to the aviary and claim the money. Was there any money? Would Jon really just hand over ten million pounds to the last person standing? What about all the dead bodies and the little fact of mass murder, how could he let the winner go and be confident they wouldn't hot foot it to the nearest police station? It all seemed unlikely to her so the real question was 'how was she going to get out of here alive?'

As she was pondering this, and getting nowhere closer to formulating a plan, the mute monkey returned to the dining room to collect the next contestant/victim. Obviously, the host had never heard of 'ladies first' as it was Thomas 'cockmunch' Dean who was beckoned to follow. He affected a 'mince' as he passed the point on the carpet where Lola had spat and she inadvertently laughed at his display. It was the first comic moment of the day and probably the last, she thought. As the door shut she turned back in her chair to face Jon and said

"And then there were two!" and raised her glass in his direction. She wanted him to talk, wanted to find out something about him, his motives, who he was, anything that might help her get out of this thing in one piece.

"Indeed...." he said in a precise way, staring straight through her with his piercing eyes. "So go on.... ask away" he somehow knew this was an attempt to gain information.

Lola much preferred the 'straight to the point' method of communication and appreciated this cut to the chase. Time wasn't on her side, the monkey would be back in five minutes or so, she needed to get on with it.

"Who are you?... I mean 'really', who are you?" she decided to keep the questions short and to the point.

Jon's eyes looked up towards the ceiling in thought and his mouth turned down at the corners. Deliberately taking a sip of wine he considered his answer carefully.

"I'm a man who has everything..." he said "...I've been everywhere, done everything there is to do. I've won a million at poker, lost twice that in Monte Carlo, owned champion horses and dived with great whites. I've done everything there is to do that gets the blood pumping and makes one feel alive. Money has never been a problem for me so I've had to find my thrills elsewhere and now I seem to have exhausted what the law will allow me to do in pursuit of feeling that exhilaration. Each time I've pushed the boundaries I've found

myself a little less satisfied with the results and so we have ended up here, tonight. This, my dear, is the next big kick."

"If that's the case, why aren't you doing one of the games? Surely it would be more 'thrilling' being on our side of the fence instead of watching from yours?"

He smiled, that reptilian grin of his that had surfaced a number of times this evening.

"How do you know I'm not in the game?" he posed.

"So you've got a task to complete too, is that the case?" she asked.

"Oh no, not in the sense that you mean. Someone has to coordinate things and I couldn't very well set myself a game to play, that wouldn't be fun. But just how much control do I have? Mr. Brown thinks he has found a loop hole in my plans and maybe, just maybe I included some? If you take everything I say at face value then I hold all the aces... but is that actually true? Maybe, Miss Cooper, I've left myself in a precarious position and a really smart person might just work out how to do more than just win the money..." and he left the words hanging for Lola to muse over.

Was he telling the truth or was this just nonsense? What was it Brown had stumbled upon? Her brain spun madly with the effort of trying to find an answer. She must find some sort of advantage, if not over Jon then at least over her competition before she left for her task. But try as she might, she could find nothing from the evening thus far to suggest a chink in his armour. It was infuriating! Desperately, she decided to ask point blank.

"Give me something to work with, I'm not like the others so give me a break, how can I win?"

"Hahaha... Oh, I do admire your candour Miss Cooper, but I think you are mistaken!" he chuckled.

"Mistaken with what?" Lola asked, a little bemused.

"Mistaken in thinking yourself whiter than the others, more morally sound, if you like. From my information, you're just as bad!"

"Like fuck I am!" she said determinedly and stared at him with a fixed jaw.

"Oh really? What about Lee Page? You do remember him, don't you?" Jon looked at her quizzically, knowing fine well she had not forgotten the boy.

Lola wasn't about to concede anything though, and although the memory pricked her quite sharply she gave no quarter. "Could have happened to anyone..." she said assuredly "not my fault he couldn't take a joke!"

Jon watched her expression keenly from the other side of the table, but her face gave nothing away. She had spirit and a bloody minded determination that might just get her through this, he thought. Just then, putting an end to the discussion, the door opened for the last time and Lola was ushered out of the room by the monkey.

"Good luck Miss Cooper" he called after her as she neared the exit. Lola turned for a moment and regarded the host one last time, would she see him again?

They left the room and began to make their way to Lola's game. As they did, she revisited the memory of the boy in the office. He was a boy too, just a boy. She remembered the first time she'd seen him, all fresh faced and rosy cheeked. Remembered how she had thought at the time that this was no job for an innocent like him, how long would it be before he either looked like the rest of those cock sure son's of bitches or had been broken by them. As it turned out, neither of those things happened.

She had not been there very long herself and was fighting, every day, against the arrogant misogynists that pervaded the company. Each time she began a new day she had to struggle, swim against the tide of abuse. Some of it focused on her class, some on her gender and most of it was sexual in content. That a woman, and a dirty scrubber at that, had the arrogance to think that she could do this job as well as them, those men of breeding and privilege, was inconceivable. They felt threatened by her and fought back with all the subtlety of a herd of elephants. How many times she'd had her arse groped in the lift, felt them leering at her from across the room, heard them talking about what they'd like to 'do' to her, she'd given up counting. It was a testament to her mental strength that she had managed to carry on, refuse to be beaten by this wall of abuse. Up until Lee's arrival, Lola had done her job quietly and efficiently, keeping away from trouble as best she could. As much as she wanted to sink her claws into their faces, drive her knees into their crotches, she managed to keep her emotions bottled. Then he had arrived, just an ordinary office junior no different to the many others the company had taken on, but he *was assigned to her. She'd seen them start, find their feet and rise through the ranks much quicker than she had. Not because they had been better, far from it, but because they were the right 'type'. Sons of previous bankers, nephews of those on the board, friends of friends at the club, that sort of thing. It had boiled Lola from the inside to see them given such an easy ride into the business. If she'd made even a tenth of the mistakes they had, she would have been out on her arse. She had needed to be perfect, twice as good as any of the men there to get half as far. Well, she had been, and they had rewarded her with her first 'junior'.*

He was twenty-two years old but looked much younger. His wide eyes and juicy red lips gave him the impression of a startled fawn and a stiff breeze looked like all it would take to knock him over. His 'off the peg' suit had been too large in most areas, typical of a first attempt to look professional. Lola despised him from the start. Not for his character, he was actually a softly spoken and diligent boy, exactly what you would hope for in a junior, but for what he represented. He was the establishment, he was just the same as the rest of those fuckers who were humiliating Lola on a daily basis. This was confirmed to her the first time they had gone for lunch and Lee had been beckoned to the 'boys' table. She herself had never been asked to join them, nor would she have wanted to, and it was a slap in the face that he'd been taken under their wing from the off. She remembered sitting there, drinking her coffee and feeling their glances in her direction. Hearing them snigger and knowing exactly what they would be saying to him. Who would be the first one in the office to fuck her had been a standing bet for some time now, Lola had been made well aware of it too. Pieterson had even shown her the betting chart they'd made up with odds for the most likely winners. She had sat there and listened to them, wondering what 'odds' Lee would be given? He would surely be favourite now, given his proximity. She had watched him laughing and giggling with the rest of them, like a puppy mimicking the older dogs and it had made her feel sick to her stomach. It was true that he hadn't looked comfortable, she also knew that he hadn't a choice in the matter. Any dissent from him, any resistance to the boys club and he may as well have packed up and left. She knew this as well as Lee had, the poor bastard was caught between a rock and a hard place, but that didn't matter to her. He was one of those 'boys', or he soon would be, and that was enough.

Lola beasted him every chance she got. At the beginning he made mistakes and she jumped on everyone. Any opportunity she had to belittle him, chew him out and humiliate him in front of the others, she took and felt no remorse for doing so. To his credit, and much to her surprise, Lee took it. Not only that but he began to get better at his duties. Those mistakes dried up and he worked almost as hard and as long as she did. He was a model student and she couldn't fault his attitude or application but she hated him all the same. Every lunch he would spend at the big boy's table and every time he did, her disgust for his 'kind' grew stronger. She would hear them discussing her with him, asking him how his 'bitch' was coming along and whether he was getting regular blow jobs from her. She heard them tell him not to worry, that soon enough he'd be her boss and he'd be fucking her whenever he fancied it. Lola heard all of this and knew that, if she was going to survive, she would have to make a stand. She needed to put an end to this or get out, it was a simple choice, and she'd worked too damn hard to give it away now.

Lee was a naturally quiet boy, had been since the first day but had come out of his shell a little recently. He would, however, do exactly what Lola told him to do, jump as high as she told him to jump. So it was no difficulty getting him into the side office with her. It was lockable from the inside and the blinds meant no one could see in. Once they'd gotten there, under some bogus reasoning or other, Lola had begun to come on to Lee. She was a very attractive woman with a wonderful figure. When she wasn't at work she was nearly always at the gym. She'd sat him down on the small sofa next to the desk and had straddled him before he knew what was happening. She started playing with his hair and whispering what she wanted to do to him in his ear. Lee had been startled by the move. Up until this point, he had been given the impression she didn't like him one bit and when he mentioned this, as tactfully as he could muster, she had told him it was just a front. Lola told him she'd lusted after him from the first day, that she wanted to feel him inside her, wanted his tongue in her mouth and his fingers all over her body. Lola was very convincing and Lee was a twenty-two year old man, it didn't take long for her to have him worked up to a frenzy. Soon he was hitching her skirt ever higher and trying, in a fumbling way, to get her clothes off whilst still kissing her and keeping the mood going. She'd managed to undo his shirt and tie and was rubbing his erection over his pants, careful not to do this too vigorously as she didn't want any early finishes! As he was undoing the final button to her blouse she suddenly stopped him. He was panting and desperate now, she had him right where she wanted him, he'd do anything she asked. It may not have been what he was expecting, maybe not what he wanted either, but he was willing enough to go along with it. Lola told him exactly what she wanted to do, what she had always dreamt of doing with him and Lee had readily agreed.

Ten minutes later she wheeled him out of the room, tied securely by the hands and feet to an office chair. Blindfold and naked with a gag in place, he had the words 'my bitch!' written across his chest in Lolas signature red lipstick. Despite the muffled pleading and tears, Lee remained tied and naked for all to see for the rest of the afternoon whilst Lola quietly went about her work. Those 'boys' all saw what she had done, all laughed too but inwardly felt deeply uneasy about it all. They were thankful it had happened to Lee and not them, relieved in fact, and viewed Lola in a completely different light afterward. Nobody touched her arse in the lift again, the 'who's going to shag Lola' chart disappeared and any whispering could be cut dead with a look. She had used their weapon against them and shown them all just what a real bitch can do. That day changed their perception of Lola completely and gave her the breathing room to excel in her job. It cost Lee his. That was the last day he worked there and she had no idea what happened to him after that. Did she feel bad about it? He hadn't deserved such humiliation but neither had she. It was a dog eat dog world that they lived in and Lola had to be the pit bull in order to survive. It was just what she needed to do, no more no less and she felt that she would have done it again. Lola was able to remove her emotions from any given situation and act in the best way for her, whatever it took. Maybe it was her upbringing that had taught her this skill? Maybe she needed to be thankful for that? She was a survivor.

They had passed along a number of corridors before arriving at the foot of some magnificent staircase. Double width and returning on both sides, she could see a huge, stained glass window at the top of the first level. This was obviously the heart of the house and Lola checked her arm band to see which way it was indicating to go from here. If she could manage to memorise her way back to this spot then she'd be in good shape to find the aviary she felt. She'd obviously paused for a moment too long and was encouraged to continue her journey by the end of the rifle making sharp contact with her shoulder. Monkey then pointed it towards the left side of the stairs and she dutifully made her way in that direction. All around her was bathed in moonlit shadows that cast eary figures across the wood flooring and giant Persian rugs. She was encouraged to walk along the side of the staircase to the back wall and in doing so, her destination was revealed. At the back of this great entrance hall, underneath the stairs, was an inconspicuous doorway. Monkey, silently, flicked a switch hidden behind the door and illuminated her path. She must follow these stairs down into what must be the basement, the bowels of the great house. It was with hesitant steps that she alighted them and found herself in the musty underbelly. All the opulence and grandeur of the upper areas had disappeared here and she was left with bare, flaky plaster walls and light bulbs with no shades, swinging in the light breeze. It was cold down here and Lola felt the chill on her scantily clad body. She hated the cold, it reminded her of her childhood. She wondered if there was a game for her to play at all or was she being brought down here to be disposed of and buried? What would the point have been if this were the case? Surely there would be easier ways to achieve this, if that was what Jon had wanted to do with them? Along the dimly lit basement, they walked until finally, the monkey stopped at an unassuming door on the right. Flicking the end of the rifle, Lola dutifully opened the creaky wooden barrier and entered her room.

She stood in pitch darkness for a moment and heard the door slam shut behind her, heard the noise of some mechanical bolts slide into place too. Then all was revealed. It took her eyes a good while to accustom themselves to the brilliant lights that had suddenly turned that darkness into a surgically bright area. When they did, she realised why they had needed to come down to the basement. It was a room of huge proportions, maybe thirty feet high to the ceiling and at least sixty feet long, she judged. Square enough in shape, it was just as wide and filled entirely with various obstacles set out in rows. One thing was certain, she wasn't going to be cold for long. In the first lane, right in front of where she was stood, Lola could see only a giant wall that needed climbing. It looked very much like a school vaulting horse, with wooden slats all the way up the side of it. Maybe twenty feet high, it had small finger holes in the side of it to climb with. To the right of this, at the other end of the room, lane two contained a bicycle and a track for it to travel down. It was clearly marked at the side with numbers that came to a finish just to the right of her, the final figure being '50ft'. Next came the middle lane, a deep and thin trough filled with water. Just as long as the cycle lane and marked the same, only in reverse and finishing back at the far end of the room. The fourth was a plain track marked on the wooden floor with two large, red 'buttons' at either end. Finally, at the far side of the room, there was an intricate balancing course with high beams, zigzag posts and thin seesaws. Two hundred and fifty feet of fairly standard obstacles to complete, this didn't look too difficult at all! She hadn't known what to expect but was pretty delighted with what she had been given.

Lola had completed any number of 'Tough Mudder's' over the last few years and this was certainly nothing to compare with those. She started stretching in preparation and wondering when the 'instructions' would arrive?

Booming from a hidden speaker and making her jump into the bargain, the voice of the host filled the cavernous room with an echo.

'Miss Cooper, welcome to your challenge. Before you are five rows of tasks that you must complete, each to be taken in turn. You will work your way from left to right and finish at the far end of the room. Each task must be completed before you can move on to the next and if you fail any one of them, you must retake it until you succeed. Each time you fail, that particular obstacle will become a little more difficult, so make sure you get it right the first time. You will have thirty minutes from the moment you press the starter button to get to the end of the challenge and press the stop button. Should you go over time, even by a second, you will not leave the room alive. Is that clear?' It was a rhetorical question as the audio was clearly pre-recorded, although it paused long enough to make her think she needed to answer.

'In the first row, you will find obstacles you need to climb over, swing from and hurdle. Failure to complete any of them cleanly and you will have to start again at the beginning. Next, the bicycle needs to be ridden the complete length of the course set out before you can get off and start the swim. After the swim you will need to perform a series of sprints, hitting the buttons provided at each end of the track until you have done nine sets. You will be alerted to the fact that you have completed the sprints by the buttons turning from red to green. When this has happened you will move on to the last row. It is a balance test and you must complete all of them without falling off. Should you fall then you will be required to start it again.... That is all. Good luck!'

And with that, the audio stopped and Lola was left to her own devices. Thirty minutes... she mused, that should be plenty. Surely the only tricky part of the test, barring what she couldn't see down the first lane, was the balance section and she figured she'd have plenty of time left to retake that part as often as she needed. She figured there couldn't be more than three or four minutes work in the middle three trials.

Taking some deep breaths and stretching her arms out above her head, Lola prepared herself to begin the task, confident she was going to be successful. Looking at the giant vaulting horse in front of her she planned her route to the top in advance of pressing the button to begin. Those holes were large enough for three or four fingers and her toe ends, it didn't look too tricky. That was the one big concern in her head, none of it looked too tricky... where was the catch? Shaking her head, she slapped both palms against her cheeks to get her mind back on the job in hand and pushed the button to start the countdown. It was time to go and do this thing, show that son of a bitch who was boss.

She climbed confidently and placed her hands and feet with care, the last thing she wanted to do was have to repeat the very first obstacle. Lola wanted to build some confidence for the rest of the course and getting off to a flying start would be just the ticket. One grip after the next, then inching her feet up afterward, she made good but steady progress. There was no need to rush, time wasn't against her. What was important was that she did this without any slip ups and saved as much energy for the last row as possible. That was the only real area she might have difficulty with. Balancing when out of puff could be trickier than she imagined. Soon she managed to reach her hands to the top of the vault and pull herself into a seated position before the descent. From here she could see the rest of the obstacles in the first row. In front of her, in order, lay a cargo net climb of similar size to the vault, a zigzag handrail, a double rope swing over a pit of something or other and a crawl area under what she presumed to be wire netting. All pretty standard stuff and it was a relief to see such things she'd done a thousand times before. She was beginning to lose faith in her belief that the host was some master sadist, that was until she looked down the opposite side of the vault that she was sat upon. Gone were the comfortable holds, not a single one could be seen but in their place, she found small wedges of wood, heavily dusted with shards of broken glass. This presented her with two choices. Inch down the side using those wedges and, inevitably, cut her fingers to bits or, let herself drop from the top to the unforgiving wooden flooring at the bottom and hope she didn't break anything when she landed. Time ticked away as she sat considering these two options.

It seemed much higher from the top looking down than it had from the bottom looking up and Lola didn't fancy the drop one bit. Besides, if she did twist or break anything, that would certainly be the end of her chances of beating this thing. She needed both her legs to be in good working order. This tipped the balance towards those unpleasant and painful wedges. She reached out a foot towards the first one and kicked at the top of it, trying to scuff the glass away. Some of it shifted and fell to the floor, the bigger pieces she was able to dislodge but not the smaller bits. They seemed to be stuck fast and no amount of force from the underside of her trainers was going to move them. Still, she thought, it was better than it had been and if she were careful then she might not hurt her fingers too badly. Holding herself by the top of the vault she found her footing on the first wedge and repeated the 'scruffing' action on the next one down to similar effect. This was time-consuming stuff but she felt it was going to be worth the effort in the long run. With the second wedge prepared she transferred her weight onto it and eased her other foot down to the next one. She couldn't quite reach it whilst her hands were still holding the top of the apparatus and so she gingerly placed her hand down onto the first wedge. Lola didn't need to put much pressure through those fingers at the moment and so, although she could feel the sharp glass under them, it didn't break the skin. Once again she performed the scuffing of the wedge with her foot, only this time it was harder to do. She didn't have such a steady base and her view of the wedge was now impeded. When she was satisfied that she'd done all she could with it, Lola placed her weight on the wedge and moved her hand down to the second one. As she did so, the pressure increased dramatically on that first grip and the glass pierced her finger tips. She felt it puncture her skin and the sharpness of the pain that followed made her release her hold on it. This, in turn, threw her balance out and forced her to cling onto the next wedge with her other hand to stop herself from falling. It too cut into her hand viciously and forced it into involuntarily letting go. Lola fell and as she did so she hit a couple of the wedges on the way down. They ripped into her hip and ribs and she bounced off them and away from the wall. When she hit the ground she was almost horizontal and landed just about flat on her side. It knocked all the wind out of her and left her gasping for air. It was one of those horrible moments where you try to take a breath but are unable to do so and feel, instantly, like you'll never be able to breathe again. It panicked her and the harder she tried the less she seemed to be able to take in. Lying there, mouth gaping like a fish out of water.

Eventually, the air she needed did start to fill her lungs and she took great gulps of the stuff and wheezed it back out of her body. Lola lay quite still for a while, making sure she was fully oxygenated before she assessed the damage the fall had caused. Would she be able to stand? Had this fall signalled the end of her challenge and the end of her life?

First up, before even trying to move, she checked her fingers. There were a number of minor lacerations and her finger ends bled and pained her. They were, she felt, usable though and this provided some comfort. Then she felt her side. Her shorts had been ripped open and a large graze, like the swipe from a tiger, had been left on her right hip. It hurt like hell but it wasn't her main concern. Lola tested her right leg for movement. Slowly bending it at the knee joint and then bringing her knee up towards her chest. It was sore but it wasn't broken in any way. Rolling onto her back, and off her left arm, she then tested her shoulder. Again, painful but not appearing to be damaged in any way. She felt her ribs with her right hand and noticed that they too were bloodied. That tiger had taken two swipes at her on the way down. Lastly, she tested her left leg, the biggest concern. It was this that had taken the brunt of the impact and it had felt quite numb as she had laid on it. Now the feeling was returning to the area and it throbbed with the rushing of the blood back into the muscles. Foot was waggled to satisfaction and the knee bent stiffly but without too much difficulty too. Hip... her left hip hurt! She rubbed it gently with her left hand and could feel some swelling beginning to form already. It was awfully sore but it wasn't broken or dislocated. Ever so carefully, Lola tried to stand and see how it felt. She pushed herself upright mainly with her hands and right foot, avoiding any pressure on her left hip. When she got back to her feet she found herself balancing on her right to avoid putting any pressure on it. Lola checked the time. Six minutes had elapsed since she pressed the buzzer, she hadn't bargained it to take any longer than a couple. She must move on, must get some movement back into that hip joint. Facing her now was the cargo net and she knew that she couldn't climb it with just one leg, she also knew that using her left was going to be agony.

Hopping, as best she could, over to the netting, Lola took a deep breath and gritted her teeth. 'get your fucking arse into gear bitch!' she hissed at herself and began the ascent. Gripping the rope hard with her hands, those cut fingers a distant memory now, she pulled her right foot up one rung of the net. It was the best she could do to keep as much pressure off that left hip, but it still hurt like hell. Once the right was in place, she stood up on it with all her weight and brought the left to the same level. Hands moved as far up as she could reach and the action was repeated. It was painfully slow, she was aware of that, but it was the only way she could do it. It was, mercifully, just plain old cargo netting. No hidden booby traps or painful little surprises and she was at least thankful for that. Rung by rung she made her way up towards the top and checked each and every part of the net on the other side for potential pitfalls. There were none. Each time she had to put any force through her left hip she squealed in pain and sucked the air through her teeth, but she carried on anyway. It was awkward keeping her balance when having to stand on her left foot as the netting swayed unsteadily but she managed it somehow. Bit by bit, she inched her way to the top and was grateful when she found herself straddling the wooden beam that signalled the end of the climb upwards. Laying on her front with her legs dangling either side she took a few breaths before carrying on. Checking the clock she noticed it had taken her two minutes to complete the ascent, must pick the pace up from here, she thought. Swinging her right leg over the beam and searching for the first rung with it, Lola's foot missed its target and instinctively her left was flung out to save her. She dropped all her weight onto that hip and a shooting pain went straight up her spine. Quickly she retrieved the right from inside the mesh and managed to find a place for it on the netting and relieve the pressure. 'Jesus Christ' she shouted into the empty room and her voice echoed a little off the walls around her. It took her another minute to descend, carefully placing her right foot down a step before following it with the tender left. Finally, she reached the floor and hopped away from the obstacle. Nine minutes had elapsed. Still, she was in good shape, those middle lanes weren't going to take too long.

It was a relief to have the handrail as the next piece of apparatus, although her fingers were cut and stinging, there was nothing wrong with her grip. She climbed up a six-foot ladder onto a box from where she needed to begin. There were about twenty feet of metal bars in front of her that made a giant 'z'. She must swing, hand over hand, along the course before taking the sharp bend in the middle. It didn't look like it had any hidden dangers to it, aside from what was waiting should she fall. Underneath the rail, after a drop of some ten feet that would surely finish off her hip for good, she saw a carpet of broken glass. Not small pieces either. These were quarter bottles and large chunks of jagged, evil looking fragments. If she fell off this then it was going to cut her to pieces. If she dropped and had to start the first lane again then she was done anyway. Forget about the time it would take, forget about what that glass would do to her body, Lola knew she'd not be able to get over those first two obstacles again. This was a 'do or die' situation in a quite literal sense. Reaching up to grab the first bar with both hands, she felt the Tigers mark on her side. It pulled as she stretched her arms upwards and made the action quite painful. It was going to hurt every time she swung her left arm but there was bugger all she could do about that, no protection she could give it. Simply, she would have to grin and bear it. Focusing on the next bar, Lola lifted her legs from the box and swung her body forwards towards it. Grabbing it securely with her left hand, wincing, and letting go with her right. She must keep moving along the bars, keep that momentum up before her grip started to let her down. Completing the first part of the 'z' was easy. She felt strong, despite the scratch to her ribs, and kept a steady pace with that swinging action. Then she got to the sharp bend in the bars and found it killed all her rhythm. That 90-degree turn took all the easy motion from her body and left her dangling dead still. It was a real effort to reach out for the next bar and try to get some movement back into her hips. Pulling forwards and backward with her hands, she could feel her grip starting to fade, not nearly as solid as it had been at the start. Soon she managed to get that pendulous action back again and made it to the next turning point. It was here that she had her first bit of luck. Without meaning to, Lola had strayed from the centre of the bars and over to the right side. When she got to the next turning point and reached out, she bypassed the corner bar completely, as the swinging action of her body took her right passed it. Momentum carried her to the first bar on the final section and when she let go with her right hand she managed to maintain that momentum through to the following section. This time there was no 'dead stop'. It was a good job too because her hands were awfully tired now. Each time she reached for the next bar she could feel there was less of her hand holding her. Each fresh bar was being held nearer and nearer to her finger ends. Had she lost momentum at the last corner she would have surely fallen by now. There were just three bars to go and she was only just managing to hold herself long enough to reach the next before her hand slipped from the last. Those damaged finger ends were screaming at her now, her whole arms and shoulders were screaming but she wasn't about to give up. She was a fucking bull terrier, she told herself, and they never give up! Half screaming, half shouting into the vast room she bullied her way to the end and dropped in a heap on the box. Dropped onto both feet and jarred that hip again which gave way immediately and left her crumpled on her side. 'Fuuuuckkkk!!!' she cried and held her arms around her chest to comfort them. All she wanted to do now was lay there and wait until her poor arms and body told her it was alright to move again, but the clock was ticking, another minute had gone by. Suddenly aware of this fact, Lola roused herself as if shocked by an electric current. In her head, she remembered some of the motivational speeches she used to listen to and tried to use these to help her.

'Pain is temporary, it may last a minute or an hour or a day, but it will subside'

'You've got to use your pain to drive you to greatness, recycle your pain. Don't cry to quit, don't cry to give in, you're already in pain, get something from it!'

'Nobody, who has ever been great, has gotten there without going through pain. If you want to win the fight of your life then you can't be afraid to fight.'

All those speeches, those words that she used to use in the gym, used to listen to during her lunch break at work, she needed them now more than she had ever done before. She needed to believe them, trust that they were right, that she could do this.

'The difference between winners and losers is real simple, failure is there every single time but the winners do it again, and again, and again, until it goes their way. They never stop! Inch by inch, bit by bit, you keep going until you reach the end...'

They were all mashed up and muddled in her head, different pieces of the same puzzle telling her the same thing. If she wanted to get through the next twenty minutes then she had to ignore the pain and get on with it. Lola had loved those 'rat races' and 'tough mudders', loved testing herself to the limit. She had always been a fighter, had that extra will and determination to succeed. Well, this was the ultimate fight right here and the challenge had been accepted. She got to her feet and stood proud. There was a fresh spirit about her and a belief that she was going to get through this, no matter what.

Moving on to the final obstacle in the first lane she surveyed the challenge ahead. That was the way she was going to look at it now, it was a challenge and she never backed down from one of those. In front of her was a mass of razor wire that she must crawl under. It went fifteen feet or so straight ahead before turning back on itself and then returning. 45 feet of crawling to do, she judged. 'Keep your skinny ass down and you'll be fine' she said to herself.

It was maybe a foot from the floor and left only a couple of inches gap to her body when she started the crawl, but it was enough. Her arms hurt from the handrail and didn't want to do any more work but they had no choice. Her hip pinched and stabbed her every time she bent her leg to propel herself forward, but it too was told to get on with it. Lola had mastered her pain and was able to push herself through it. She stopped her emotional response to what her body was telling her and simply did what she needed to do. It hurt, that crawl, and there were points where she caught her back and bottom on the wire. Snagged her clothing and cut her skin, but she didn't stop for a second and made it all the way through to the end.

Hauling herself up to her feet again at the end, Lola clapped her hands together hard and chalked another obstacle off the list. She'd beaten the first lane and believed entirely that she would beat all the others too. Time check - 18m 30s left on the clock.

Waiting for her at the start of the next lane was the bicycle. It looked an ordinary enough piece of equipment and with only fifty feet to ride Lola couldn't see why it had been included. Where was the difficulty? It wasn't until she got on the thing that she noticed a couple of subtle differences. For one, the chain wasn't attached to the back wheel, it went straight down from the pedals to some place under the floor. There was a large slit for it to go and return, but she couldn't see what it was attached to underneath. Secondly, the bike was fixed by each wheel to two pieces of metal on the floor. There was a groove that ran directly in front of them, all the way down the lane to the finish. Lola began pedalling and the action of doing so made her hip throb, it also propelled the bike forward at an incredibly slow rate. Finding a pace that was tolerable for the amount of pain it gave her, she noted her progress along the course. Each foot was clearly marked at the side of the bike and she was able to judge how far she was going against the clock. At her present rate, which was about the best she could do, she was travelling exactly one foot forward every ten seconds. Now she understood what the bike was there to do, eat the clock. Ten seconds per foot, fifty feet to travel, 8m 20s for the course. That meant she'd have less than ten minutes in which to complete the rest of the obstacles. It also made her doubt that the swim and the run would be quite as easy as she had imagined. Speeding up wasn't an option so she had to take her medicine and watch as the clock ticked down and she moved ever so slowly towards the end. It seemed to take an eternity and the sweat she was producing ran into those scratches and stung like a bitch. As each minute went by, some more of the wind was taken from her sails. It was frustrating as hell, but there was nothing she could do about it. That pain in her hip, sharp and biting at the start, had relaxed into a dull ache, her body getting used to the rotary action it was being told to produce against its will. Lola ground it out, pushing a steady 70rpms and eeking her way to the finish. There were no hidden penalties to worry about, no glass Tigers to take a swipe at her, the only torture here was watching the seconds disappear on the clock. When she finally did make it to the end of the course she looked anxiously at the time she had remaining. 9m 57secs.

Quickly hobbling over to the 'swim' section, she tried to shake the cycling motion out of her legs before she plunged into the trough. When she did she found herself submerged up to her chest in a thick, clear substance that seemed to hold her exactly where she'd jumped in. It felt like wall paper paste, had the consistency of it too and was very difficult to make any headway in. At the beginning she tried to propel herself as quickly as she could, mindful of the time that was passing, but this proved to be exhausting and counter productive. It took her a good half minute to realise that the slower and more deliberately she moved her limbs, the quicker she managed to pass through it. Any fast movements almost brought her to a standstill. This was another task designed specifically to scrub time and cause her greater frustration. Patience wasn't one of Lola's virtues and the mantra 'slow and steady wins the race' had always seemed stupid to her, but that was exactly what was required here. Careful movements brought greater length to her strides and the more she kept her discipline, the quicker she moved along the trough. She couldn't see the clock as it was behind her now, but she could feel the seconds ticking by. It was hard to concentrate on those steady inches of progress when she knew how little was left for her to finish, but it was the only way. When she did finally arrive at the other end and hauled herself out of the gelatinous liquid, which stuck to her clothes and clung to her skin, she saw four further minutes had elapsed - 5m 53sec. It had been very steady work but the force required had taken its toll on her body none the less. Lola was tired, very tired now.

When she tried to run to the next obstacle her feet slipped and skidded on the hard wood flooring. That paste had clung to her shoes too and made them feel like she was trying to run on ice. Lola collapsed to the ground, landing knees and hands first, and barked out a frustrated and pained cry as she did. It took only a moment for her to decide that the shoes and socks would have to be removed and she discarded them as quickly as possible. Lola used the socks to wipe her lower legs clean of the paste before clambering to her feet and passing on to the run. There was a small sign next to the first red button that read 'press to begin the task'. In front of her lay another fifty feet of flooring, marked out into five sections and each a different colour. There were small holes in the floor, about an inch apart, all the way along the course and they ran the width of the track. Lola didn't like the look of them one bit.

She pressed the button and began to run to the other end. Normally, nine lengths of a fifty-foot course wouldn't take her any time to complete but she was tired and hurt. Her body ached badly from the falls she'd had and she was deep into her energy reserves. With a hobbling gait, she made her way down the track and pressed the button at the other end before turning to repeat the run. When she did so, just as she was about to step into the second 'ten-foot' section, it filled with spikes. She came to a juddering halt, her right foot just an inch before and her body almost overbalancing. With her arms outstretched and her left foot in the air behind her, she tried desperately not to fall into the next section. If she stood on those nails then the game would surely be over. She'd never be able to complete the run, let alone beat the balance test that was to come. She hung there, teetering on the edge of that section, trying with all her might to arrest the momentum that was pulling her body forward. It felt like she had a rope attached to her shoulders and someone was gently increasing the pressure to pull her forward. She felt her body go past the point where she could retrieve it, beyond her balance, and the decision was 'what do I fall on?'. As if it were in slow motion she fell forward and, consciously, refused to bring her left leg through to stop her. She was going to land on her hands, it was the only way she could think of to give her a chance of winning. Those spikes were going to be driven deep into her flesh by the weight of her body and it was going to hurt! That's what she knew, but she also knew she had no other option. It took great will power to keep that leg from coming forward and as she fell, her body held flat as she could manage, she kept her hands as close to her shoulders as she could. With only a foot or so between her body and the floor, the spikes retracted as quickly as they had emerged and Lola hit the ground only a millisecond later. It was a good job they did, as her hands failed to stop her face and body hitting the floor with a thud. It took some of the wind out of her and shook her up a bit, but it was a good deal better than landing on those nails.

As soon as the spikes had retreated from the second section, some more appeared in the third. Lola got to her feet quickly and moved to the end of the second ten foot mark, waiting for the spikes to go back into the floor before progressing. She rubbed her hands, which had taken the brunt of the impact, and was pleased she hadn't broken her wrists. Behind her, in the first ten, she heard a noise that confirmed those spikes were now chasing her as well as impeding her progress. Hers was the only section that was free of them. When the nails were withdrawn again from the third area, she stepped into it and a second later saw them reappear behind her. 'So that was how it was going to work' she thought, it was a 'bleep' test with a sinister difference. She had to keep up with the track in front of her and avoid the spikes behind. Lola made it to the second button and pressed it to complete the run. When she turned she saw the second section had already been filled with the spikes, it had speeded up! She hobbled her way to the edge and they disappeared just as she got there. This time, whenever she got to the end and was about to wait for the section to become flat again, they retracted as soon as she arrived. When she pressed the button to finish the third set, those spikes in the second ten withdrew as soon as she turned and she had to hurry to get into that section. This time she had to keep a jogging pace all the way along to avoid getting caught by the spikes behind her. Four buttons pressed, only five more to do. That fifth run was a 'fast' jog and each time she pushed off and landed on her left foot the pain shot straight up her spine and made her wince. On the sixth, she was almost caught by the nails, half way along she felt the edge of one against her heel as she left the section. This made her spring into the air and she nearly stumbled when she landed again. Lola fell into the button at the end and pushed off of it to get some pace into her body for the next run. It was a near sprint this time and she could feel those nails chasing her down the track, like a dog snapping at her heels. She was a dog though, she was a bull fucking terrier and they never gave in! 'Pain is temporary... Fear is not real...' those motivational speeches ran through her head as quickly as she ran down the track. Pressing the button after her eighth run she threw her body forward and pushed off with all her might. Pinning her ears back and thrusting her arms out in front of her, Lola squeezed every last ounce of energy she had out of her body and flew down the track. That dog, that black dog that chased her with teeth of steel ran fast to nip her heels. Ran hard to bite her feet. But it didn't catch the bull terrier and she hit the final button and ran straight into the wall behind it.

'Time?' Her first thought, when she knew she was safe was to check how long she had to go. 1m 55secs were on the clock. She had time, there was enough left to get to the end. What she didn't have was any energy to do it with. Lola, doubled over and gasping for breath, couldn't move an inch until she had some oxygen back in her muscles. She didn't even look at the next task as she sat there panting, didn't want to know what it contained before she had given herself some time to recover. It was another fifty feet of obstacles and they were all about balance, that's what she knew and she gambled that she could do it inside a minute. This gave her some forty more seconds to breathe and try to compose herself. That would have to be enough. She watched the clock closely and took great gulps of air, shaking the lactic out of her legs as best she could.

1m 10sec. Lola dragged her body upright again and slowly made her way to the start of the final task. From one end to the other, the entire floor area was covered in broken glass. She laughed to herself when she saw it. What did it matter, if she fell off then she wouldn't have time to try again anyway. It could be covered in fluffy pillows or Samurai swords for all the difference it made. She had to do this first time or not at all, that was her only option now. First up was a beam just wide enough for one foot to fit on and it was fixed some six feet off the ground. Lola had to climb up onto a small platform to begin. 59 seconds to go, the clock had started flashing and the numbers had turned red, as if she needed reminding. With her arms outstretched, she made her way along the beam to a round post at the end. It must have been about ten feet in length and was a gentle start to the course. Both feet firmly planted on the post, 50 seconds to go, she now had a series of similar wooden posts to hop onto. They varied in height and took her diagonally left and then right. Each was placed just an inch or two too far for Lola to stride across. She was forced to jump. Thankfully, there was enough room to get both feet on each one and she was able to use her right foot to do the jumping and landing with. She was still breathing hard and the sweat was pouring off her head. She had to wipe her eyes to keep it from bothering her. Lola found the lower posts harder to judge and wobbled on a few of those but managed to keep her balance. 37 seconds. She knew she had to be quick and decisive, it was no use taking any time over these things. That final post led her to another beam that was set up as a seesaw. Quickly she edged her way to the middle and waited for it to drop and rest at the other side. Impatiently she put too much pressure on the bar and it bounced when it hit the bottom. She had shuffled forward in anticipation of completing it and the judder from the bar made her turn her body sidewards and nearly threw her off. Lola swayed forwards and backward a couple of times before managing to regain her centre of gravity. Precious seconds ebbed away as she did so and she felt the pressure of time mounting. That buzzer at the end of the course still looked very far away. 29 seconds. At the end of the seesaw, about half way along, she found some parallel bars. This was a much-needed break from the balancing and she made light work of it, scratching off another ten feet as she did so. 18 seconds. At the end of the bars, she found a post to put both feet on and compose herself before the second to last challenge. It was a large, wooden log about eight feet in length and it was designed to roll should you put a foot anywhere but the very centre of it. She hated these things! Speed was the key but, with only a post at the other end to stop herself she couldn't go too quickly or she'd fall off the end. Taking a quick, deep breath, Lola scampered lightly across the log and felt every tiny movement under her toes. Each time it shifted slightly she had to adjust her next step to counteract the movement. It tried to roll, did its best to throw her to one side or the other and she held her breath the whole way until she felt her feet on the post at the end. She stopped, just, and blew out her cheeks, eyeing the final piece of equipment. 11 seconds to go. It was the same task as the one she'd just completed, only this time there was no post to help her. She would have to jump two feet across from where she was, land on the rolling log and make her way to the end. It was impossible! How could anyone manage to do this? she thought. 9.... 8.... 7.... There was no time, no turning back, no second chance.

She leaped as lightly as she could, trying to hit the very centre when she landed. 6.... 5.... Her foot must have been a millimetre out as the log started to rotate to the right and she threw her left leg forward, judging how much off line she needed to be to stop the log roll. She landed a little too far left and it twisted back on itself to start moving the other way, only quicker this time. Lola's body contorted, her legs were above the log but her torso had been thrown out to the right. Momentum was all that would keep her from falling and her right foot lurched forward trying to find any part of the log to push off from. 4.... 3.... she hit the log on the right-hand side, full but way off centre. It was enough to get a good push from and she knew her next step wouldn't make contact. Lola was falling to the right and couldn't do anything about it. With all the strength she had, she launched herself forward like a triple jumper at the end of the pit and cleared the glass trench by a matter of centimetres. Landing on her side she slid forward towards the wall and reached up a hand to hit the buzzer...

Chapter 8 - Daniel keeps his head

Daniel sat on the chair contemplating his fate, he'd never killed anyone or even thought about doing so and he wasn't thrilled at the prospect. However, he was less thrilled with the alternative and was, as he sat here now, determined to get to the end of this thing. Sitting here, knowing what had happened and what was probably going to happen, his life of poverty didn't seem so bad. Sure he'd lost all those luxuries and trinkets, had loved the high life he'd become accustomed to, but when faced with the very real prospect of dying, they didn't really matter one bit. It was certainly true, or it felt it right now, that your health was the most important thing you can have. He'd never really believed it before but then it had never been presented to him in such a stark way. Still, unlike those poor bastards with cancer or other such diseases, Daniel still had a chance to keep his health if he could get through the next part of the 'game'. It wouldn't be right to suggest he was grateful for the fresh perspective this experience had brought him, but it was certainly a valuable lesson. Whether or not he'd manage to keep this new philosophy with ten million pounds in his pocket was another thing entirely.... Ten million quid, was there really that sum waiting for the winner? As far as he could tell, Jon had been fairly honest with them up to now but would he seriously hand over the cash if he got to the end? Clearly, money wasn't an issue for the host, this country house for a start was a testament to some considerable wealth. Still, in order to make them participate he would need a carrot to dangle, wouldn't he? Really, it was useless dwelling on this train of thought. Whether there was or not, Daniel had to get to the aviary alive regardless.

Looking up at the clock he noted there were three minutes left before the door would open. Time to get himself prepared and check how he was feeling. Standing up on those thick bandages caused a little pain, but nothing too bad. He would definitely be able to walk and maybe even run, should the situation require it. They also provided him with a noiseless platform from which to creep, and he was happy with this. Creeping could be a distinct advantage in the next phase of the game. Everywhere he'd walked so far he had stepped on wooden flooring and even his trainers had made a squeaking sound. These soft wraps virtually eliminated any sound from contact. To demonstrate this to himself, Daniel walked around in two or three circles to confirm. His hands, he flexed them to see, felt good and strong. Not only did the bandages allow him a decent grip of the spanner but they made a strong fist for fighting. Physically he was tired, but pretty much recovered from the climb and he felt like he would not be found wanting should it come to a battle. There was, rising within him, a good deal of nervous energy to carry him through and he had experienced what the adrenaline had contributed to his performance and was confident his body would supply just as much should it be needed again. He checked his arm band to see which way he ought to be going when the door did open and found some more good news. There had ceased to be a full compliment of competitors and his chances had, statistically at least, become a lot better. He had no idea by the lights which had extinguished, who it was that had failed, but he hoped cock munch was one of them. At least, that was his initial reaction. Thinking about it more carefully he came to the conclusion that, should he need to kill anyone, cock munch might be the easiest one to overcome. Both physically, and as a human being, Daniel felt he'd have the least trouble with that mincing bastard. Anyway, it didn't matter who was left, he had to get by them and win the game regardless and that was what he was going to do!

Ten seconds to go. Daniel picked up his Mamba bag and slung it over his shoulder, feeling the snake wriggle angrily inside. Holding he spanner in a tight fist, he prepared himself for an immediate assault as soon as the door swung open. He wasn't about to be caught off guard at the first moment. Breathing rapidly he counted the seconds away, 3... 2... 1... Those bolts slid mechanically across and found their housing with a weighty clunk. Daniel waited for the door to swing open... but it didn't. It just stayed in exactly the same position waiting for someone to turn its handle. He'd bargained on the dramatic, maybe some smoke to accompany the release of the door. It would swing open and all hell would be let loose from the other side. That it just sat there waiting for him to physically turn the handle was a bit of an anticlimax. He chuckled to himself nervously about the difference between expectation and reality. Having to open the door himself felt much worse, much more terrifying than it happening out of his control. Daniel edged carefully closer to the shiny brass knob and allowed just one fingertip to touch it. Half expecting some electrification as he did so. Nothing happened. Well, I can't just stand here all night, he thought to himself. There were about two hours left in the game and he had no idea how far or what obstacles he would face on his way. Time to move, time to get serious about this.

Standing adjacent to the opening, right hand raised with spanner at the ready, he gently turned the knob in his hand and felt the door 'give' a little when the latch bolt past its housing. It was now free to open and he re-gripped the knob a number of times to psych himself up for the next event. Pulling it swiftly open, enough to bring his weapon into play should he need it, Daniel lurched forward into the empty space the door had left. As he did so he passed from the bright light of the room behind him into what seemed like the darkest pitch outside. He was blind for a second or two and it panicked him. Stepping further out he swung the spanner madly in front of him, making contact with nothing but his thigh. All he could hear was his own heavy breathing and the sound of his heart pumping strongly in his chest. It felt like it was trying to escape his rib cage completely.

As the seconds passed and he stood motionless, waiting for an attack, his eyes began to adjust to the gloom of the corridor he was now standing in. When he had entered the room this corridor had been dimly but quite well lit. Obviously, the host had thought it much more atmospheric to cut the lights for the next part of the game. With his bright white bandages and reflective gym top, Daniel felt distinctly disadvantaged and wished he'd changed back into his old clothing. He was half thinking or returning to the room to do so when he remembered that he'd mutilated his trousers to create the Mamba bag. As this passed through his mind the door to the room closed itself and he heard the locks twist into place. Nothing for it, just have to carry on as I am, he thought.

His initial panic and conviction that he would be subjected to bloody murder before he'd even had the chance to see what was happening had left him now. Being able to see what was around you made a big difference to one's state of calm. He was stood near the end of the corridor and his arm band was pointing directly to the right. That he couldn't go right was a pain but he guessed that the band was displayed in 'crows flight' and not the actual geography of the house. This left him with no other option than to follow the corridor until he was given the opportunity to turn. There was one barely lit lamp, fixed to the wall at what looked like the end and very little in between. Daniel made his was softly towards it. Each step was ever so carefully placed to ensure no sound was made and he was pleased his heart had decided to allow him some peace from the frantic pumping of moments ago. Steadily he made his way, stopping dead still whenever he thought he detected a sound. His senses were so keen he would have heard a fly walk along a feather pillow. It's amazing how much you think you can hear when there is not a single sound being made. Passing a dead relative, framed in gilt on the wall, he turned and could have sworn the musty old painting had changed its pose to follow him down the way. Any and all of the shadows were sinister, threatening figures, painted in a translucent darkness that menaced his brain. There was nothing and no one to be fearful of in this corridor but that didn't stop his mind inventing some. That thirty-foot walk to the end of the passage was probably the longest and most stressful walk of his life.

When he reached the end and peered anxiously around both corners, Daniel checked the arm band to confirm which way he needed to go. It was still telling him to go in pretty much the same direction it had before and so he turned to the right. When before he had known there was nothing behind him - although this didn't prevent him from checking every second or two - now he had no such comfort. There was the passage he was travelling down and a very similar one, just as dimly lit, to the back of him. He was, and felt, very exposed. It was another fifteen feet or so before he came to the next opening and the next decision on which way to go. When he arrived at this point he realised that the route he was now travelling wasn't the route that had taken him to his room. Before him, opening out in a truly grand and, at this moment, grotesque fashion, was the main hallway. This would be where a normal host would greet their guests and have their coats taken by a servant. He was sure that, in the daylight hours or properly lit, this was a magnificent arena in which to be welcomed to the house but now, in this gloom and under these conditions, it was horrifying. He stood for some time appraising the area.

From his position, adjacent to the main staircase, he could see most of the room and guessed that what was obscured by that enormous panneled stairway was a mirror image of his side of the hall. There was a symmetry to the windows at the front and the whole thing, when looked at in terms of its ceiling, was square. Huge double doors of great height were flanked either side by framed glass that cast moonlit shadows across the dark wood floor, extending to the foot of the stairs. Each of these windows was heavily barred in steel to prevent escape and these too, played with the architecture within, changing form as the clouds passed the moon outside. All it needed, he thought, was a foot of mist to cover the ground and it would be as perfectly frightening as anyone could imagine. Two enormous stuffed bears, stood proudly on their plinths, occupied the corners of the front wall and one of them appeared to be sporting a bowler hat. If it were for comic effect, it was lost on Daniel at this time. To his left, he could see two doors leading out the back of the room, to where he did not know. They looked the same as the one he had exited some moments before and there was no chance he was going to try them to see what they possessed. Maybe they were the rooms to the others 'games'? Maybe they conceiled a competitor just waiting for the opportunity to smash his brains in? Maybe they were just some rooms at the back of the house? Whatever they were, he wasn't about to find out. That band on his arm was indicating that he should pass directly across the hall to the other side, and that was exactly what he was going to do, once he had gathered his pluck. What was preventing him was the openness of the area. There was no way he could creep around the stairway and keep out of view. Anyone with a vantage point, and there may well be somebody, would see him coming a mile off. Creeping past those closed doors and keeping to the wall until he was unable to do so was only mildly more appealing than moving swiftly from his position directly across to the foot of the stairs. His brain saw danger in every move that was open to him, but move he must.

Edging out of the relative comfort of the doorway, Daniel, crouching, pinned his back to the wall and moved silently along it towards the back of the hall. It may have been a longer way round but it felt a lot safer than waltzing straight across the floor to the foot of the staircase. It was dark in the edges and he felt protected by this. As he made his way to the first corner he stopped and listened for danger but there was nothing to hear. This silence made him even edgier. Some background noise, maybe a bit of wind from outside, a storm perhaps, would have given him some cover and stopped his mind from inventing sounds that weren't there.

At the first of the doors along the back of the hall, he stopped again and considered what was the best plan to employ. Open it and risk an attack from a competitor that was lurking within or pass by and not know whether there was anything to fear from within? He judged that, up to this point, it would have been impossible for anyone inside the room to have any idea he was outside. He'd made absolutely no sound to give himself away. If he could open the door silently too then he might gain an advantage, might just catch them off guard. At some point along the way he was going to have to fight, this was certain, best be the one that picks the time and place, he concluded. Holding the brass knob with his finger ends he twisted it a millimetre at a time. He could feel the tension in the mechanism and had to apply more force to turn it fully around. At no point did the door yield as he was expecting it to. Despite the fact that his wrist was almost turned completely, the door remained fixed in place. Applying a little pressure with his left shoulder it became apparent that the door was either bolted shut or the handle only worked from the inside. Either way, he would not be getting through it to see what was on the other side. Carefully, he allowed the knob to twist back into its original position and was relieved that the whole process had been accomplished with the minimum of noise. He doubted, even if there were anyone inside, that they had been alerted to his presence. Checking the hall behind him for stealthy assailants, he then moved on to the next. Repeating the process he found the result to be the same. Two locked doors.

Sliding along another ten feet of panneled wall he found himself in a corner. That giant stairway rose above him by some fifteen feet or so and he was enveloped in the darkest space the hall had to offer. He would have to make his way from here to the foot of the stairs and the exposure that would bring filled him with dread. His body wanted desperately to stay exactly where it was, wait the whole thing out in this corner, but he knew he must continue. He remembered some speech he'd heard once and tried to use this to bring life back to his static body. 'Fear is not real, it is a product of our thoughts of a future that does not at present, and may never exist. Fear is an illusion, fear is a choice!' Fine words indeed, he thought, but his fear was of a future that most certainly did exist and would happen. As he argued with himself over the validity of this statement his left hand, unconsciously, came to rest on a handle at the side of him. It startled him out of his stupor. It was another door, here at the base of the stairs and he'd completely missed it in the darkness. Chances were it would prove to be just like the other two, but he would have to try it and see to be sure. Taking a breath, he placed two fingers on the very end of the handle and pressed softly downwards. It didn't move one inch and the damn thing felt like it had seized up. Placing his whole hand upon it, straightening his arm and pushing down with force it resisted, for a moment, before giving way. As it did so, Daniels' hand slipped off the end of the handle and it jumped back up into place, making a hell of a racket as it did so. 'Fuuuck!' he screamed in his head and pushed himself back into the corner. All that care, that noiseless creeping he'd done to get to this point and he'd completely fucked it up with this one slip of the hand. How could he have been so stupid? Sweat dripped down his forehead as he stood there listening into the dark, expecting someone to come or something to happen...

Daniel waited there a good while in expectation but nothing came of his slip. No one rushed from the dark to attack him or called out that they knew he was there. Once again he was bathed in that hideous silence. If he'd have taken any notice of his armband, checked it for directions or time, he would have realised someone was indeed so very close to him. Flashing, unseen amidst the panic of the situation, was his and the second of the competitor's lights.

Watching from his dark corner, searching for movement from the room in front of him, Daniel saw the shadows dance across the flooring. It must have been a cloudy night outside as the light that passed through those windows and created the menacing floor figures would, with regularity, disappear completely for a second or four. Each time leaving the room in darkness. This gave him hope and courage for his next manoeuvre. If he could time it right, judge just when it was going to happen, he'd be able to pass across the bottom of the stairs in relative cover. Steeling himself, he began to make his way towards the middle of the room, keeping the panneled stairway as close to his side as he could. As he neared the foot of the stairs, peeking through the slats under the banister, that flashing light resumed a constant glow once more. Daniel had missed its warning, failed to see that another was close by, but they had not missed him!

Crouching at one of the large wooden posts that flanked the beginning of the stairs, he waited for the right time to move. That moonlight shone brightly through the windows and illuminated the room, he couldn't risk passing just yet. As he cowered in anticipation, he checked the direction on his device once more, half hoping it would tell him to turn around and go back... It didn't. That arrow still pointed towards the other side of the room and there was no other way to get there. It seemed to take an age for the next bit of cloud cover to arrive and he had grown fidgety waiting for it to happen. When it did, without hesitation, he scampered quickly across the flooring and around the other post, stopping immediately after he did so to listen. His heart beat at a terrific rate and he had a hard time listening over its thumping in his chest. When no danger presented itself, in either sight or sound, Daniel moved quickly to the back of the room again and found a mirror image of the other side. Everything, aside from the doorway under the stairs, was exactly the same. As was the result of trying the two new doors on the back wall. That arrow still pointed for him to continue moving both back and right but there was no doorway or corridor to allow him to do so. He moved tentatively forward until he was adjacent to the corridor he'd first entered the hallway from, finding its corresponding partner halfway up the wall, but it was closed off by a large, steel gate. Chained and padlocked, this was not the way out of the hall and there were no more exits to be found this side of the room. His heart sank to the pit of his twisting stomach as he realised he must climb the stairs to continue his journey. It was the last thing he wanted to do, and probably why Jon had planned it this way. Maximum stress and ample opportunity for an ambush. At least the armband would give him some warning if he did pass close enough to another. It had taken him over twenty minutes to navigate his way to this point from the corridor and all of that time had been wasted. On the band, he noted the time that was remaining, 1h 35mins.

Clouding over, the room was pitched into darkness once more and he used this welcome opportunity to make his way to the foot of the stairs once more. Peering around the large and ornately carved post, Daniel surveyed what he could see rising above him. Those stairs must have been ten feet wide and carpeted all the way to the edges. Brass poles running the length of the bottom corners kept the carpet in place and were in keeping with the age of the house. It was a nice touch but Daniel was not in a position to appreciate the faithfulness of the decor in relation to the period of the property, at this moment he was just wondering whether one of them might make a better weapon than the one he had in his hand. Unless he needed to pole vault someone to death then he judged they would not. Counting, he found there to be 28 steps from the bottom to the landing above him and from his position he could not see whether there was anywhere to quickly hide when he got to the top. All he could see was a dark area that was more than capable of hiding any number of murderous things. Waiting for clouds seemed useless too. They wouldn't hide his progress up the stairs and even if they did, it would take him far too long to climb them to rely on darkness for the whole ascent. Like it or not, and he didn't, he would have to just grin and bear it. Taking tentative steps, keeping ever so close to the banister on the right-hand side, he made steady progress. That banister afforded him no cover but it did seem to provide a little comfort, something to lean against and crouch next to, anytime he imagined he heard a noise.

As befits a two hundred-year-old stair case in a creepy old mansion, nearly every one of them made a creaking noise when he stepped on it. Try as he might to be as light on his feet as possible he couldn't eliminate gravity and his thirteen and a half stones in weight was too much to prevent the wood from moaning. Each step and each fresh squeak from below caused him great anxiety. Surely he was giving himself away terribly here? If there were anyone waiting in the shadows they would be fully aware of his progress and readying themselves for an attack the moment he got within reach. Crouching, as he was, didn't offer Daniel the best body position to defend himself either, but it felt much safer than walking upright with spanner aloft and so he continued the agony.

Three-quarters of the way up he could now see some of the landing area. There was a great, stained glass window at the top of the stairs with two smaller ones either side of it. There was some light coming through but because the moon was at the front of the house, it was still very dark. Those different coloured stains cast horrible shadows of blood reds and greens. Furniture wise, he could see a large oak bench underneath the windows but very little else. Thankfully, there didn't appear to be anywhere for someone to hide for a surprise attack and the closer he got to the top, the emptier the landing looked. Daniel made it to the last step and checked the left side of the landing before peeking around the top post to the right. What he saw was less than a delight, but no more than he was expecting. Dimly lit passage ways with recesses to hide in and plenty of places to wait in ambush. Along the right hand one, the one he must travel, Daniel could see what looked like the figure of a man, stood tall to attention. He judged, and hoped, that this was a knight in shining armour. Maybe there was a better weapon to be had, a mace perhaps or a sword? If his heart didn't give out before he got to the figure, he'd be sure to look.

Maybe he was the first contestant here? Maybe he'd been released before the others and this was his opportunity to find a good hiding place to wait for them? This new idea emboldened him a little and caused Daniel to re-check the hallway beneath him. All was silent... horribly silent. There were still lights on his arm band, so there must be others around somewhere, but this place seemed as devoid of life as it could be. That idea of him being the first to make it up the stairs and have the chance of finding a place to hide pushed him forwards. Daniel moved around the top post and quickly across the landing to the back wall under the window. There was no point in crouching here and so he stretched his body upwards and felt his spine thank him for the relief. Entering the new passage his eyes were fixed on the 'knight' in front of him. For a second there, he thought he saw it move. It was still a good twenty feet away from him but Daniel brought the spanner up in readiness all the same. As he did so he noticed his band and stopped dead...

One of the lights had turned from red to blue. He was sure it was red only a moment ago and had changed in the last ten seconds or so. What did it mean? It felt like such a long time ago, a lifetime in a way, that Jon had explained it all to them. What was it indicating when it turned blue? His nerves were shot and his brain frazzled from the stress of the situation. He couldn't think clearly and clarity was what he required. What did it mean??? If it flashed then it meant you were within ten feet of someone, he knew that much but turning from red to blue was a mystery to him. Daniel held his left hand to his face and pressed it into his eye. For some reason, he thought this would help him concentrate. Inside, he was shouting at himself for being so stupid that he couldn't recall what had been said. If it turns blue then it means you're cold? Why on earth would it matter if you were cold? It made no sense. Wait! Something in his brain finally clicked into gear. It wasn't because you were cold, it was cold because you'd removed the damn thing! He'd got it, one of the others had removed their armband... Now he needed to work out why?

They'd been told they couldn't win if they took their bands off, so why had this person chucked it all away? It made no sense to him. Moving forward another four steps or so brought the answer. That blue light started to flash.

Another four feet or so in front of him was a recess in the wall. He couldn't see what was in it yet, but it was the only feature within ten feet where someone could be hiding. It must be a room running off the passage and there must be a person in that room. He would have seen someone in the corridor otherwise. What's more, that person in the room knew he was coming. They'd known how close he was and removed the band. They could be anywhere in the room and had a distinct advantage over him right now. Daniels pulse raced and his body filled with adrenaline. Fight or flight? Should he burst into the room and face what was waiting for him or turn the other way and run? Maybe he should remove his band too and even up the contest? It wasn't his style. He was a boss, he was the one that would dominate the room and this attitude had been ingrained over the years of practice. What he was going to do was front up and take what was coming. It actually felt like a relief to finally be in that position. After such a long time hiding and creeping around waiting for something to happen, now it was here he felt less anxious. Like someone who'd been given bad news by the doctor after waiting two weeks for the results, it was better to know.

He edged out into the centre of the corridor, not needing to fear the shadows anymore, and looked into the recess. There was an open doorway and wrapped around the handle was an arm band. 'Son of a bitch' he said audibly and any doubts about whether he would be able to kill another human being were banished in that moment. He was ready to bludgeon whoever it was in the room and not stop until the life had completely gone from their body. He was fired up and trembling with energy. Daniel, as befit his nature, burst into the room with his hand clenched tightly on the spanner. Running into the centre of this unfamiliar space he nearly fell over the dark leather sofa, managing to stop himself just before he overbalanced. Using it as a 'lean to', he turned to defend his position. As he did so, the near pitch dark room was suddenly illuminated in bright, burning light. That contrast blinded him and he swung the spanner in front of him and shielded his eyes with his left hand. A flash of silver appeared in front of him and he threw his body backward instinctively. It wasn't quite quick enough to avoid contact and, as he fell over the sofa, Daniel felt a blade cut through his shoulder. If he hadn't have been quite so agile it would have been his neck. Tumbling over the cushions and rolling onto the floor behind, Dan jumped up sharply and found his eyes had adjusted a little to the new, bright environment. What he could see, standing the other side of the couch, was an outline of a man with a dirty great sword in his hands. Daniel, in his evasive manoeuvres, had lost his weapon somewhere in the cushions and as he moved forward to see if he could retrieve it, a swipe from the steel blade sent him reeling backward again. That extra bit of time allowed him to fully come to terms with the light and he could now see what, and who he was up against. Thomas-cockmunch-Dean, the dirty little bastard! They were caught in a stand off, Thomas had him pinned behind the sofa and defenseless but couldn't, from his position, get close enough to take another swipe at him. Each stood appraising the other, Daniel furtively scanning the room for a make shift weapon to defend himself with.

"Well well, look who made it through the game, Mr marketing! Have to say I'm surprised, didn't think you'd get past the climb..." and he paused to let the implication of what he had said sink in.

Daniel stopped still, dropping his guard and forgetting himself for a minute. "How... How do you know about my game?" he stuttered quizzically.

"Know about it? I designed it dear boy!" and he laughed menacingly.

Daniel stared at him blankly, not able to compute the information he was receiving. "What the hell are you talking about? How could you have... you're..."

"Oh Mr. Ferris, do try and catch on, it's really not that difficult. I'm the brains behind it all. This whole thing was my idea."

Daniels mind raced back to when they were in the dining room and what had been said. "But he killed your dog..."

"We killed 'a' dog you idiot, not my dog. Do you know how easy it is to get hold of a shitty little mutt? A few water works and a bit of pleading and you all took the bait without question."

Daniel was clearly struggling to make sense of this "So who the hell is Jon then?"

"Jon? He's my bitch!..." and he laughed again "I'm the brains and he's the brass. He paid for all of this, this is his house, but I was the one that came up with the idea. Delightful isn't it?"

"But why? Why make yourself one of the contestants? Why risk your life?" Daniel couldn't get his head around the mentality of the man. Why would someone go to all this trouble and put themselves in such danger?

"For the fun of it Mr. Ferris, the sheer hell of it! How many people know the feeling of hunting another human being? Of pitting themselves against worthy opponents and coming out the victor in the ultimate game? What money does, as you well know, is ruin one's enjoyment of life. Anything I want I can have and that kinda takes the fun out of it. When there's no risk involved then you lose the thrill of winning. Life becomes so dull. Putting everything on the line is the only way to truly feel alive again."

Funnily enough, Daniel could understand. He'd never really been happy with his life and the things he'd bought himself, those things he had dreamed of, had given him no joy. He too had felt very much 'alive' this night and wasn't about to chuck in the towel just yet. "So you think you're going to win then?"

"Oh, I'm sure of it. Have to admit I'm pretty disappointed more of you didn't get through, but what can you do? Had to bend the rules a little to get Lola passed her game, but only having one scumbag to kill wouldn't have been much of a test. You're going to die here Mr. Ferris and then I'm going to go find that gutter whore and chop her up into little pieces too" Thomas made a sudden jerk to the right as if he were going to come round the sofa and quickly moved left again. Daniel didn't fall for it and held his ground.

"Just a minute..." he said, and held his hands out in a steadying fashion. "Let's just suppose I got the better of you. Would I be able to win this game? Is there really £10 million waiting in the aviary for me?"

"You're never going to get there but ok, let's suppose" and he rested the blade of the sword on the back of the sofa "We've played pretty fair up to now, haven't we?"

"Well not really..." Daniel returned.

"Ok, so there might have been a few things we didn't tell you, but essentially, the game is the game. If you make it to the aviary and you're the last person alive then I can tell you that there's a case waiting with the prize in it. Whether Jon will let you leave with that money is a different matter. He may well be a little peeved over the fact that you've killed his boyfriend but the money is there, I promise you that. However, the object of the evening was to watch you suffer in the games and kill the survivors one by one, and that's exactly what is going to happen." Thomas tapped the side of the blade lightly on the leather sofa and grinned.

Daniel looked around the room for something that might help him. It was a relatively small, square room with book cases around the walls and a fireplace behind him. Quickly checking over his shoulder he was disappointed to find no heavy pokers or coal shovel. There was nothing in the room he could spot to use as a counter weapon to Thomas' blade. As he was checking the place for some assistance he noticed that the door had been closed and bolted. Thomas must have done this when he turned the lights on. It all looked pretty grim. He couldn't very well stay behind the sofa forever, waiting for Thomas to die of starvation, but he couldn't see what he could do. As he arrived at this miserable conclusion Thomas, wishing to get on with the murdering, dragged a small side table across to the back of the sofa and stood on it. Any second now he would jump over and take a swipe at him, Daniel was sure, so he made a break for it and ran to the book case over at the back of the room. Picking up the largest hardback he could find, he held it out in front of him and wished he had a better plan. Thomas casually hopped off the table and wandered over towards him.

"There is one thing I'd like to know before you die, if you wouldn't mind?" he asked sincerely.

"Go on..." he was grateful for the extra moments of life.

"You said before your game that Jon had missed something... Well, Jon didn't plan this thing, I did and it's been bothering me ever since. What exactly do you think I missed?"

Daniel smiled and was about to admit that he'd just said it to irritate Jon and get inside his head, when he felt something wriggle behind him. He'd backed himself up against the book case and the pressure of his body had squeezed his little allie into life. Holding out a hand to indicate he come no closer, Daniel said: "Stay there and I'll show you!"

Thomas looked amused by this and confidently rested the blade across his shoulders, adopting the pose of a man accepting the proposal.

Daniel turned half his back to Thomas and pulled the bag round to his stomach as he did so. "You're going to kick yourself for missing this..." he said as he undid the top of the bag and drew the head of the Mamba out in front of him, shielding it from sight.

"I'm sure I won't, but I'll entertain you anyway," he said.

Quickly removing the tape after making sure he had the head firmly secure in his grip, Daniel tapped the snake on the nose a couple of times to make sure it was properly pissed.

"Come on Mr. Ferris, I haven't got all night..." Thomas said impatiently.

Pulling the rest of the snake out of the bag he whipped around and threw it at Thomas' face. He only had time to take one hand off the blade before the snake hit him and uncoiled around his shoulders. Before he could grab the beast with his free hand the Mamba struck, one, two, three times in the face, injecting massive amounts of venom as it did so. It took three attempts to remove the snake from his body and throw it down on the ground. Thomas, screaming in anger, slashed at the serpent as it wriggled on the flooring, trying to get away. His first attempt nearly cut it in half and his second, a more measured swipe, took its head off and embedded the end of the sword in the wooden floor. Daniel saw his chance and was upon him before he managed to pull the blade free. Thomas was no match for Daniel physically and, in seconds, he was knocked unconscious on the floor. Already Daniel could see the venom taking effect. Thomas' face was swelling badly at the injection points and it wouldn't be long before he was paralysed by the venom. Death would probably take another ten minutes or more, but he wouldn't be able to move during that time anyway.

Suddenly an idea came to him. Racing over to the door, he threw back the bolt and opened it, taking the armband that Thomas had left on the outside handle.

Running back over to his prone body, Daniel attached the band to the prone man's left arm and attached his own band to Thomas' right. Next, he took the shoe lace he had tied the Mamba bag with and wrapped it around his arm, just above the elbow. Pulling it as tightly as he could to cut the circulation off, he knotted the ends and watched. Both lights had turned red again and were flashing. Daniel judged that the arm with the tourniquet would show no pulse and cool quicker than the other one, thus giving the impression that the owner of each band had died separately. If it worked, he would then have a distinct advantage over the masters of this game. He would, essentially, be a ghost.

Pulling the side table across from where Thomas had stood on it, Daniel sat down and removed the blade from the floor. Not only was he invisible to the host, he now had a proper weapon to defend himself with. It wasn't as good as an automatic rifle, but, if he were stealthy enough, it would give him a fighting chance. He sat and watched the bands, hoping to see one of the lights extinguish before the other. Also watching to see if the other light started to flash. It took about five minutes for the light on the tied arm to go out. Pleasingly, the other one was still going strong. Thomas had roused from his unconscious state and was moaning and making a terrific racket as the venom was now coursing through his system. Tissue around the points where he'd been bitten had turned black and his breathing had become extremely laboured. He posed no threat in this condition other than giving his position away with the noise. It would have been a mercy to put him out of his misery with a swift cut of the blade, but Daniel was not in a merciful mood. He was, however, keen to shut him up. He didn't feel like he had murdered Thomas, the snake had done that, and taking the blade to finish him off didn't bother him either. It was an act of kindness really, he pursueded himself. Actually, it was an act of self-preservation. He wanted the silence to return and now that the light had gone from one of the bands he need wait no longer to extinguish the other.

Putting his right foot on the chest of the dying man, Daniel rested the hilt of the blade on his neck. Applying pressure, he dragged the blade its full length and cut deeply into his flesh. Blood pumped from the carotid artery and pooled around the head and shoulders. It wasn't a pleasant thing to do or see, but it had to be done. Only one other light remained on the band and Daniel knew exactly what the next step should be. He felt he had a good chance of winning this from his position, all he needed to do was find Lola.

Chapter 9 - It's you, not me!

Slumped in a crumpled mess, half resting against the wall, half sprawled out on the floor, Lola was catching her breath. She dare not look at the timer, not yet. Had she made it? She couldn't even be sure she hit the button when she had lunged for it. It was one of those situations where, if you didn't look then you couldn't have lost, and she didn't want to know just yet which it would be. She felt banged up, beaten and physically wrecked all over. Her hip hurt the most but it was a pretty close call with the rest of her body. She let her body slide down onto the floor and tried to arrange her legs in a more natural position, one where they wouldn't hurt her so much. Wincing in pain as she did so, she managed to pull them around and lay flat on the floor. If she tilted her head back far enough she would be able to see the timer but she didn't want to know just yet. If she'd made it then she needed to recover for a while, if she hadn't then she was going to die anyway, so may as well take a breather. Either way, she felt it necessary to let her body find itself again.

Carefully she started checking herself for any serious problems. Those two tiger scratches were sore and stung when touched, they had that glistening look to them from the beginnings of the bodies repair work. It didn't help that she was still sweating profusely and each drop that made it to the raw wounds felt like she was being thrashed with a nettle. That hip was still the major problem but she didn't think it was going to get any worse now. Tomorrow she'd not be able to walk, but for now, it was just a case of limping through the discomfort. Those cuts on her fingers had stopped bleeding and didn't feel bad at all, she'd have full use of her hands and that was important. Over all, although her entire body ached, she felt in pretty good condition to carry on... the question was, could she? Had she passed the test?

It was time to look and see. Lola couldn't put it off any longer. Rolling herself over onto her front and dragging her knees up, she pushed herself into an upright position that looked like she was praying, and in a way, she was. Clasping her hands to her face and taking a deep breath, she opened her eyes and brought her gaze up to the timer across the room. It read '0m00sec'. Lola's heart sank and she felt a knot twisting in the pit of her stomach. Her head started to swim with the understanding that, after all her effort, she had run out of time and lost the game. She sat for a few moments crouched over herself in despair and a few tears dropped from her eyes and bounced off her cheeks to the floor. She was broken.

From the speakers that were placed within the room she heard a crackle, the channel had been opened and she sat awaiting her fate. This was the point where he would tell her how she would die and she wondered just what horrible way it would be.

"Congratulations gutter trash, you made it!"

Lola looked up at the speaker, her hands still over her mouth. Was this a joke? Was he playing the cruellest of tricks on her?

"You hit the buzzer with half a second to go you lucky bitch! Now you need to get yourself ready for the next part of the game. Go attend to your wounds and the timer will tell you when the door will release you"

And that was all he said. Lola just sat there with her mouth open. She had been overcome with the belief that she had lost and now she was equally wrecked by the reprieve. Where one or two tears had trickled off her cheeks in defeat, a flood now came in relief of victory. She sat, her shoulders shaking, and wept, letting all her emotions out and draining herself free of that tension in her body. When she finished, when there were no more tears to shed, she wiped her face and found herself angry. This bastard was toying with her. He'd broken her again and again, to a point no one had managed before and she was going to make him pay for this. Lola screamed hoarsely at the top of her voice 'Bastard!!!' and heard the word echo around the cavernous room. She didn't know whether he was listening or not, it didn't matter, she just needed to let out that primal emotion. Only then could she be calm herself and begin to think about the next stage of the game. Looking over to the timer on the wall, it had been reset and now registered 25m 15sec. Underneath she saw that a hatch in the wall had been opened and within it, there were a number of items to inspect. Dragging herself to her weary feet and hobbling over to the wall, she looked to see what goodies had been left for her.

Most prominent amongst the items on show was a baseball bat and the sight of it made her laugh out loud. She instantly recognised it as her own and it had a very special place in her memory. Jon had done his homework alright, she thought and was instantly taken back to the day she bought it. She was seventeen years old and had just watched her mothers coffin slide into the furnace. Along with the rest of her 'family' they'd said their goodbyes, although Lola was the only one not to shed a tear. She'd gone to the crematorium purely because she felt she ought to and to make sure that everything had gone off properly. Her brothers and sisters, the snivelling bastards, had wailed at the passing of a woman that had given them a life to forget, if they ever could. Pain and suffering was all Lola associated with her, she was the catalyst for all of that and she was glad to see her passing. It was time to move on, time to draw a line under this chapter and begin her new life, and she knew just what she had to do to achieve this. Whilst they had gone back to their home in a taxi, Lola had walked. Through the streets she knew so well, past the familiar shops and straight to one shop in particular. She'd seen it in the window of the shop a hundred times before, had fantasised about what she might do with it but had never had the courage. Today was different, today she didn't give a shit.

Inside the shop, the attendant had told her it was a solid willow bat, good quality and cheap for what it was. She had picked it up and swung it a couple of times, careful not to knock anything off the shelves as she did so. It was a little heavy for a skinny, malnourished 17-year-old girl, but she found the weight reassuring. It was just the job, she'd take it. Lola had walked home through the park, ignoring the calls from the boys playing football, in a dream like state. She appreciated the sky, the flowers and trees, all of the life that she found there, maybe for the very first time. She felt free and that had given her wings to rise above the scum and the dirt that was all around her. She could see a better world and she was going to make it, knew in her heart that she was going to win, once and for all.

When she arrived back home, to that pit that had caged her for seventeen years. That place of countless acts of violence and degradation. She instructed her siblings to gut the place. Handed out bin liners to be filled with everything that signified that old life. Her eldest brother was 24 now but still lived at home, as did the rest of them. All pathetic wasters in Lola's eyes and all incapable of seizing this opportunity to change. Well, she wasn't going to let it pass by. They were told to clean and tidy, get rid of the old and make the place as bright and welcoming as possible. Stained net curtains, ashtrays and filthy throws, all removed and taken to the bins. Windows washed to let the sunlight in, carpets cleaned and cleaned again. Every surface was scrubbed within an inch of its life whilst Lola busied herself in her mother's old bedroom.

When she had finished what she needed to do, she reappeared from the room with a single, tatty suitcase that didn't actually fasten properly but rather gaped in the middle. Cheap, old and worthless, it fit in perfectly with the rest of the place and encapsulated her old life in a nut shell. Watching, her siblings said nothing as she passed by, suitcase in one hand and baseball bat in the other. Lola opened the front door and placed the case just outside. She then took a chair from the table they occasionally ate at but mainly did drugs on and sat by the door, which she bolted. She knew he'd come back, all she needed to do was wait. He was the latest of the abusive bastards that had taken advantage of her family and, to Lola, he represented all of them. Many men had been and gone, all leaving their particular mark, and it was about time one of them paid.

Minutes ran into hours but she never moved, never said a word, just waited, expecting. When he finally did arrive, drugged or drunk or both, he bashed into the door, expecting it to open. Only then did he notice the suitcase outside and realise what it meant. Furiously he pounded on the door and vowed to knock seven shades of shit out of the lot of them. Lola allowed him a minute or so to work himself into a fury before she released the bolt. He kicked the door open and stared straight at Lola who was waiting for him. Gave her the look she'd seen too many times before. Those evil, blood red eyes fixed directly on her. She allowed him time enough to say one thing.

"Who the fuck do you think you are you little bitch?"

As he lurched forward to grab her, she swung the bat with all her might and smashed him just under his arm pit. Lola heard the cracking of his ribs and the contact it made felt so satisfying. It knocked the wind right out of him and he collapsed in the doorway in front of her. Lola held the bat high above her head and brought it down across his shoulder blades, the force of which made him smack his face on the floor and bloodied his nose in the process. He screamed out in agony and coughed some blood onto the floor. Lola knelt down next to him and pulled his face up by the hair on his head.

"Shut your fucking mouth and listen to me..." she hissed "when I've finished with you, and I haven't even got going yet, but when I have, you will pick up that case and fuck off. If you ever come back here again, if I ever see you in this estate again, I'll fucking kill you" and she spat in his face.

He didn't walk out of there that evening, he barely crawled. She busted ankles and fingers as well as ribs and teeth. She saved the sweetest revenge for last. As he was crawling out the door like a dog, as she had told him to do, she swung the bat one last time. If he ever did function as a man after that is any ones guess, but Lola believed she'd done the world a great favour in seeing to it that he didn't.

Lola left the house that evening with nothing but the clothes on her back and that baseball bat. It was a symbol of a new life for her and she'd kept it ever since. That retribution she brought about wasn't entirely for her, she wanted to give the rest of them a fighting chance. Remove the last excuse for not making something of their lives. Whether or not they grasped this opportunity she would never know, she was done with them and had paid up in full whatever debt she owed. She went and never looked back.

Placing the bat on the floor, almost reverentially, she moved through the rest of the items contained within. They were composed of various bandages and tapes with which she could patch up her battered body. There were even a couple of pills to take the edge off her aches and pains and she swallowed them down with the bottle of water provided. Boy did that water taste good. When you are truly thirsty, when you're empty of all fluids, water is the most wonderful drink in the world. It feels like life returning to your body and she gulped and savoured every drop. Getting to work on her body she managed to cover and tape her tiger scratches well and they felt instantly better for it. Those pills were the only thing she could do for her hip and she used the surgical tape to wrap her finger ends. All in all, now she'd had a good few minutes to recover, she felt pretty good. Tired and battered, but ready to fight again when she had to.

Checking the timer she noted that there were less than five minutes to go before the door released her. Lola retrieved her shoes and cleaned them as best she could with the gauze that was left over. Tying them tightly over her feet they felt protective and good. She would be swift and silent in these and that thought gave her hope for the next part of the game. Just before the door released Lola noticed the scissors she'd used to cut the tape and bandages with, they weren't any good as a main weapon but as a surprise... well, they may just come in handy. She tucked them into the back of her lycra bottoms and was now ready to go!

3...2...1... Those bolts slid open and the door was released. They made enough noise to alert a passer by as to her whereabouts and, because of this, she hesitated before reaching to pull the door. That first, and last, time she had used the bat she had been waiting for her victim. She had expected him and he was surprised by her, that wasn't the case here. She was nervous and edgy, not in the least bit composed. Only now did she look at her armband to see how many dots were still 'in play'. Two was certainly better than four, but it was still going to be difficult to get the better of whoever was left. Of all the people she *didn't want to meet, James was the one that stood out. It would be a pleasure wrapping that bat around his head after what he had done but his quiet and controlled attitude had unnerved her. She was used to the brash, cocksure bastards like Daniel and Simon, she'd spent her life getting the better of those types and was confident she could do so again, but James was a different proposition.*

Carefully, she pulled the door open a crack and peered through the gap. She could see nothing in the darkness outside but nor could she hear anything and this helped calm her a little. Allowing a good amount of time for her eyes to adjust before she pulled the door any further, Lola was ready to slam it shut at any moment. But her precautions were not necessary, there was nothing hiding in the shadows waiting for her. Eventually, she opened the door enough to slide her slender frame through the gap and assess the area. Damp concrete and stone, musty smells and a subterranean chill greeted her. Where there were a number of lamps lit on the way to her room there was only two left illuminated now. One of which was outside her door and the other seemed to be coming from the top of the stairs she'd walked down earlier. There was only one other door to be seen in the basement and that was directly across from hers. She moved over to it and tried the handle. It didn't give and she judged that it must be locked from the inside. Was there another contestant held within it, ready for release? If so, they would have heard her door unlocking and be prepared for an attack. But she would also be given the same warning. It was useless just standing there waiting for something that might never happen and so she moved on quietly towards the stairs. She needed to get back to the main part of the house and figure out where to go from there. Lola crept along the corridor, bat at the ready and eyes like flash bulbs seeking out any movement in front of her. Eventually, she made it to the foot of them and stopped.

They were just a set of stairs... She'd walked down them not much over an hour ago but the prospect of walking back up them again filled her with dread. At the top, there was a door and she knew that outside that door, a door she must exit, was the cavernous expanse of the hallway. Once she left this basement she was then 'live' in the game. Lola believed that, just as she had no idea where the others had been taken, they would have no clue she was down here. This meant that as long as she stayed within the basement she was safe. But the fact was, at some point, she would have to leave. Checking her arm band she saw that there were 1h 43mins left before the midnight curfew. Having gone through what she had in her room, what was the point of just sitting here and waiting to be killed?

'Come on girl... you can do this!' she told herself, although how much she believed it to be true was debatable. None the less, baseball bat firmly in hand, she started to climb the damp stairs towards the door. Had he put her down here because it was the only place large enough for her game or because it was a reminder of where she came from in life? This would have been the servant's area, damp and squalid, in stark contrast to the majesty of the house above. Cast down with the rats in this subterranean dungeon, that's where he thought she belonged? Well, she'd show him, she'd show all of them what she was made of.

Step by step, each as tentative as the last and her eyes fixed on the landing at the top, Lola made her way out of the pit. She was breathing quickly and finding it hard to keep her attention on her feet as well as the top of the stairs. At one point she missed the next step and stubbed her toe, having to reach out for the wall to steady herself. She very nearly let out a little cry of pain too but managed to swallow it back down inside her. There was only one dim lamp to guide her way but it was enough to see where she needed to go. Without being aware of it, Lola had slowed her pace towards the landing to a virtual crawl. Three steps to go and she would be at the top, five feet or so from the door. She clasped the bat with both hands and held it out in front of her, ready to smash anything that came within range. Only then did she notice the little flashing light on her band. It took a moment to register but when it did the realisation petrified her. There was someone outside the door!

Lola's initial reaction was a physical one. Her legs turned to jelly and she nearly buckled at the knees. Then the brain took over. Were they waiting outside for her? They couldn't be, they couldn't have known she was in there... They would know now though. If her band was flashing then theirs would be too and she was standing in a very vulnerable position. It was no use retreating back to the corridor, she judged, what she had to do was get behind that door and prepare herself to smash the shit out of whoever came through it. This was her only course of action and she needed to get into place quickly before the bastard came through. If he caught her on the stairs she was a sitting duck. Lightly but speedily on her toes, she made it up the last of the steps and moved into position, watching the door keenly as she did so. Adrenaline rushed through her body as she waited with her bat raised above her head. She waited for the door to burst open, prepared herself to bring that wooden bat down as hard and as fast as she could, the first sight she got. She waited...

Her arms were trembling and she felt like her whole body was shaking with energy but nothing happened. Why the hell wasn't he bursting through the door to come and get her? This pause in proceedings was utter torture and she felt like screaming 'come on then... come and get me!' but she held her tongue as she held her pose. Then, after what seemed like an eternity, she heard the handle creak and saw it move ever so slightly. Suddenly, the damn thing snapped down and she nearly jumped out of her skin. It flicked back up in place as quickly as it had fallen and the door remained closed. Jesus Christ, she thought, what the fuck is he playing at?

She stood, stock still and ready to pounce, waiting for the handle to fall again and someone to come bursting through the door. They must know she was waiting for them now? In the dim light her senses, thanks to the adrenaline, were super keen. She could feel the blood pulsing through her body, felt like she could hear it too. What she definitely did hear was the sound of the outsider sliding back against the wall and slightly away from the door. What were they doing? Daring not to move, hardly taking a breath either, Lola waited. Those seconds felt like hours but the handle never moved.

She did hear 'him' move again though, heard him pass the door and continue along the wall outside. After a few more steps and just as her senses stopped picking up his movements, the light on her band stopped flashing. Maybe he decided it was too dangerous to come through the door? Whatever his reasoning, Lola was glad of the respite. With the constant light, she felt she could relax her pose and let the bat come to rest on the floor. She needed that break too, her arms hurt from holding it for so long above her head. She carefully dropped herself down onto her haunches and thought about her next move. That outsider could be finding some place to lay in ambush, knowing she was trapped here behind the door. She'd have no idea where he was hiding but he'd know she would have to come out soon enough. It was a bad position to be in and there wasn't a thing she could do about it. What was the best thing to do?

There was a good hour and a half to go, more than in fact, so why should she try and go anywhere? Why not wait it out here? It surely couldn't take more than five minutes to get from here to the aviary, wherever it was. This place was big but it was only a house, not the bloody Pentagon. There were two blokes out there with weapons, why not wait for them to find each other first. Hopefully, one would be seriously injured in the act of killing the other and make her job a whole lot easier. Whatever happened, she had a fighting chance against one of them, much less so against two. Sit where you are girl, she told herself, wait for another light to go out first. Lola lowered her backside down to the floor and leant her back against the wall behind the door. May as well get comfortable whilst you wait, she thought.

Resting the stick on her lap, she rested her eye lids too but kept her ears pinned. As she sat there she felt the light touch of dust drifting down her face, she could smell it too. Opening her eyes she noticed, from the lamp above her head, little puffs falling from each step, ascending the staircase. That outsider must be climbing up to the next level, that must also be the way to go to the aviary, she thought. Resting her eyes again she waited and allowed her body to relax and recover. She was tired, dog tired.

Lola woke with a start, like one does on a late night bus and you're unsure if you've missed your stop. Confused and a little panicked, she clutched the bat instinctively before checking her band for the time. 41m 35secs. She stared at the timer for a good few moments, unable to compute the information. Discombobulated was the perfect word to describe how she felt and it was a while before her brain fully awoke and began to work again. How on earth had she managed to fall asleep? Anything could have happened! She was angry with herself for letting her guard down and leaving herself open to attack. Lola was angry right up to the point where she noticed the lights on her band. There was only one left... Again, this information, as simple as it was, took a long time to sink in. At first, she thought it a mistake and kept staring at it, waiting for another light to flicker on again. Then she thought she must have been mistaken in thinking she was ever one of those lights, but knew, actually that there were only five to start with, so she must be. There really was only one conclusion to be drawn, the outsider had killed the other and died in the process. It had to be that way, there was no other explanation. As she sat there running this over and over in her head to check it for sense, make sure she was correct in her thinking, she also came to the positive conclusion about what this meant. She had won. Without having to engage in any fights, without having to kill anyone along the way, she had won the game. All she needed to do now was find the aviary and she had 40 minutes or so to do that. Her confusion and anxiety subsided to be replaced with euphoria, a wonderful sense of absolute joy.

Lola pushed herself up with the bat, her body had seized somewhat whilst she had slept and it was painful trying to get some motion back into her limbs. That hip was stiffer than ever but it didn't matter now. She took a moment to shake the life back into herself before reaching for the handle. Purely out of disbelief at her luck, she checked the armband once again for the lights. Still only her own was lit and so she confidently pulled the door ajar and left the basement behind her.

Following the advice of the arrow, she limped her way up the stairs and turned right. In front of her was a dark corridor with the figure of a man standing to attention half way down. That sight arrested her progress before she realised it was just a suit of armour. Even though she knew she was the only one left, she was still cautious and clung to the bat with an iron grip. Climbing the stairs had hurt and she had used her arm on the bannister to help keep the pressure off her hip. Now, on the flat corridor, she had nothing to hang on to for support so she reasoned that the bat was wasted held aloft and far better employed as a makeshift walking stick. Lola found it comical that she was walking like a geriatric, reliant on an aid to ease her discomfort. She'd seen people walk with sticks many time before and never look like they needed to. They had always given the impression of someone shamming for attention or benefits and she couldn't see what use a stick would be anyway. Now it was an absolute godsend and made her progress bearable if not pleasant. She vowed never to scorn those people again.

As she approached the knight in shining armour, she mockingly saluted his presence and said "Evening guv'nor"

"Evening Lola..." came a reply from directly behind her followed by the touch of cold steel on her neck. She froze to the spot. "Drop the bat and stay perfectly still!"

She let her stick fall to the floor and her eyes fell also to the band on her arm... one light! She said simply "How?"

"Now that is a tale to tell, let me show you," he said and ushered her into the room in which he'd been hiding.

Daniel sat her down on the little side table, close to Thomas' body, the sight of which made her feel quite sick. He indicated, with a wave of his hand, both armbands and the makeshift tourniquet on the dead man's bicep. "This is how, I had the opportunity to 'kill' myself and I took it. The better question, Lola, is why?"

She looked at Daniel, looked him all over, regarding his injuries and his physical condition and wondered if she could make a break for it. She thought he was going to kill her and take her band before the light went out. Something in the way she was looking gave her away.

"Don't try it..." he said calmly "there's no need for you to run, I'm not going to kill you"

"Oh, so you're just going to let me walk to the aviary and collect the money then? That's very nice of you" her voice held a good deal of sarcasm and she looked disbelievingly at the man with the sword.

"Actually, that's exactly what I am going to do. But I think I have a good reason for it." and he told her all he knew, and what he surmised, about Thomas. "You see, he was the brains of the whole thing. This was 'his' game and he wanted to hunt us down... but he failed"

Lola listened sceptically but tried to hide her emotions from Daniel. She felt she needed to 'play along' if she wanted to get out of this alive. "So why remove your band? I don't understand. Why not wait for me to arrive and try to kill me?"

Daniel was frustrated with her inability to grasp the situation the way he saw it. "Look at your band," he said, "which light is still on?"

"The second one" she replied, simply.

"That's right... and mine was the fifth. Mr Dean's over there was the third one, don't you see? When Jon told us that he didn't know who's was who's he was lying. Brown, Cooper, Dean, Evans, Ferris... B, C, D, E, F and they corresponded to the lights on the band. Now I do believe that there are no cameras in the house. I've checked this room thoroughly and can see none. Why? I've no idea but it must have been by Thomas' say so. However, it's clear that they, Jon and that monkey, know exactly who's light is who's. If I'd killed Thomas and retained my band then I'm pretty sure they would have stopped the game and come to *kill us both. However, I made it so my light went out first, then Thomas' a little while after. Looking like we both died in the fight between us. I've been waiting here for either you or them to turn up. Do you see now?"*

Lola considered what he had said carefully before replying "So you want to send me to the aviary like a lamb to the slaughter? Thanks a bunch!"

"Nooo! Listen to what I am saying!" he said in exasperation "We've been behind the game the whole time. They've held all the cards and we've had to do what they said, play their stupid fucking games. Who knows if there's any money in the aviary or not, whether any of us 'could' win this from the start?... Honestly, I don't care about that anymore, I just want to live. Don't you?" he asked.

She was starting to see what he was driving at. "Go on..." she said.

"Now that I'm dead, or they think I'm dead, they won't be looking for me. That gives us an advantage. We need to work together if we want to get out of here."

Lola agreed that, given what she had just learned, it was unlikely that there was any pot of gold waiting for her at the end. "So what's the plan?"

"Well we can't make you 'dead' as well and they're going to be expecting you to turn up sooner or later - what took you so long to get here anyway?" he asked suddenly before carrying on "so... you're going to have to go to the aviary. We don't know for sure that they won't simply pay up and let you go, they have told the truth about some things tonight, maybe they were on the level about this?"

Lola scrunched her face "Do you really think so?"

Daniel paused for a second, considering whether to lie "Well no, not really. If I'm honest with you I'm expecting them to try and kill you when you walk in the room"

"Brilliant!" she mocked "so what's the fucking plan then? Because it's not looking good for me at the moment. I'd be better off taking my chances hiding in the house"

"Firstly, they'd know you were somewhere, even if you took the band off. Second, there's two of them with guns, you'd have no chance. So I'd forget about that if I were you." Daniel shook his head, her failure to play along with

his ideas was annoying him. "What you need to do, poppet is go to the fucking aviary..."

She interrupted him mid-flow "Call me 'poppet' again and I'll ram that fucking blade up your arse!"

Daniel stopped and stared at her for a couple of seconds "I could just kill you, that is possible you know..."

"That wouldn't be very smart now would it?" she ventured "you'd give yourself away if you did!" and she forced a smirk in his direction.

Daniel shook his head again "Are you going to fucking listen or not? Jesus, you're hard work!"

Lola laughed "You better have something good to say nob head, or you can count me out"

"Right... Shut up for a fucking second and I'll tell you" and he quickly held his hand up to counter the objection she was going to make to the 'shut up' instruction. Lola decided to let this one go, this time.

"Here's what we are going to do. You go to the aviary and claim the prize. Outcome A is that they were being honest about it and you get the money and walk away. This means that they have accepted what's happened and it gives me the best chance of walking out of here too. They won't be expecting me and they won't be prepared. I'll find you later and you can bung some cash my way as well and we're both happy. Outcome B is that you go to the aviary and there's no cash. They are going to kill you and you need to beg for your life. If this happens, you tell them about me. Tell them how I managed to 'die' and that I thought 'Outcome A' was what was going to happen when you got there. You tell them you know where I'm hiding and you'll show them, if they'll spare your life. It'll save them the trouble of searching the house if you can, so they may go for it. Besides, what threat do you pose to them? What will actually happen is that you'll bring them here. I'll be waiting in ambush for them along the way and when I jump out, you help me as best you can with these" and he produced the surgical scissors from his shorts.

Lola laughed and pulled out the same scissors from hers "Great minds eh..." she said "so that's the grand plan then is it? Not exactly nailed on to work. What if they just kill me anyway? What if they smell a rat and are ready for you to jump out along the way?"

"Well, you can tell them you didn't know I was going to do it, if that happens. Guess it depends on how good an actress you are? And you're assuming Outcome A isn't going to happen"

"It still sounds pretty shaky to me, you're taking a lot of things for granted."

Daniel rested the point of the sword on the floor and sighed "Forgive me..." he said "I've had a whole twenty minutes to come up with a way of us getting out of here, sorry it's not bullet proof!" it was his turn to apply the sarcasm "If you can come up with anything better in the next five minutes then feel free to enlighten me"

"Sorry..." she said, and meant it "it's not a bad plan and it could work out if we're lucky" she tucked the scissors back in her pants and sat forward, resting her elbows on her knees.

"There's still a chance they'll just give you the money..." he said, but didn't look or sound convinced.

Lola started to cry, she hid her face in her hands and wept "They're going to kill me aren't they?..." she sobbed.

Daniel, feeling the hopelessness in her voice, moved forward and rested a hand on her shoulder to comfort her. Tenderly he said, "Hey... you don't kn..."

Before he could get the words out she'd hooked her leg behind his and jammed her fingers up his nose. Daniel was flat on his back and staring at the point of the blade.

"How's that for acting?"

Chapter 10 - The Organ Grinder and the Monkey

"Whether you 'like' it or not is of no importance plonky..." Jon spat this remark over his shoulder as he watched the monitor that showed the position of the contestants in the house. Ruby, the hired monkey, didn't like it one bit. All the expense they had gone to, why had they not fitted the place out with cameras? It made no sense to him and he had made his feelings clear.

"You're not here to provide an opinion, you're here to do as you're told sunny Jim!" Jon was dismissive of Ruby's thoughts on the matter. That he had ventured them in the first place had deeply irritated him.

"I've done everything you've asked, haven't I?" he grumbled, "I just don't understand why we haven't got 'eyes' on them?"

"Because, my little fucking washed up squaddie, that's the way Thomas wanted it to be. You're not expected to understand, you're not getting paid to fucking chip in with your own ideas and, let's face it, it's not like you're any fucking expert on anything other than screwing things up. So if you don't mind" he said in feigned reverence "shut the fuck up and do your job!"

Ruby scowled at the back of Jon's head but said nothing in reply. What he wanted to do was smash the bastard's skull in, but he resisted the temptation and sat himself down on a chair behind him and watched the TV instead. He hated him, hated the way he spoke to him, had done from the moment they had met but he needed the money. An opportunity like this would never come again and it was his chance to make amends for all the things he'd done. Put everything right again, well, as right as it could be after what had happened. Another hour or so and it would all be over. He'd never need to listen to this arsehole again. All he had to do was keep his cool.

It was a large, Victorian addition to the house, tagged on the back and quite beautiful in its own way. Lots of glass and metal work, high ceiling and a fresco of an exotic landscape on the wall that divided it from the house. It was from this that the room had gotten its name. It wasn't an 'aviary' at all, more a sunhouse or large conservatory, but the brightly coloured birds painted in amongst the foliage had secured the room it's identity. Growing almost to the height of the room were a number of plants from far flung places, only able to flourish thanks to the enhanced atmosphere created within by that glass. Large fans hung from steel beams that straddled the canopy and looked for all the world like they should be driven by little punkahwallah. It was a grand place to 'take tea' and have one's elevenses with the vicar or visiting dignitaries. Tonight its sole purpose was to act as the finishing line to a terrible game where no one was supposed to win. In daylight, it was a delightful place to spend one's time, here in the darkness of the late evening it had taken on a much more sinister tone. Illuminated by numerous lamps and the intermittent light of the moon, those giant plants cast ever changing shadows across the flooring and furniture. Thomas felt it added to the atmosphere of the night and had insisted on the 'game' finishing there.

Jon was sat by the table watching the three dots move around the screen in front of him, drinking some more of that Richebourg and wishing there were cameras in the house so he could see what was happening. He'd wanted them, had said so when they were planning this, but Thomas had said no. He'd been most insistent about it. Cameras in the rooms so he could enjoy the torture of the games, Jon liked that, but none in the rest of the house. He'd said it would spoil the 'thrill' of the hunt for him. That, with those in situ, the feeling of danger, of pitting oneself against the others, just wouldn't be there for him. It was the reason he - Thomas - had come up with the plan in the first place and it would be ruined if he felt that safety net. If Jon could see what was happening then he would be able to intervene should things look like they were going wrong, and that would always be in his mind. Thomas had won the argument, as he always did, and Jon had gone along with his wishes. It was his birthday present after all.

Jon didn't care much for danger, this 'hunting' was not what turned him on to the idea. If it were up to him they would have all died in the games or been made to fight each other to the death afterwards. There would have been no involvement on their part if he'd had his way, he just liked the cruelty. It had been such a delicious idea at the start but he was weary of it now, he just wanted it over. Those years of planning and waiting had taken the shine right off the experience for him but Thomas had loved the details. It had grown into more than a sick game for him, it had taken over his every thought. Jon had lost him to it and was sick of the whole affair now. Had he enjoyed the 'games'? He had to admit that he had, but they could have done the same thing with a bunch of tramps they'd picked up from the streets and done it years ago. All this detail had left him cold.

They'd met at prep school, twenty years ago or more, and had fallen in love. Jon with Thomas' machiavellian mind, Thomas with Jon's money. They had a shared love of the macabre and a total disregard for the feelings of others. People were then, and even more so now, just vessels for their own sick brand of entertainment. They didn't have any 'worth' as human beings and they were treated with the utmost indifference. Only when they could be manipulated, humiliated, stamped on, did they hold any interest to the pair at all. He remembered the first time they had 'played' with someone and how much fun they had had too. It was back at the school, only a matter of weeks after they had found each other, that their career in ruining people had begun. Thomas had liked the look of the school chaplain, a weak and God fearing man in his thirties. Ineffectual and dithering, he was often teased by the boys who could see how hot and bothered they made him. Really, if he hadn't been a filthy pervert who couldn't stop himself from fiddling with kids, then he'd have been fine. That had been the origin of the theme that had run through their games from then on. That they would use peoples weaknesses to bring about their destruction. His weakness was for young flesh and Thomas had been exactly the sort of cherry lipped thirteen-year-old this dirty old bastard couldn't help himself with. All it took was a smile and an offer to stay back and help tidy the chapel and his fate was sealed. Like some Nabakovian vision, Thomas enchanted him and he was powerless to prevent what would become his destruction. Even back then, Thomas had loved the feel of a cock in his mouth and Jon had enjoyed watching from behind a curtain. Pictures were taken, threats made and the silly man of God had been theirs to play with for however long they wished. They made him sweat for a month or two, made him pray for his unworthy soul, but soon became bored with the snivelling shit. There's only so much fun you can have with a man as racked with guilt as he was. They copied the photographs and sent some to his wife and others to the local paper. 'Hornby School Chaplin Commits Suicide' ran the headline, this was obviously preferable to 'man of the cloth fucks kids at expensive prep school' well, preferable to the father of two anyway. He'd had a choice, face the music or face his maker, he'd chosen the latter, as they thought he would, and would now be burning in the pits of hell for his sins. That they had brought about the death of the man was of no consequence to them, nor was the fact that he had left his wife and kids fatherless. It was his weakness that he had paid for, not theirs. Find out what motivates someone and you have them at your mercy, this was the lesson they had learned and it had been a defining moment in their lives.

"It looks like the spider is about to catch the fly," Jon said, looking over his shoulder to engage Ruby in what was happening on the monitor. Daniels light was getting ever closer to where Thomas had planned to wait. He hadn't really wanted to bring Ruby back into a conversation, he found him dull and stupid, but it was much less fun experiencing it on his own. He was used to sharing these moments with Thomas and felt a little lonely sat there without him.

"And what if the fly catches the spider, have you thought about that?" Ruby questioned.

Jon had thought about it, it had kept him awake for days but Thomas had been so bullish about it, so sure that he was going to win. With false conviction, he repeated the lines Thomas had quoted when asked the same question. "Lambs to the slaughter darling..." and his voice trailed off to a near whisper. He was nervous, suddenly very unsure about this and lacking the bolstering effect that Thomas' conviction had always given him. He'd always been the weaker of the two but had sailed on the waves of Thomas' confidence.

Those two lights were getting ever closer. Jon knew Thomas had a plan, knew that he would have covered all the bases, it was his forte after all, but he still felt horribly anxious. Playing the role of his master, in an attempt to quell his fears, Jon adopted a cock sure attitude. "You just watch... That fifth light will disappear soon enough" and he tried to show Ruby his signature 'smug' grin.

"Sometimes you think you have control when all you have is chaos" Ruby murmured.

"Philosophy!" Jon cried in mock appreciation "how wonderful... and what would a washed up fucking pisshead like you know about it?" he jibed "Oh, that's right, you failed in your duties and ended up losing everything you'd worked for, didn't you?"

Ruby stared directly into Jons eyes, didn't waiver for a second "That's right, I failed and it cost me. You've no idea how that feels, but maybe you soon will?"

Jon stared straight back and, without hesitating, responded to the warning "And you're putting yourself in the same league as Thomas? You? A fucking partially trained monkey think you're in some way on a par with him?" and he laughed hysterically.

Those piercing jibes didn't hurt him, he didn't care what Jon thought about him, but the memory of what he was alluding to did. He remembered the day very clearly, he should, he relived it every time he closed his eyes. It was a baking hot, cloudless morning, pretty standard conditions for the territory, and there was nothing out of the ordinary about the orders they received. 'Activity 10 miles north, sweep the area, high risk' - it was the sort of thing his troup had done maybe fifteen times or more and they'd rarely encountered any problems. Usually, by the time they got to the position, whatever had caused the command had moved on somewhere else. He was deep into his tour and only had another 10 days to go before he could go home, this was always the worst time. You got edgy, you saw things that weren't there and invented danger where there was none. Ask anyone, the most anxious time is always the time you can see the finish.

It had been a pretty trouble free tour, his group had lost no one to IED's or enemy fire. Whilst other troups had been suffering losses and mourning brothers, his men had seemed to lead a charmed life. Wherever they went, they missed the trouble. Sometimes by days, sometimes only hours, but they had missed it all the same and felt blessed because of this. Maybe they even got a little complacent, believing in their guardian angels, or whatever they thought was looking over them.

They'd set off with the intention of securing the area and there wasn't supposed to be any civilians to muddy the waters. Anyone they found there was to be treated as hostile and dealt with in such a way. He was the eldest of his men and seen as a father figure by many of them. He'd come to the army later in life and even though he wasn't any more experienced than his kids - that's what he called them because they were to him - his life, before he joined up, had hardened him and given him an authority the others respected and appreciated. He was their leader and always took the advanced positions in such missions. It was no different today.

Growing up on the rough estates of south London, Ruby was always the first one in. He was bigger than most his age and expected to fight, like Ray Winstone in 'Scum', he was 'the daddy' and relished the role. Schools gave up on him early and they stopped reporting his truancy, just happy he was causing trouble elsewhere. Petty crimes, shop thefts and muggings were all over his arrest sheets and he made his way into borstal at the earliest opportunity. There really was nothing else for kids like him and he carried on this way right up until the day he found out he was going to be a father. Something about that had triggered a switch in his head. Ruby had never known his own father and he'd blamed all his problems on that fact. It wasn't his fault, he had reasoned, if he'd had a dad to guide him he would have been a different boy. Just an excuse, which he knew fine well, but one that had suited him to use. Absolve him of any responsibility for the things he had done. Knowing he was going to be a dad was the wake-up call he needed. It was like he had been plunged into an ice bath and could suddenly see the worthlessness of his life so far. That excuse for his own wrong doings had come back to haunt him. He couldn't let his own child have the same reason to fail. Now he had a real dependant and a woman who wanted him to change too. Before that, all he could see was the same road he had been travelling, stretching out inevitably in front of him. He was blinkered, like a horse, and his vision narrowed to the point where there were no other options. Now those blinkers had been removed and he wanted to take a different path.

He got himself a job, a legit one, away from the drugs and violence, away from the temptation to make easy money. He took pride in earning his crust, a man feels clean when he's worked hard for his money. They got a flat away from his manor and he cut his ties with those 'friends' who were nothing of the sort and soon forgot about him. Things were working for them and they were happy. She, Anna, didn't want or ask for anything other than a good man and this purity gave him strength. When the baby came, when he stood over her with his boy there in her arms, he felt like a king. All he wanted to do was provide and protect them, give them the best he could and this brought him a fresh pressure. No qualifications, no talents for anything legal, his scope for earning the sort of money he wanted to, give them the sort of life he felt they deserved, was limited. He needed them to be proud of him the way he was proud of them, needed to be a 'big man' again but in the right way. He was big, strong, fit and afraid of nothing, the army was a perfect fit for him. All he needed to do was wait until his wrap sheet was clean and join up.

Nobody had ever been able to order him around before, but he'd had no reason to listen. Now he had a cause and this made it easy. He found himself perfectly suited to army life and the army loved him back. He was exactly the sort of man you wanted to go into battle for you. And so it was that those skills that had caused him such trouble as a young man were revered here in the forces. Ruby had the respect of the men as well as his wife and son. If he'd had a better education behind him he would have risen quickly through the ranks but it didn't matter, he was making enough to feel like a real provider.

Then came the war and that fateful day. They'd travelled up to the site and found a deserted village. Taking nothing for granted they swept the houses one by one, Ruby leading the way. It had seemed like another call for which the action had come too late, all was quiet. He remembered the heat of the midday sun beating down and the glare that made the distant view shimmer. He could see that his boys were relaxed and this had worried him, what if today was the day they needed to fight? He'd gathered them together for a pep talk, tried to knock the lax attitude out of them and told them to finish the job right, like soldiers! He remembered that phrase 'like soldiers'...

He'd been taught to fight for his country, fight for his boys. Never to compromise the safety of the unit and act swiftly when the situation required it. He'd been taught to kill and believed himself more than capable of doing so. He was prepared to kill for his troup and his country but he wasn't prepared for what he found that day. As he entered that ramshackle building, one of the last to be cleared, poised and ready to fight, he found himself facing the enemy. It was a boy, a dark haired and frightened little boy. Maybe a couple of years older than his own son, that's all, and he was concealing something under his coat. They'd heard stories of children being used in this way, strapped with explosives and a trigger. Ruby had waved his boys back, commanded them to retreat to a safe distance whilst he dealt with the danger. He'd shouted at the boy to show his hands, take them out of his coat so he could see what he was hiding but the child had started to cry and call back in his own language. He was just a boy. Ruby had been taught to fight men. He remembered his finger hovering on the trigger of his gun, the sweat dripping off his nose. He'd thought about his own boy, playing football in a park or maybe even 'army' with his friends. He was the reason he'd come here in the first place. His finger hovered...

Ruby raised a hand to the boy to show he was putting down his weapon. He spoke in hushed and soothing tones, as best he could, and tried to make the boy understand he wasn't going to hurt him. All he needed to do was show him his hands, show him what was inside the jacket. His face was dirty and his nose bubbling, the child had such large, dark eyes, glassy from fearful tears. Pleading and terrified, his speech was excitable and erratic, as were his movements and he never once let Ruby see what he was concealing. Ruby had knelt on the floor of that house to try and show the child he meant no harm. He was looking into his eyes, those deep, pooled eyes, when he heard the crack of the rifle.

"I've seen things you'll never see... things no one ever should," he said.

"You've seen the inside of too many bottles of whisky, that's all" Jon said and he sneered at the man behind him in disgust.

Ruby's head had fallen to gazing at his lap, he barely heard what had been said and cared even less. He was lost in his thoughts of the boy and how his life had unravelled afterwards.

"I'll tell you one thing you haven't seen..." Jon said "you haven't seen your son growing up, have you? Well if you ever want to see them again then you better do as you're told and cut the attitude"

Ruby gripped the handle of the rifle tighter at the mention of his family. "You don't talk about them!" he said, through gritted teeth.

"We know where they live plonky, do you?" It wasn't a wise thing to say to Ruby, Jon didn't understand the 'motivation' game like Thomas did.

Ruby jumped up from his chair "You go anywhere near them and I'll fucking kill you, I promise you that you evil little bastard!" and there was no mistaking the sincerity and conviction in his voice.

Jon felt his cheeks flush and his blood cooled inside him "calm down squaddie..." he mustered, his voice wavering "remember why you're doing this"

Ruby couldn't forget, it was his one shot at redemption. One million pounds for one day's work and all he had to do was follow orders. He hadn't known what to expect but for that sort of money, he'd imagined it to be both illegal and life threatening. So far it had only been disturbing and twisted, he could deal with that. However, at the mention of his family, he'd nearly lost his control of the situation. He didn't care what happened to him, had given up on himself ages ago, but his family meant everything.

They'd found him propped against a bin out the back of some city dive bar. Pissing on the bags of rubbish and barely keeping his balance as he did so. He didn't remember much about that first meeting, hadn't remembered much about the last year to be fair, but when he woke in a hotel bedroom the next morning he had found a letter pinned to his clothing. There were some fresh clothes ready for him to wear and an invite to breakfast. Sceptically, he'd played along as he was curious and hungry. Their proposition was a simple one, he'd get one million pounds for one day's work and there were to be no questions asked. He wouldn't have believed a word of it if it hadn't been for the story they told, his story. They'd known everything about him, his childhood, army career and what had happened afterwards. They'd known details he didn't even remember himself or had tried to forget, and they also knew what was most important to him now. Something he didn't think was even possible, given his situation. That he wanted to give his family the life they deserved, that was all he'd ever wanted really. He hadn't seen his wife or son for over a year now but they occupied his thoughts every single day. What had happened between them haunted him almost constantly and he wanted to make good what he had made bad.

It had begun, that road to self-destruction, the day he saw the boy killed in front of him. That moment had stuck with him and, like a broken record, he couldn't move on from it. That was the finish of the war for him, the finish of his army life. He had no more to give. What he had witnessed was beyond what he was prepared for, beyond anything anyone could be prepared for, and it had broken him. They, the army, had been very good about it. He was taken out of duty and sent to the shrinks to get his head straight. PTSD is what they had called it, Ruby had never been one for fancy names, all he knew was that it was a living hell. Every time he closed his eyes he was taken back to that moment and no matter what he did, he couldn't change the outcome. Sometimes he dreamt about it and the kid's face became his own sons, he'd call out 'daddy' and just before he managed to get to him the shot would ring out again. Sometimes he'd be stuck to the spot, trying to shout his men down but no words would come out. Again and again, he'd relive that day in a thousand different variations and it always ended the same way. When reality was there, in those waking hours that felt like weeks between rest, he was tormented by the knowledge that he'd failed to stop it, failed to prevent what had happened. He was exhausted by it, never really sleeping, never feeling awake either, just getting through each day in a horrible daze. They'd tried to medicate him, round the edges off those daily nightmares and wrap his brain with some chemical duvet, but he resisted. As hideous as it was, it was his reality and he needed to deal with it. Gone were those days of excuses, he didn't make them anymore and he wasn't going to go back to that way of thinking. What had happened was his fault, he felt, and he would have to deal with it, accept the responsibility for it.

They sent him to a fancy hospital with well-meaning people of various vocations. All of them sympathetic to his situation, none of them understanding what it was like to experience what he had seen, what he was responsible for. Nurses, doctors, occupational therapists, social workers, he'd seen them all and they had all had the same thing to say... they 'understood'. But the truth was, they didn't and they never could. He spent his first month trying to get through to them that there was nothing that could be done to 'fix' him and all that got him was extra medication and more one to one sessions. Going over what had happened with a stranger was the last thing he wanted to do. Month two saw him clam up completely. This new attitude towards his rehabilitation brought a levelling off of the meds and a relaxation of the intensive sessions, they had felt he was making progress. It wasn't until the third month that he realised how to play the game. He attended the right groups, got involved in the 'art therapy' and presented himself as an active and cheerier member of the ward. Weekly meetings with the chief head fuck (psychiatrist) to review his progress were opportunities to bullshit his way to freedom. Throughout his time in hospital, the one constant that he had presented was that he wanted to go home to his family. It took him three months to work out how.

Keeping up appearances was the hardest thing he had to do. Knowing he couldn't let them see that nothing had changed, knowing that his only way out of here was to convince them he had. They had boxes to tick and all of these were based on what they wanted to hear, that's all psychiatry is. They used to 'cure' homosexuality by giving people electric shocks until they said they weren't gay anymore. It really hasn't moved on any further than that. These days they've replaced the electricity with pills and charts, little tests that you need to pass to prove you're well again. All bullshit really, nobody knows what's happening in your head and Ruby worked this out for himself. Whether he stayed there a lifetime or left the next day, nothing would change the way he felt about what had happened, so it was a case of choosing which path he wanted to follow. He smiled more because that made him look less depressed. Interacted with the other patients, to show that he was sociable again. Ate well and told them he was sleeping well too, they liked that sort of thing, it was 'normal'. When he spoke about his feelings to the staff he told them about a future and claimed to have reconciled the past. Future planning was a big tick in the 'well again' box. He pretended to take his meds with no issue and kept his room tidy and clean. All of these things he knew they wanted to see, needed to believe in order to pass him fit for a return to society. That it was a lie didn't matter to anyone. They'd get to stamp their records with a success and he'd get to go back to his family, it was a win for all concerned. When you're looking for negatives you'll find them in any nook or cranny and it's the same with positives too. They wanted to see progress, wanted to see him be 'well' again, so it wasn't hard to convince them they were right. It's called confirmation bias, he'd read about it in one of the books they had in the office. People will see what they want to see and use this to prove themselves right. When he first arrived they had wanted to see 'broken', and he had duly obliged. During his stay, they had looked for signs of repair, and seen those too. Now, after a good amount of time had elapsed, they were looking for 'fixed' and Ruby had given them what they wanted. He left with a prescription and some handshakes. Many thanks for the hard work done and plenty of pats on the back for the staff, he was sure. Was he any different? No... but the important thing was that they thought he was. And so he finally got what he wanted.

He'd missed them terribly and they had missed him too, but the man that had left was not the man that came back. There was a large part of him missing and what had come in its place was difficult to deal with. Those nightmares persisted, as the daymares did too and they rendered him useless for any meaningful work. Being stuck at home only exacerbated his feelings of worthlessness and drove him crazy. What was left was a man who couldn't stand himself and this loathing needed to come out. He was irritable and picky, the least little thing made him fly off the handle. He started drinking to try and blot out the pain and that drinking made him mean. He couldn't stop thinking about the boy and couldn't stand people telling him it was alright. It wasn't fucking alright and he hated them for suggesting it. No one understood how he felt, how the nightmares terrified him. How the days seemed like months and all he could do was drink to get through them. He hated going to sleep even more than he hated being awake and this all made him impossible to live with. He could see what he was doing to his family but he was powerless to change. What had happened would never go away.

Maybe a month, could have been four, he really had no grasp of time at that point, she left and took his boy with her. Back to her mum's house and Ruby hadn't tried to follow. As fucked up as he was, he knew she, they, were better off without him. After that, he sunk further and further into the sand. He didn't care about anything anymore, especially himself, and set off on the road to destruction. His pension paid for the booze and he drank the whole damn lot. Pretty soon he was waking up in shop doorways with bruises and cuts from fights he had no recollection of. Wishing that one night somebody would go too far and finish him. That's when they had found him and given him the chance to make things good.

Ruby sat down again, furious but in control. Jon turned his attention back to the screen. Thomas' dot turned blue, what the hell was he doing? Jon didn't want to play anymore, he was out of control and didn't like the way this night was going. Why had he taken the damn band off? He must have a plan, Thomas never did anything without a plan. Jon told himself to keep the faith, but he didn't like it. What he wanted to do was take the rifle from Ruby and go shoot the bastards, but he knew Thomas would never forgive him. This was his grand idea and woe betide anyone who spoiled it.

Daniels dot passed the blue one and came to a stop. Jon knew that Daniel had a spanner and Thomas a sword, Daniel was banged up and Thomas fresh as a daisy, but he was still nervous. Watching, waiting and praying for that dot to go out, it was painful for him. It seemed to take an age to happen, but when it did Jon was overcome with relief. Daniels dot disappeared, he was dead!

"Ha!" he cried and jumped up out of his seat "That's my bitch!" and he turned to Ruby, excited like a child. Ruby didn't share this emotion, he wanted the pair of them dead.

"There's still another player to go..." he said

"Yeah, and he's going to chop that little whore up too, you'll see" and again, he was giddy with the thrill of it all.

"You're a couple of real sick bastards" Ruby mumbled.

"We're a couple of fucking legends is what we are. You couldn't conceive such a game as this, it's completely beyond your capabilities. This is a sport for the gods, not the cannon fodder" he was practically euphoric, drunk on the success of the plan.

Ruby stared at him in disbelief. They were mad, perfectly mad and completely out of touch with reality. He'd met some crazy people in his time but this was way beyond anyone he'd known. "You do know you're insane, don't you? I mean properly bat shit crazy!"

Jon laughed in his face "you could never understand what we are doing here, the genius of it, and I'll thank you for keeping a civil tongue, you are in our employ after all. You do still wish to get paid I presume?" and he resumed his superior pose.

"I better get paid" Ruby muttered under his breath, although he wasn't sure it was going to happen. Truth be told, he'd never been convinced that he'd get the money they'd promised, but what did he have to lose? Even if it cost him his life, so what? He wasn't really living anyway and all the goodness, everything that made life wonderful had gone a long time ago. It had been a gamble from the start and one that didn't appear to have a downside. Get paid or get killed, either was preferable to the living hell he was going through every day.

Jon was skipping around the room, laughing as he went. He was, in both the old sense and the new, 'gay'. Ruby watched him mince about the place, how different he appeared now, free from that anxiety, almost human.

Coming back to his seat and refilling his glass, Jon eyed the screen, "where's that little gutter whore hiding? She's going to have to come out and play sometime" and he noted her position on the monitor hadn't changed. "No good sitting there forever little tramp, you're going to have to move if you want to win the game" He wondered what plan Thomas had for Lola, where he was going to confront her and he waited for his dot to make its move.

They both waited in silence for the next battle to commence, but neither dot moved an inch. As the minutes passed, Jon became more and more annoyed with the situation. "Why the hell isn't she moving?" he asked, rhetorically. Ruby said nothing, he just checked the time. Not long to go now, whatever happened out there, it would be over soon.

As they watched and as Jon wondered, something entirely unexpected happened. Thomas' dot turned from red to nothing at all. Jon stared at the screen, not quite understanding what was, or rather had, happened.

"Where's his light gone?" he asked Ruby, in earnest, hoping for a favourable explanation.

Ruby, taking interest in the game for the first time, answered with the only conclusion he could think of, "he must be dead..." and he said this as a matter of fact.

Jon, becoming a little frantic at what he saw, or didn't see said, "but that's impossible... he killed Daniel, we saw that. How can he have died now? it doesn't make sense?" and his eyes questioned Ruby.

"He hasn't changed position since Daniels light went out, in fact, they were both in the same place. Daniel must have wounded him badly enough to kill him and it's taken this long for him to die... That's all I can think..." and he stopped talking and watched the other carefully.

Jon became deeply agitated, pacing in front of the screen and willing the light to come back. It must be a malfunction or maybe his armband had broken? Any and many excuses whizzed through his mind and his world seemed unsteady and unfocused. "It's wrong..." he stammered "it can't be... he can't be..." denial, that was the way to deal with this. Refuse to accept the truth. They had planned this too well, it couldn't have gone wrong, they didn't make mistakes.

But he had, he had given Daniel a chance and he had taken it. Thomas was dead because he failed to see danger when it was in front of his eyes, his ego had killed him in the end.

Jon paced and muttered, still disbelieving the facts on the screen. Still waiting for the light to reappear and signal that all was well again. But it didn't.

Ruby, sat with the rifle in his lap and ready to pick it up and use it any second, watched with some joy, as the other, that superior bastard, moved from one point to another in absent agitation. "He's dead!" he said, with finality.

Jon stopped and looked at him like a ghost. All the colour had drained out of his face and he looked like a lost child. Slumping down into his chair, those words from Ruby seemed to have finally broken that spell of denial that had held him these past few minutes. He sat, only half on the seat, with his head drooped down. His whole body had lost its air and he appeared half the size as he sat there in silence.

Ruby kept a close eye on the man. After denial, there would surely be anger and that might just be directed his way. He was ready, should he make a move. But he didn't, not for a good while. There was just no life left in him. As Ruby watched, he noticed on the screen behind him that Lola's dot had started to move.

"Hey!" he called, and Jon looked up. "Lola's on the move," he said and pointed to the monitor.

Jon clasped his hands to his face and rubbed it vigorously. He then slapped himself a few times to bring the life back into his body. Suddenly, he stood and picked up the chair he was sitting on and raised it above his head. Ruby readied himself, finger on the trigger of the rifle but there was no need. Jon smashed the chair down onto the floor and, in a fit of uncontrolled rage, repeated the action until the was nothing but splinters and broken pieces, scattered across the floor. As he did this he screamed at the top of his voice, letting everything inside him out into the room. When he had done, calm returned. Jon stood himself tall, pulled his suit back into place and smoothed back his hair. Collecting his glass, he took a light sip of the wine, to show he was back in control, back to being the master again. "Let her come..."

"So what are you going to do when she gets here?" Ruby asked, thinking he already knew the answer.

"Give her the money of course!" Jon said, with a little twist in his voice.

"You've got it here? And you're just going to let her walk away with it?..." Ruby was dubious about both these points.

"Oh yes..." he smiled "see the briefcase on the table over there" and he indicated it with a nod "contained within is five hundred thousand pounds cash and the documentation to access a private bank account with the rest of the funds. It can be checked online so she is sure that it's waiting for her and there are also the keys to a car outside. When midnight arrives, those doors will unlock" he pointed to the double width glass doors at the back of the aviary "and she will be free to leave..."

Ruby, noting the sadistic smile on his face, didn't believe there wasn't a catch somewhere "So that's it? She can just leave with the money?"

Jon's face changed and suddenly took on a serious look "She can leave... but she won't get far!" he said, deadly "Do you honestly think I'm going to let that little bitch go with my fucking money after Thomas has been killed? Did you really think any of them could possibly win from the start?" he stared straight at Ruby "That was never the point of the game!"

"So what's going to happen then? I suppose you want me to shoot her in the car park?" This was what Ruby had thought was going to happen in the first place, but he was confused by the briefcase.

"Goodness me no!" and his face turned again to one of playful mischievousness "how inartistic... how crude you are" and he scowled disapprovingly at Ruby "contained within the case is an explosive device, for your information. Once she leaves the boundaries of the house it will set off a five-second timer, enough to get clear of this room, and Boom!..." he made an exploding gesture with his hands and laughed.

Ruby looked at him questioningly, he didn't get it. "Why go to all that trouble, the money, bank account, car? Why not just shoot her when she gets here?"

Jon shook his head and blew some air out through his nose in disgust "Why do any of this in the first place? Why not just line the bastards up and shoot them?..." he ventured, rhetorically "because, my stupid blunt instrument, where's the fun in that? We decided that, in the worst case scenario, the funniest thing to do was to make them, whoever it was that got here, believe they had actually won. Money, bank account, car, everything they needed and it all had to be authentic. Then, when they relaxed and were on their way... It's a matter of style squaddie, something your like simply doesn't understand" and he looked him up and down like he was the lowest form of life.

Ruby, as cool as a man could be, picked up the rifle and aimed it at Jon's head. "You know," he said "there's a hole in your plan"

Jon stared back at him, unflinching "Oh really? Pray tell what that might be?" he asked, and looked much less concerned than Ruby thought he ought to.

"You've gone to great lengths to make sure there is nothing to link anyone involved to this house, to you, but the reverse of that is true too. What is there linking this house to me?"

"What do you mean?" Jon asked, quizzically.

"Well, what's to stop me killing you now and taking the money? Ten million being a much nicer sum than the one you said you were going to pay me and given the fact that nobody knows we're here..." and he took the safety off the rifle.

"Oh, I see..." Jon said, casually "You think we hadn't planned on that? Hadn't credited you with enough savvy to take that chance, should it arrive. How silly you are!"

Was it a bluff or had they really catered for this situation? "Well, you've three seconds to tell me why before I blow your head off, so you better make it a good tale!"

Jon stood firm "I told you Thomas was a devil for the details didn't I?..." and he picked up his Richebourg and took a flamboyant sip "well, safely residing in a drawer at my solicitors is an envelope. If they don't hear from me before ten o'clock, Monday morning they are instructed to send that envelope to the police. Contained within it is all the evidence they need. Full details of what has happened here and your part in the process. You're complicit in the kidnapping and murder of the others, along with the murder of myself, which is what you're planning to do, yes?"

Ruby smiled "Absolutely..."

Jon smiled back at him "You see, you'll never get away with it plonky. They'll hunt you down in a matter of days"

Ruby laughed and kept the gun pointing directly at Jon's head. "No they won't," he said.

"Ha! You've no chance of getting away dickhead, we've got your passport. Where do you think you're going to go without that?"

Ruby, still smiling, still aiming the rifle at Jon's head, said: "I've no plans to 'go' anywhere..."

Jon stopped smiling.

"You've forgotten one thing Mr know-it-all... why I agreed to do this in the first place." his aim was steady and his finger poised. "You think you're so clever, covered all the angles, but you've forgotten my 'motivation' haven't you?..." and he waited for the other to respond.

"Your family, you're doing this for your family..." he stuttered, unnerved for the very first time.

"Exactly, and I've got until Monday morning to sort them out. That's all the information I was looking for. That you'd had something over me was a given, all those careful plans and all that information you gathered, you had to have taken this into account, I just needed to find out what it was and you've just told me, you dumb fuck!"

"Wait!.... wait a minute..." Jon blurted, hands outstretched in front of him "they will find you, you can't disappear, not these days..."

"Let me tell you a story Mr Big shot, and I'd advise you to listen carefully. You know all about what happened with the boy, how my life went to shit after that and I lost the one thing that mattered most to me. You did your research well, found what I wanted the most and offered it to me. But you didn't understand me..." and he looked Jon square in the eyes "you failed to understand me because neither you nor Thomas are 'human'. You're a couple of fucking psychopaths that don't feel anything for others, don't have those human emotions. Well, I do and do you know what? I'm tired! Tired of the nightmares and the headaches, tired of drinking myself into the gutters to numb the pain. I'm ashamed of what I did and of what I have become. Can't do this anymore, I just haven't got the will. You don't know what it's like to lose the one thing that was everything to you, the only thing that made you 'good', and know it was your fault. Know that you failed them when they needed you most. Every day.... every fucking day I wake up and wish that I hadn't, wish that I could have some rest from the torture. All I want is to make amends. That was why I agreed to this. It was my last opportunity to do something good for them, and if I did... If I could, then I could go to my rest in peace. So I've got until Monday to take this cash to my family and get back here. Yes, the police will come, armed with that envelope and what will they find? Everything you said they would and an extra body, my body. Do you think they'll look any further? If they tried, who would they be looking for?"

Jon's face had dropped and he looked ashen "They'll notice the money missing..." he tried.

"Will they? How do they know it was here in the first place? Even if it was, who could have taken it? Everyone you told them about is here and dead... No, Jon, I don't think so. They'll be happy enough just to clean this mess up and tell stories about it to the press."

"Wait... wait!" he said, desperately "It's only half a million, I'll give you five, ten if you see this through with me."

"You think I would trust you? Do you think I ever have? Besides, half a million is plenty for my girl, she'll do well with that." and he smiled again, but a different kind of smile as he remembered his wife and the goodness that she had. For the first time in as long as he could remember, Ruby was happy and peaceful in himself.

"But..." Jon tried again to stall him but it was too late. Ruby, finger on the trigger and as steady as a rock, squeezed on his outward breath and blew Jon's brains all over the TV screen.

Chapter 11 - One little Indian, left all alone...

That bullet passed through Jon's right eye and straight out the back of his head. Not only did it cover the TV in blood and pieces of brain, it made a hole right in the middle of it and smashed the screen. Bollocks, Ruby mused, he'd have no idea where Lola was now, or when she might be arriving. However, he thought, she would be making her way here thinking she was the only one left and not worrying about the others. Shouldn't take her too long. He placed the rifle on the table beside him and stepped over to have a good look at the body. Should he move it or leave it where it was? If Lola was cautious, and she could see the body from the doorway, she might be able to bolt back into the house before he had the chance to get her. Best move it to somewhere a little more out of sight. Checking the room, he saw a large, wing back leather seat at the far end and decided that, given how gloomily that area was lit, he could prop Jon up over there and he'd not look dead until you got pretty damn close to him. That would both draw her in and keep her attention on Jon whilst he manoeuvred himself around the back of her. Picking him up by the ankles, Ruby dragged his limp body around the outer edge of the room and over to the chair. With the aid of a cushion, he did a pretty good job of making him look relaxed and quite 'alive'. Walking to the doorway to check his work, he was pleased with the effect it created. She'd have no idea he was dead until she had crossed a good part of the room to see. That would give him plenty of time to ambush her. All he needed to do was cut off her exit and she had no chance.

He'd thought about just emptying the money from the briefcase, taking the car keys and smashing his way through the doors. They were electronically bolted, like the rooms, and obviously programmed to unlock at twelve o'clock, but they were mainly glass. It wouldn't have been difficult to smash enough of a hole in one to squeeze through to freedom. Problem was, Thomas and Jon had planned everything to such a degree Ruby didn't trust that those doors weren't booby trapped. For the sake of another twenty minutes or so, why take the risk? Better to sit and wait it out. He was practically home and dry.

Taking a throw from the sofa near the doors, Ruby drenched it in soda water and used it to mop up as much of the blood and bits as he could. He didn't want to risk it drawing her attention and spooking her. It wasn't a nice job, but there was only a small area visible from the doorway and it didn't take long to complete. When it was done, and he was happy with the way the room was dressed, he took the rifle and found a position behind one of the exotic plants that dominated the corners of the aviary. He sat and he waited for the 'winner' to arrive.

Lola handed Daniel the sword and said: "You better be a lot sharper than that later, or we're both dead!" There was no point killing him, not that she wanted to anyway but if he were telling the truth about Thomas then he was probably her only hope of survival. If he were lying then he didn't matter, alive or dead.

Daniel just looked at her, relieved she had decided to go with his plan and not chop his head off instead. "Don't worry about me, I'm ready" he said.

"You don't fucking look it... what did they do to you?" she regarded the, now, blood soaked bandages.

"Snakes and ladders..." he said cryptically and hauled himself to his feet "best get going, they'll be wondering what you've been doing in here for so long."

"Yeah, funnily enough, I'm in no hurry to get there..." she said and picked up her trusty baseball bat. As she walked to the door, she looked over her shoulder at Daniel who was hobbling across the room. She needed to see something in his eyes that she could trust, something to give her confidence to go through with this.

"Good luck" he said. He was serious and honest, she felt a bond between them and she believed him. It was enough. Lola turned and walked out the door.

Into the dark passageway, she went, following the arrow on the armband. Passing the armoured knight, she kept silent this time, lest he come to life and grab her. After the night she'd had so far, nothing would surprise her now. Well, nothing but a handshake, ten million quid and a free ride out of here, that would be a shock. She wasn't counting on anything as simple. Making her way to the end of the gloomy corridor the arrow still pointed straight ahead, but there was no 'ahead' to go. In front of her was a wall with a barred window. Looking out, she saw trees in the near distance and underneath, the roof of what must be a conservatory. Or was it the aviary? To her immediate right, she found a narrow staircase leading back to the ground floor. This must be the way, she thought and the fact that she was so close to the end scared her. With trembling legs and that aching hip, she edged her way down the stairs, one by one. There was no light on the stairs themselves, but a dim flicker of a lamp shone from the corridor at the bottom. Each step hurt, she felt like her legs were going to give way and she panted, trying to get enough oxygen into her system.

Short breaths that hardly filled her lungs at all. If Daniel were telling the truth about Thomas, then Jon was most likely going to kill her. It wasn't an inviting thought to have, she was tempted to return to the room and suggest a different plan, but her brain couldn't come up with one. Maybe he'd been lying about Thomas and she was just yards away from a fortune and freedom? But why would he do that? Because he didn't trust them... "Fuckety fuck bag!" she said quietly. She was too tired to work out what was what and it annoyed the hell out of her. Pull yourself together girl, she said in her head this time, balls it out!

Peering into the bottom corridor she saw the usual panelled walls with paintings and an oak chair for sitting in contemplation. One large rug ran the length of the floor and she stepped lightly on it. Some fifteen feet in front of her, along the right-hand wall, was the opening to what must be the aviary. Two large wooden doors were all that stood between her and the end of the game... maybe? Lola made her way along and hesitated for a moment. Her hand didn't want to reach out to the handle. Taking a deep, deep breath she blew out her cheeks and grabbed it. With her other hand, she gripped and re-gripped the bat, holding it slightly behind her, as if to keep it a surprise. Releasing the door, she pushed it open ahead of her and it swung quietly into the dark room. Lola crept forward into the space that the door had vacated and peered inside. She was expecting it to be well lit and populated with at least the host and the henchman, there was no one to be seen. To the left of the doorway was a large, oak table with chairs around it. To the right, a smaller table some distance away with a briefcase on it. Other than that, all she could make out were large plants and shadows. Moving a little further, stepping into the room itself, Lola scanned its contents again. Towards the back, shaded by one of the thick, tall plants, she saw a chair and a figure. He was looking directly at her but had made no sound nor moved an inch at her arrival, was it the host? As she moved further still, to get a better view, she turned to look behind her, checking either side for danger. Aside from more plants and a huge mural, all she could see was a broken TV screen. It failed to hold her attention and she turned back to the figure in the shadows.

"Hey!" she called, "is that you?"

It was a stupid thing to say given that, whoever it was, it was most certainly 'them'. Still, no reaction came and she was forced to move further into the room. Lola made it about half way along the large oak table before she managed to recognise the figure in the chair. She also noted a fixed expression and a missing eye. Quickly she raised the bat and spun around. Closing the door and sliding a bolt in place, some ten feet back from her, was the monkey, rifle in hand.

"Oh fuck..." she said and lowered the bat to the floor in resignation.

"Evening Lola, glad you finally made it, I've been waiting here a while now" and he smiled at her.

Lola was shocked to hear him speak, even more so by his accent. He was a London boy, sounded just like the people she'd grown up with. Not a toff like Jon.

"Well I'm here now," she said "what's the deal?" and she jerked her head backwards to indicate the dead host in the wing back chair.

"Why don't we get you comfortable first and then I'll tell you all about it," he said. "grab that chair and pull it to the middle of the floor, away from the table" he used the gun to illustrate what he wanted her to do.

Lola obliged, she didn't see what option she had. It was a heavy oak chair, good quality with thick arms and legs.

"Now put the bat on the floor and kick it over to me please" all the time keeping the gun trained on her chest.

She carried out the instructions and waited for more in silence. She felt utterly deflated by the situation.

"Now sit down and use these to secure your legs to the chair." he tossed over two long zip ties that fell at her feet. Ruby waited for Lola to pull them tight. "Now..." he said, and placed the gun on the table, "make a fucking move whilst I tie your arms and I'll knock you out!"

She had no doubts as to how serious he was, she was also quite pleased he hadn't just shot her when she'd walked in the room. "I'll not move a muscle," she said calmly and placed her arms the length of the wooden rests.

Ruby took another two ties from his pocket and secured her wrists to the chair. He then bent down and checked the ankle ties, pulling them three notches tighter than Lola had. She winced a little as the ties bit into her skin but said nothing. Ruby picked himself up and retrieved the gun.

"Can I ask you a question?" she said solemnly.

Ruby nodded "Go on"

"Why didn't you kill me when I walked through the door?"

He looked at her kindly "Three reasons..." he said "Firstly, I'm not a murderer. That piece of shit over there doesn't count. Secondly, you're one of my kind. We grew up in the same shit hole, with similar experiences I'm sure. Lastly, I've no need. Once I've done what I need to do, I'll come back to the house and let you go. Nobody knows you were here so you can get out of this and go back to your normal life." Actually, he knew the police would be coming and that they would have all her details. Without her body here, they'd be looking for her. If they found her then they'd assume she had the cash and that suited Ruby down to the ground. Keeping Lola alive was a further protection for his family. She was the ideal scapegoat.

"Thank you," she said genuinely, and smiled at him "so go on, what happened to laughing boy over there, lovers tiff?"

Ruby mulled it over for a moment, thinking about how much he wanted to say. "That sadistic fuck got what was coming to him."

"Not a friend of yours then?" she prompted, wanting to get something she could use.

"Ha!" Ruby laughed, "none of what happened tonight had anything to do with me. I was just here for the money, like you, and that's all I'm going to take."

Lola felt he was opening up a little and wanted to keep him talking as long as possible. Maybe there was still an angle she could play? "So there is money then? The whole ten mil?"

"Oh yes," Ruby said and walked over to the briefcase. Opening it, he threw stacks of cash onto the table. "Five hundred grand in cash and the rest in a bank account for the winner"

"Well I never..." she said, surprised.

"Yeah, but you'd never have gotten out of here with it alive" Ruby laughed "the sick fucker put a bomb in the case. You'd have been blown to kingdom come half way across the car park."

"Son of a bitch!" she said, "so why have the money in the first place?"

"That's what I said, apparently we're not as 'artistic' or clever enough to understand. Well the bastards dead, so I guess he wasn't quite as clever as he thought?"

If it were true about Thomas, which she was almost convinced it was, then monkey man must have known. Lola had to get him to say before she could play her trump card. "So nobody could win from the start then, he just wanted us to kill each other and then blow up the last survivor, is that it?" She looked deliberately perplexed by this.

Ruby looked a little suspiciously at Lola for a second... "No, the point of the evening was a man hunt for Jon's boyfriend. He was supposed to kill those that beat their game and were released into the house. But it didn't go to plan, he got himself killed by Daniel. Leaving you as the sole survivor..."

"But I'm not..." she cut in, using her most sincere voice and expression.

Ruby stopped removing the money and looked up. "What?..." he asked "what do you mean? We saw both lights go out. First Daniels and then Thomas', they're both dead"

"They're not... well, not both of them. Thomas is still alive" and she kept her pretension up.

Ruby looked stone faced now, "what are you talking about?" he said, demanding an answer.

Retaining her innocence, Lola explained how she'd fallen asleep in the stairwell and how, when she had woken, only her light had remained. She'd thought she was the only one left but... as she had followed the arrow up the stairs, she had heard noises in the room to the left side of the corridor. She'd crept alongside and seen Thomas, acting completely insane, butchering Daniels dead body and talking to himself about 'only three to go!'. She had managed to get past without him seeing and made it here to the aviary hoping to get the money and run before Thomas came along. That had been her plan.

"He's lost it you know... I mean totally bonkers!" she said, "you can't leave me here with him in the house."

Ruby didn't doubt a word of what she had said, it had been a most impressive performance. But he didn't understand how Thomas had made himself dead? Lola said she didn't know either, but had seen both arm bands on Daniels body.

"Maybe he put them on him and chopped one arm off before the other?" It was offered as one who was making a wild guess, but Lola had known how Daniel had managed it, so simply switched it around for Ruby's benefit. He took the bait. He couldn't allow Thomas to live, that would jeopardise his chances of pulling this off. Thomas was the brains and if he found Jon dead then he'd go after Ruby, or his family, probably both. As he stood there, considering what to do next, Lola made a plea, "Untie me and let's get out of here together. You can have the money, I don't care about that, I just want to get the fuck out of this place alive"

Ruby was considering this when another thought popped into his head, 'what if she's lying?' She'd seemed so genuine about it, but those people Jon and Thomas had collected were a bunch of bastards that would do or say anything to win. That's why they were here in the first place, their greed. Suddenly, he doubted everything. There was still ten minutes left before the doors opened, best to go and check it out. Picking up the rifle and checking the cartridge, he looked at Lola quizzically, appraising her honesty.

"Tell you what," he said "you stay here and guard the cash whilst I go and see if you've been telling the truth. If you have then I'll let you live..."

Lola tried to make out that this was a terrible idea and she feared that Thomas would kill him. Tried to convey to Ruby that she was definitely on 'his' side. Secretly she knew this was the best possible outcome for her. If he killed Daniel then she had been telling the truth, she'd just got the two mixed up, easily done! If Daniel killed Ruby then the plan had worked and she would be leaving with a share of the money, as they had agreed. Either way, she got to live through this and there was a chance she'd get paid. Brilliant.

"Don't do it, don't leave me here like this. Let's just get out of here together" she said, but knew fine well that he couldn't leave Thomas alive. Goodness, she really should have been on the stage, she thought.

Ruby smiled, he believed it was a nonsense story from a desperate woman but it needed confirming none the less. "I'll not be long, sit tight" and he unbolted the door and left the room. Lola allowed herself a little smile when she was sure he had gone.

Daniel, back in the murder room, had been a busy boy since Lola had left. He needed the element of surprise if he were to overcome both the monkey with a gun and Jon with who knows what? He'd reckoned on about five minutes at the least, ten at most, to get himself ready. Grabbing the horribly disfigured body of Thomas by the ankles, he dragged him over to the sofa, layin him the length of the thing to check its size. Happy with the proportions, he then tipped the sofa onto its back, revealing the underneath. Using the sword, he cut a flap in the bottom cover which allowed access to the inner structure of the seat and was pleased to find what he had hoped to see there, a space large enough to tuck in a body. Actually accomplishing that task of heaving a dead weight body into a sofa's belly was no mean feat, the damn thing kept sliding back out as soon as he got one part in. However, once he thought to turn Thomas to face towards the bottom and use his spine to hold him in position, the task became achievable. Carefully returning the seat to its natural state he was pleased to see the dead man completely hidden inside. Now what he needed to do was 'dress' the other body he wanted them to find. They wouldn't know for sure if Lola was telling the truth or not, so finding his blood drenched body laying prone in the middle of the room just might give him the advantage he needed. If he could give those bastards a conundrum, a room with one dead guy instead of two, he felt that might just throw them off guard. When they came to check him and wonder where Thomas was, he would strike as quickly as he could. He hoped that the monkey would do the checking and that Jon would be without arms, at least of the gun variety. If that were the case then he had a chance. It was a long shot but he didn't see any other way to go. There were precious few areas to hide in ambush. Presenting them with a scene they wouldn't expect was the best he could think to do. Taking the body of the snake, and placing a small waste paper basket just at arm's length from his head, Daniel lay with his back to the door, some ten feet into the room. He placed the sword on the ground and lay down on top of it to shield the weapon from view. Taking the snake and squeezing it from its tail to its severed head, he managed to cover his neck in a decent amount of thick, dark blood. With the same technique, he squeezed what was left in its body over his side to try and give the impression that Thomas had successfully hacked him to death and left the room after. With the snake now relieved of its precious fluids, he packed its body into the basket and pushed it away from his head, behind the table they'd used to sit on. Now all he could do was wait for them to come and be ready to spring to life again as soon as the big guy got close enough to check him out. He hoped his arm didn't go dead in the time it took for them to get there.

Ruby was back in 'army' mode, leading the recon and sweeping the areas for enemy targets. It felt natural to him and all his training and experience came back the instant he left the aviary. His sense heightened by the stress of the situation, he was unusually stealthy for a man of his size. Moving lightly along the corridor, switching from one wall to the other, rifle poised and ready to engage. He wasn't the type to sit and wait for trouble to come to him, he always preferred the proactive approach. Besides, he was relatively confident that Lola had been telling him lies. She'd been incredibly convincing in the tale she had spun but just a little too eager to get herself out of those ties. Ruby never underestimated the enemy and credited Lola with the guile to engineer an opportunity to strike. If he'd untied her, he was sure she'd make a play for the money and he couldn't take any chances on that front. Nor could he afford to leave Thomas unaccounted for. If he were alive then he'd be hell bent on avenging the death of Jon and there was no way he was going to jeopardise his family in that way. Not for the sake of a five-minute mission. Slowly he made his way down the corridor towards the room in question, the only real danger point being the knight half way along. It wasn't easy to see, but the closer he got the less likely it became that Thomas might be hiding behind it. He passed the thing with his back to the opposite wall, watching the suit carefully, ready for any movement. This wasn't 'Scooby Doo' and the suit of armour failed to spring into life as he went by. Ruby smiled at the childish reference his brain had made at this moment of stress as if providing a little light relief from the tension. Next up came his destination point, was she lying? He was about to find out.

Daniel didn't hear him coming down the corridor, he'd been too quiet but he felt him. Somewhere inside him, there was a sense, an ability to detect a difference in the atmosphere. His mind and body were so keyed up by the situation and yet he must remain utterly still up to the point of attack. His right hand was on the handle of the blade and tucked the length of his side, he checked his grip and readied himself. Controlling his breathing was the most difficult part. His body yearned for more oxygen and he was desperate to take great gulps to satisfy it but had to ration himself to the lightest of inhalations. Thankfully, with the lights off, it would be near impossible to detect the rise and fall of his rib cage from any distance other than close enough to strike. He lay there waiting for his opportunity, praying he would get one.

Ruby stood, back to the opposite wall and surveyed what he could of the room inside. It was dark but he could see a figure on the floor inside pooled in blood. It was hard to make out but it looked like Daniel. With his body in this position, he couldn't see his arms, couldn't verify whether he had both bands on. Not that it mattered, the accuracy of the story didn't matter now, all that did was finding Thomas, dead or alive. Edging closer to the doorway he moved from one angle to another, scoping out as much of the interior as he could before entering. It was a dangerous area to 'clean' and if he'd had a hand grenade he would have chucked it inside to do the dirty work for him. He could feel his body's reluctance to go any further, his brain told him it was folly too. Against all the training he'd had and quite the opposite of his better judgement, he stepped into the room. Reaching out with his left hand, he flicked the light switch to illuminate the area. Nothing happened, the room remained pitch dark. Bollocks, he muttered to himself. From the items of furniture contained within there were few places to hide but that didn't mean Thomas wasn't. One large sofa presented the best opportunity, and he must pass over half the room to view the other side of it. Checking the sides and turning his head to listen for any outside noises, Ruby prepared himself to move over towards it. He was breathing heavily now and the noise he was making annoyed him. It would mask any little noises from elsewhere. He wasn't as young as he used to be and his body was letting him down on this front. Steadying himself, he prepared to move swiftly over to the back of the seating to see. That figure on the floor was definitely Daniel and it looked like Thomas had made short work of him. Daniel had died first, he'd seen that on the monitor, and the way it looked here he couldn't see how he'd managed to inflict enough damage on Thomas for him to die of his injuries some five minutes later or so. Maybe Lola had been telling the truth after all?

Daniel heard his footfall as he came into the room. Knew that he was checking the area and would soon be coming closer to look behind the sofa. It was then that he must strike. He heard his light steps on the floor. One step, stop... one step, stop... it was torturously slow and he had to stop himself from going too early. Patience was the key. Whomever it was, they had obviously fallen for his trick and all he need do was wait for the right time. As the man got closer, inch by inch, he could now hear him breathing and knew it was just one of them. If the other was waiting outside with the gun then this could all go to shit pretty quickly he thought, but quickly dispelled this from his mind. What he needed to do was stay focused and deal with the problem in hand. Whatever happened after that would need to take care of itself. For now, he had but one problem, the man who was very nearly stood behind him. What he couldn't do was give himself away before he had a chance. Timing was the key.

Ruby inched his way warily across the room, gun barrel oscillating from one end of the sofa to the other. If there were an attack coming then it had to be from behind the seat and he was primed for it. He was nearly in the centre of the room now and could see the base of the wall behind the seat, not much further to go to clear the area. His heart was beating faster than he thought it ought to, harder than he liked, thumping away in his chest. 'Where are you, you mincing little bastard' he thought and stepped a little closer still. All his senses were trained on the sofa now, he'd blocked everything else out of the equation. If anything moved from behind it he'd blast it to kingdom come! Raising himself up onto his toes, craning his head to try and see over the back he heard the faintest of noises from the side of him. Shit! Turning as quickly as he could, all he could manage to do was force the gun out in front of him as his eye detected something coming towards him. There wasn't time to get it into a position to fire so he used it as protection. With a crack of metal upon metal, the rifle was knocked clean out of his grasp and slid across the floor away from him. As the figure went to strike again he fell on top of it and grabbed the arm that held the weapon. Daniel flailed underneath him and tried to work his arm free to strike again but Ruby was too strong. As soon as he had managed to get a controlled grip on his arm it was over for Daniel. Sat on top of him with his knees either side, he smashed Daniels hand down onto the floor. Once wasn't quite enough to free the weapon but a second blow against the hard wooden flooring released it from his grip. Once that had happened Ruby turned his attention to Daniels' throat. Daniel fought to get his hands away and Ruby's fingers slipped off a couple of times because of the thick wet blood around his neck. Soon though, he managed to get a proper hold and squeezed with all his might. Daniel was younger and fitter than Ruby, but he didn't have his bulk or power and could do nothing to release him. Even pushing both hands into his chest to try and force him off didn't work. It gave him an extra breath or two, but failed to remove his hands, the man was just too strong and heavy. Ruby's fingers were vice like and he kept applying the pressure. Daniel could feel the oxygen leaving his brain and his vision failing. His world was speckled with tiny stars and the darkness was creeping ever inwards from the edges of his sight. Pretty soon he would be unconscious and all would be lost. Desperately, he grabbed one of Ruby's hands and yanked it sidewards. Slipping on the viscous red liquid, Ruby's hand was freed for a moment and Daniel managed to gulp down some air. Ruby caught his left wrist and twisted it, the pain from earlier wounds shot through Daniels body and he was powerless to prevent the monkey from pinning it under his knee. Daniel let out a scream of pain and exasperation as the fight seemed lost. Ruby tried to grab his right hand to do the same and Daniel, instinctively, pushed it down behind his back. It was a purely defensive move and Ruby decided to go back to the strangling instead. With his right hand tucked under his bottom, Daniel found salvation in his back pocket. Working them free from the pressure of Ruby's body he gripped hard and drove the surgical scissors deep into Ruby's neck. Only the base of his fist prevented them from driving any further but they had gone far enough. Piercing the outer skin easily they punctured the jugular vein on their way to stopping at his trachea. Fresh, hot blood pumped from his neck and spilt down Daniels' arm, covering his bandages and dripping onto his face. Ruby released his grip and clasped both hands to his wound. Kneeling up, he removed the scissors and felt the pulsing action squirt blood between his fingers. Daniel pushed him with all his might and managed to topple the giant lump over. Ruby hit the floor and rolled over, still holding his neck to try and stem the flow. Leaving one hand on his wound he started to crawl towards the sword that lay some six feet away from him, he wasn't done yet. He was losing power with every second that went by but his determination to finish the job carried him through. Daniel saw, as he crawled away from the man, what he intended to do and looked around for something to defend himself. He only needed a few seconds before Ruby would be too weak to pose a threat, but he had to find those seconds. Rolling onto his hands and knees, he started to crawl to the door and found the rifle was blocking his path. If he could make it to the gun he would be safe. Turning, he saw Ruby reaching for the blade and getting himself shakily to his feet. His oxygen levels hadn't yet replenished and he felt dizzy and sick, crawling was his only option and he was slow to do that. Ruby was upright now and using the sword to steady himself, was staggering his way over to Daniel. 'Crawl you bastard!' Daniel shouted inwardly and dragged his weary body ever closer to the gun. He could feel the man behind him, each step making the floor flex and filling him will ever increasing panic. Reaching out with his right hand to propel himself forward he placed it down awkwardly on a wound and the whole thing gave way beneath him. Sprawled out on the ground, just a couple of feet away from the gun, he looked over his shoulder to see Ruby stood above him. He was drenched in his own blood, all the way down to his shoes that had left horrible red tread marks on the ground behind him. It was too late to reach the rifle and Daniel put his arms up in a cross to protect his face from the blow. Ruby, bent at the knees, picked the sword up and held it above his head... Held it there for a second or two before falling, head first on top of Daniels prone body. The weight of the impact, of Ruby's great mass, knocked what wind he had right out of him and he lost consciousness.

"Evening darling, how was your day?" Lola called sarcastically when she saw Daniels figure appear in the doorway. "Fucking hell!" she exclaimed when he moved further into the light of the room and she could see the amount of blood that covered him. He looked like Carrie's twin brother on prom night. Daniel said nothing, just edged his way into the room, furtively checking the spaces for danger, rifle at the ready.

"He's dead!" Lola said abruptly, having observed the other's behaviour. "The butler did it," she said ironically "he's sat in the chair at the back of the room minus his brains"

Daniel looked over to where the body was propped "shame, would have liked to have killed the bastard myself" although actually, he was mightily relieved.

"Do you even know how to use that thing?" she asked before adding "so you killed him then?" she wanted to be sure they were the only two left.

"Oh yeah, he's dead alright. Silly old fucker shouldn't have messed with me..."

His attempt at macho bravado didn't quite carry the authority he'd hoped and Lola didn't buy it either, but she was pleased it was over. "Come on then, get these ties off me and let's get out of here."

Daniel walked over to where she was sitting and looked at the zip ties around her wrists and ankles. "Got you fastened in pretty good, how come he didn't kill you?"

"Promised him a blow job and a Sunday lunch... What the fuck does it matter? Get me out of these ties and let's get out of here!" she was annoyed with the slow progress on the freedom front. She also knew he'd not seen the money yet and wanted to get released before temptation started to play with his better judgement.

"Hang on a second princess, I just want to get the facts straight before we get going," he said and stroked her cheek with his bloody fingers "you don't unmuzzle a dog before you know it's not going to bite you"

"First up, call me 'princess' again and I'll fucking kill you!" she was furious "Secondly, I'm not a fucking dog and we had a fucking deal! I've kept my end of the bargain, it's time you kept yours. Take the bastard ties off and let's get out of here."

Just then, his gaze diverted to the large pile of cash on the table and the briefcase next to it. Leaving her struggling in the chair, he walked over to take a closer look. "Well I never did..." he muttered under his breath, "they weren't joking about the money after all" and he thumbed through the cash to check how much was there. Further inspection of the case told him the rest of the story. "Car keys, bank account and a good few hundred grand in cash, this evening has certainly taken a turn for the better"

"Remember our deal Dan," she said, more in hope than expectation.

"And why should I exactly? You're in no position to offer me anything anymore, you've served your purpose. Sorry, but I'm sure you'd do the same if you were in my shoes"

He was quite right, she'd have left him there to rot just the same as he was doing with her, but she wasn't going to admit that "you're not wearing any shoes, nob head!"

"You see... It's that kind of attitude darling that makes me think I can't trust you. Sorry, but I'm going to have to pass on the whole 'sharing' thing, I'm sure you understand" and he started packing the money back into the briefcase. It was gone midnight and the doors at the back of the aviary had automatically unlocked. There was nothing barring his way.

Lola knew he wasn't going to untie her, it didn't matter what she said. She had no cards to play now and would have to watch him walk out the door with the money. "Ok," she called in resignation "ok... the money yours. Well played, you won the game and you've got the spoils. Just do me one favour before you go"

"Thank you, Lola, glad to see you're not a sore loser, what is it?" he asked.

"Leave me something so I can untie myself when you're gone. All I want to do is get out of here and go home. That's not too much to ask is it, I did help you after all" she played the role of the defeated contender to a tee.

Daniel thought about this for a moment. If she got out, how much of a threat would she be to him? He'd have to flee the country anyway, killing two people doesn't go down well with the law no matter how good the reasons, so she'd have pretty much no chance of finding him even if she had the funds to go look. He finished packing the case whilst he mulled it over.

"Go on then, I tell you what I'll do. This table is about the same height as your arms, I'll leave you my surgical scissors and if you can manoeuvre your way over here then you should be able to cut yourself free." It would take quite a long time for Lola to perform this task, if she were able to do it at all, so he felt this was a pretty safe option. It also felt better than leaving her to starve to death, tied to a chair. He'd killed two people who had tried to kill him, that was self-defense. He wasn't a murderer and didn't want to start now.

"Seriously? is that the best you can do? I'll never be able to get this chair over there. Come on Daniel, give me a fair shot" and she sounded almost pathetic at the finish.

"That's all I'm going to offer you and you're lucky I'm being so generous," he said smiling. Closing the catches, he chucked the cars keys up into the air and caught them again with a flourish. He was the cat that got the cream with the added bonus of rubbing it in the face of another cat that could do nothing about it. Daniel placed the scissors, freshly wiped clean of finger prints, elaborately down on the table's edge and walked to the doors.

"There's something I know that you don't," she said quietly as if speaking to herself.

"Nice try Lola, but I don't think so if you had anything to offer you'd have used it by now. Guess this is goodbye princess..." and he used the word as a final insult, the icing on his victory cake. Opening the doors, he turned once more and winked at her before stepping outside.

Lola called out after him "What did I say I'd do if you called me that again?" and she counted in her head, bracing herself.

Daniel, ignoring her threat, started to walk to the car that was waiting some ten feet away.

The blast from the case cut him in half at the waist. It sent his upper body skyward and his middle scattered in all directions around him. It blew the contents of the case all over the car park and everywhere there were lumps of burning banks notes spattered in blood. It was so fierce and he was still so close to the doorway that the wind it created blew Lolas chair clean over, shattering the windows of the aviary and sending shards of glass all over the room. When she opened her eyes she realised what it had done. She was laying on her side, still fixed to the chair and the damn thing hadn't weakened one bit. Solid oak, it had lasted maybe two hundred years of service and falling over with her slender frame inside it had done nothing to loosen any joints. Try as she might, and she certainly did, there wasn't an ounce of give in it. Lola, once she had finished her initial frantic shaking and pulling, laughed.

And then there were none.

Printed in Great Britain
by Amazon